THE RELATIONSHIP CONTRACT

To Barcelona with Love Trilogy

Book 2

Marcella Steele

Quotes

"**G**rowth involves giving up the stories of your past, so you can write a new one." ~ Marianee Williamson

"Love is like a virus: It can happen to anybody at any time." ~ *Maya Angelou*

"Age does not protect you from love. But love, to some extent, protects you from age." ~Jeanne Moreau

"Love follows you. It goes where you go. It does what it wants, even if what you want is not to be in love." ~ Abby Jimenez, *Part of Your World*

"Life really does begin at forty. Before that you're just doing research." ~ Carl Jung

Contents

Prologue

O nce upon a time...

Ah yes, romantic fairy tales. Those delightful little fantasies that convinced generations of girls that their biggest life goal should be waiting around for a man on a horse. A *white* horse, naturally—because symbolism matters when you're being rescued from poverty, captivity, or inconvenient comas.

Here's the thing: We now know these stories were written by men. Shocking, I know. Women weren't exactly encouraged to publish back then—too busy scrubbing floors and not having opinions. But those medieval maidens probably kept watch anyway, hearts fluttering at every distant hoofbeat. *Is that him? Is my happily-ever-after finally cantering over that hill?*

Plot twist: The prince might've been riding to rescue a young *man*, but that version never made it past the gatekeepers of ye olde publishing house. And the radical idea that a damsel could rescue *herself*? Please. That story wouldn't see daylight for another few centuries.

By forty-nine, I'd fully embraced my inner cynic. Life had thoroughly beaten the sparkle out of me, like a piece of fabric pounded against riverbed stones until all the color bleeds out. I'd forgotten what hope even looked like—that shimmery feeling of infinite possibility that comes so easily when you're young and haven't yet learned better.

And then something miraculous happened. A sequence of events so unexpected, I started wondering if I could write myself into an entirely different kind of fairy tale.

Now, you might protest, "But fairy tale heroines can't be past twenty-nine!" It's practically a *law*. To which I say—and my mother would back me up on this—I've never been particularly good with rules. Besides, I was about to discover something the original fairy tales never mentioned: The *real* magic doesn't happen when you're young enough to believe in princes. It happens when you're old enough to know better—and brave enough to rewrite the narrative.

I wasn't always so brave; my fairy tale required more than a few drafts, but I'll let you in on how it unfolded.

Once upon a time, there was a middle-aged damsel named Sofia Drake. Even though she was pretty, kind to small woodland creatures, and had raised a prince of a son, she had lost her sparkle—her mojo, if you will. She'd kissed a LOT of frogs since her husband had run off with a handmaiden, but surprisingly, none of them became her prince. All the middle-aged would-be princes rejected her in favor of a younger model, because 1) they'd already had the minivan version and were

in the market for a hot, red sports car, or 2) they were finally ready to spawn an heir. Lucky for men, their timeline was wide open. Unlucky for Sofia, whose ovaries were now shriveled prunes.

Oh, but the younger princes... they formed a line to court her. However, she discovered they only desired a piece of her—the piece below the waist... under the petticoat... intent on making the beast with two backs. Well, you get the picture.

All alone in her tower, she cherished her work, dedicating her life to helping the townsfolk in their daily battle with melancholy (and disorders not yet named). But while she toiled at her job, available to be called upon at any hour of the day or night, her company downsizing left her out on the street.

Discarded like an old, used up horse put out to pasture, she felt useless without purpose or direction.

As in all fairy tales, things were looking bleak for Sofia, until a real prince of a man came along. A young, handsome prince of just thirty-five, named Ryan Hunter. But Sofia, not a woman of twenty anymore, no longer believed in princes. Fearing more heartbreak, she sent him away. Instead, she gathered her courage and set out on an adventure alone to a faraway land called Barcelona, desperate to chart a new course.

But the omniscient overseer of this fairy tale had another plan in mind for Sofia. Call it a fairy godmother intervention, if you will, but fate snatched the reins, resulting in her and Ryan crossing paths on the journey. Slowly but surely, Ryan proved to her that while he might be young, he truly was her prince—or at least, a really good guy who loved her a lot.

Sofia blossomed like a bud opening to the warmth of spring in this new land, inspired by its beauty, antiquity, and the new sensations this foreign place brought forth within her. She found herself all sparkly and new again, glowing with love, as if a fairy godmother had cast a spell and whisked her into an elegant ball gown. Poof—she shed fifteen years in the blink of an eye, or at least it seemed, obliterating all obstacles to lasting love with her prince.

So, the happily-ever-after must be around the corner, right? Not so fast, dear reader. Just when the castle was on the horizon, the horses galloping into the sunset, a fork in the road appeared—the diverging paths ahead determining their future. Ryan, envisioning a future with children, rode straight to the signpost marked PROCREATION—FAMILIES ONLY. Sofia watched in horror, gazing longingly at the other sign: HAPPY COUPLES, NO HEIRS ALLOWED.

Her fairy tale bubble burst, menopause circling like a ghost as the clock struck midnight, and those fifteen years reappeared like a magic trick gone wrong. Unable to follow her beloved, she hung her head and turned back, riding alone into the darkness from whence she came.

But Ryan proved his true mettle. He grabbed the reins, heels digging at the horse's flanks, and sped like the wind until he reached her side, pleading with her to join him on the path for couples. Sofia was not convinced he truly wanted to make her his princess, for she could not give him the offspring he desired. Her love for Ryan was stronger than her own needs, desiring only his happiness.

But Ryan's love, equally powerful, moved him to sacrifice an heir rather than lose Sofia. In desperation, he offered a proposal on bended knee. "Sofia, I beseech you to give me sixty days to prove that my heart is true—prove there is no obstacle that our love cannot conquer."

Sofia, overwhelmed by his offering of pure love and sacrifice, cast aside her doubts. She fell into his arms, praying that fairy tales might indeed come true after all.

Together, they set out on a new path, the horses' hooves cutting a swath in the grass of an uncharted course, vowing to make a fresh start and test their love in another foreign land called London.

Most fairy tales have a finite, predictable ending, but this one is far from typical. The reader will need to be patient to learn the outcome, because this story will take some unexpected twists and turns as Ryan and I weave our own alternative happily-ever-after.

Chapter One

Sofia

"We will now board flight 2247 to London." I looked up from my laptop screen, saw the line forming for group one, and scrambled to gather my coat, possibly too-large personal item, and an overstuffed, wheeled, carry-on case. The holy trinity of over-packing.

"A night flight is the way to go, babe. It's far less crowded," Ryan had told me when I'd driven him to the San Francisco airport two weeks ago. A night flight meant attempting to sleep upright with the aid of a neck pillow that never failed to leave me walking off the plane like an extra in a zombie movie. So, I started to argue my point, when he offered a solution. "Don't worry, I'm booking you a business class seat. You're going to sleep like a baby."

Speaking as an independent, grown-up woman, I responded, "I can't let you do that." Who was I kidding? I would pawn my ex-husband's wedding ring for a business ticket. In the end, it had been easier to give in when I learned that he was booking the flight with his miles. I realized that dating a man whose job sent him flying around the globe, accumulating miles faster than he could spend them, turned out to have its unexpected perks. Guys should post that on their dating profiles. Photos with a hot sports car conveyed that the dude was having a midlife crisis. But a picture of his airline miles account might earn him a swipe right.

There was only one problem with this plan. Ryan had to be in London for work before I could leave San Francisco. It would have been nice to set off on this new adventure together—a bookend to match our encounter on my first trip to Barcelona. Then again, Ryan was a distraction I couldn't resist, so having two boyfriend-free weeks to prepare for my journey turned out to be a blessing in disguise. But now, as I strolled down the gangway with the other lucky Group-One passengers, separated from the economy class crush, excitement fluttered in my chest. In just twelve hours, we would be reunited.

"Welcome aboard!" The flight attendant's tone was so perky I wondered if she'd been recruited from a Disney theme park—the British version. Her words reverberated through my mind as I tried on the sounds in various regional accents; the Queen's English and possibly Cockney, but I wasn't certain. I had a habit of mimicking accents when visiting places outside California. The last time I was in London, I'd sounded like Mary freaking Poppins. Yes, it was that long ago.

"Can I show you to your seat?" Her eyes performed a quick reconnaissance mission, from my head to my sneakers. Was there a dress code for business class? Nostalgia—or perhaps superstition—had me choosing the same long, blue skirt and matching blouse I'd worn to Barcelona nearly two months ago. Thankfully, the bloodstain on my blouse had come out in the wash. Memories of Ryan nearly breaking my nose when he'd whipped open that bathroom door came rushing back as I passed the lavatory, and I had to suppress a laugh. When horribly embarrassing incidents happened, people always promised that someday you'd look back and laugh. But even then, the sheer absurdity of us literally running into each other had us both collapsing into hysterics.

Following her lead, I wheeled my suitcase toward the front of the plane, resisting the urge to squeal like a teenager when I glimpsed the seating area—palatial compared to my usual sardine-tin accommodations. I was practical—frugal with money—the kind of person who went to the grocery store armed with the sales flyer in her purse and created spreadsheets containing flight prices organized by dates and airlines. Naturally, I always flew economy, which left me envious of those with either money or a reckless disregard for credit card debt. But this time, I had no reason not to indulge in the guilty pleasure of traveling like someone who didn't clip coupons.

After stowing the carry-on in the overhead bin, I slid into my place at the window. Only it wasn't simply an upgraded seat. It was as if I had my own private suite, spacious enough to spread out and unload the contents of my aforementioned overstuffed bag. I'd come prepared for the long flight with fuzzy slippers, a change of clothes, a USB heating pad, a zip-lock bag of medications for any ailment, and this time, I included a first-aid kit—just in case disaster struck twice.

I tucked my book into the compartment and examined the complimentary amenities bag, tearing it open like a kid at Christmas, thrilled to find a toothbrush, mouthwash, lotion, and sleep mask. Was it odd that receiving free stuff on an airplane was now my marker of luxury? Maybe, but my bar was low. It just seemed cruel that I'd have to go back to coach seats after this trip. How had I ever survived being treated like cargo?

"Champagne?" Miss Perky materialized with a tray of fluted glasses—actual glass, not the flimsy, plastic, multipurpose cups that doubled as both beverage container and a toy for restless toddlers.

"Of course," I said, like it was routine for me to drink champagne on a Tuesday.

"I'll leave the menu on the console. You can give me your order when you've had a chance to look at it." She looked down at me with a broad smile, her posture impeccable, towering above me at about five foot ten. I had developed a talent for judging height, because when you were barely five-foot-four, it was necessary to make fast friends with people who had the altitude to reach that box on the top shelf at the market. She looked like she'd stepped off the cover of an airline magazine. Probably thirty-something, legs like a giraffe, narrow hips, and a waist a man could enclose in his hands. Her blonde hair was sculpted into a perfect bun that had clearly made a bet with gravity and won.

Since my usual seat resided in airplane Siberia, by the time the meal cart reached me, my options typically dwindled to one questionable entrée that bore a resemblance to cat food. Now I had an actual menu, with options that made my mouth water in anticipation.

My thoughts turned to the little things I could do to thank Ryan for the treat. When that became too stimulating to bear, I opened my *Guide to London* book and began skimming through the pages. It had been twenty years since my last visit—I remembered Big Ben, fish and chips, and a ridiculous number of roundabouts that had nearly claimed my life because I'd failed to notice the oncoming traffic. In my defense, everyone had been driving on the wrong side of the road.

Glancing around the cabin, passengers were settling in for the long-haul flight, some typing furiously on their laptops like they had to get in one more email before going off the grid. The man in the row next to me already had his sleep mask positioned over his eyes, his fingers tapping to music playing through headphones.

When the engine roared and the plane thundered down the runway, lifting like an overweight bird, I pressed my nose to the window. The city sparkled below through the crisp night air, with thousands of twinkling lights. Everything that had been home began disappearing as we pierced the clouds.

As we gained altitude, I felt the release—as if I were shedding my carefully orchestrated life and gliding toward the excitement of something new, however terrifying. I closed my eyes and began to imagine...

"Have you decided on your meal?" I jolted, eyelids flying open. Miss Perky had returned, still sporting that industrial-strength smile. I wondered if she was allowed to let it slip from her face. Was it a requirement listed in the hand-book for attendants in business class? Having flown econo-my, I knew that 'perky' wasn't in the rule book.

"Oh, yes." I reached for the menu. "I'll have the leek soup to start, the duck a l'orange for the main course, and... choco-late mousse for dessert."

"Good choices." She glanced at the book on my lap. "Is this your first trip to London?"

"Not exactly, but it's been twenty-five years, so I'm re-freshing my memory. Though I imagine Big Ben hasn't relo-cated since then?" I squinted at her name tag as she leaned in to adjust my stubborn footrest. "Elaine, right? You must know London well—assuming you're from there?"

She produced what I could only describe as a theatrical laugh—a string of enunciated "ha-ha-ha's," that sounded like a soprano warming up. "Believe it or not, I've seen little of the city despite all my flights there. Layovers are usually just a day, and I spend them unconscious in my hotel room."

"That doesn't sound fair. It seems like this job would be the perfect way to see the world and have some fun between flights."

"I have my moments." She followed the comment with an unmistakable Cheshire cat grin, which left zero doubt that she had plenty of entertainment, even if it might be limited to the four walls of her hotel room. "How long will you be in London?"

"A few weeks, I'm not sure yet." *Me—the ultimate plan-ner—winging it?* "It's sort of open-ended. I think I'll be in Europe for two months, traveling to various places." I hesitated, because how could I explain I was choosing to spend my severance package on this trip to Europe instead of job hunting—that I was hurling myself into a new life, a new relationship, without a clue about the direction this would lead?

She tilted her head with curiosity. "Business or pleasure?"

I barked out a laugh. "Definitely pleasure. I'm joining my boyfriend." The word still felt foreign on my tongue. After years spent in romantic exile, being part of a couple seemed surreal. "Ryan works in London part-time—his main office is in San Francisco, where we met. So, I'm basically following him across an ocean." I shook my head. This was coming out all wrong. "Not that I'm desperate or anything. I mean, I lost my job, but the timing worked out perfectly because Ryan suggested I come live with him. Well, travel together, since he moves around constantly. We're returning to Barcelona at some point because that city holds special meaning for us—" I cut myself off, cheeks burning. Apparently, my anxiety had me spiraling out of control, transforming me from an articulate professional into a babbling teenager who just discovered her first crush.

Her eyebrows shot up, while her forehead remained suspiciously smooth. "Ryan? That wouldn't be Ryan Hunter, would it?" Her voice climbed several octaves.

"Yes... do you know him?" Something cold twisted in my stomach.

"Know him? Um. Not personally, but he's one of our frequent flyers." The way she scrutinized me made every hair on my neck stand at attention. "He's your boyfriend?"

I nodded, shrinking into my luxurious seat like a deflating balloon.

This time, her smile looked painted on, her tone as artificially sweet as high-fructose corn syrup. "If you need anything else, just let me know." Watching her slim figure trail through the aisle of the cabin, I wondered if I was projecting or if the twist in my gut was justified. Anyone who knew Ryan might take one look at me and wonder, *Really? Him... and her?* I had questioned that myself when we first met. Despite his unwavering attention, I wasn't sure if I would ever get past the age difference when someone like Elaine was sizing me up.

When Ryan and I were alone, it was just too good to waste time worrying about how the world viewed me. In his eyes, I was perfect. He didn't notice the saggy bits or dimpled skin. According to my best friend, Madison, I had a figure most women would kill for and could pass for a forty-year-old on a good day. Most days were not that good, but I'd made peace with the crows feet and that little belly pooch that refused to disappear. After all, at one time, it was a baby bump, then a beach ball. I'd earned that lump.

Still, a thought niggled its way into my brain. There was something suspicious about Elaine's reaction to me. Call it women's intuition, but somehow, I just knew. Had she hoped to snag him for herself? I couldn't blame her; Ryan was the very definition of tall, dark, and handsome. His image should appear on a Pinterest board titled: Hot Guys with Dark, Curly Hair and Piercing Blue Eyes. How many flight attendants and restaurant hostesses had set their sights on him?

Elaine's smile had seemed to slip a fraction when she served me dinner. Even the restaurant-quality meal didn't improve my mood. I watched two movies, hoping the insecurities would retreat into a manageable size so that I could wrestle them back into the compartment of my brain meant to stay hidden. But even as I stretched out with my blanket and pillow, I knew I wouldn't be sleeping like a baby.

In the cabin's darkness, I stared up at the ambient blue light, my mind swirling with the events of the last few months. It seemed surreal that in a few hours, Ryan and I would be living together, testing our relationship over the next sixty days. Possibly, it was the fatigue crashing over me, or the fact the plane was bouncing on turbulent air, but the uneasy feeling in my stomach had me rifling through the pockets to find the airsick bag. This wasn't how I did things. I wasn't the woman who jetted off to Europe without a detailed itinerary, backup plans, and a PowerPoint presentation. There were far too many unknowns for my comfort. Since I didn't have my trusty poster paper, I counted them on the fingers of one hand.

1. How did I know we could live together for two months? We'd been with each other almost every day in Barcelona, but that wasn't the same as navigating cohabitation twenty-four seven.

2. What if he changed his mind, or we imploded spectacularly before our trial period ended?

3. Even if #1 went well and #2 didn't happen, what would I do with myself while Ryan was working? Become a professional tourist? Learn to make proper tea?

4. The most terrifying scenario: What if we made it through all sixty days, I fell even more in love with him—raising the stakes of this experiment exponentially higher—and it still ended?

Was I making a terrible mistake? God, I needed my poster paper to sort this all out, but it was a little late, since I was already hurtling through the heavens toward the unknown.

My gaze fixed on the black sky that lay beyond the porthole-sized window until the droning hum of the engines drowned out the nagging thoughts, and sometime later, I drifted into the relief of sleep.

By the time we landed, I was more than ready to leave the plane—and Elaine—behind. London, and more importantly Ryan, was waiting for me. I told myself that everything would be fine once we were together and I could wrap my arms around him, feel the solidity of him. His belief in us always anchored me when I became untethered.

He had left me with the instructions, "I'll have a driver meet you at the airport. Look for a sign that has your name. Go straight to the hotel suite and get some rest, just a couple of hours, or you won't be able to adjust to the time there. I'll be in meetings, so I'll catch you in the afternoon."

He could be so bossy. I hadn't known whether to thank him or salute. But now, as fatigue set in and I spotted my name held aloft by a stout man matching Ryan's description, I sagged with relief. I couldn't imagine lugging my suitcases to a train, then trying to find a taxi. What if I fell asleep on the train and all my stuff was stolen? The thought of losing my comfortable jeans—the ones that had taken months to break in—made me want to cry. And what if I lost that expensive lingerie I'd bought especially for this trip?

A lady racing to the exit nearly tripped me with her roller bag, which jolted me from my thoughts and stopped me from careening down the 'what-if' hill. When nervous, I played that damn 'what-if' tape in my head, but I was supposed to be confident and optimistic on this trip. At least that's what I'd promised Ryan.

"Miss Drake?" I heard him call out my name, the sign prominently displayed.

I maneuvered through the chaos of departing passengers, nearly colliding with a tiny, yapping escapee from a pet carrier while its frantic owner pleaded, "Muffin, be a good boy and come to Mama!" as the dog led her on a chase between travelers' legs.

"Please, it's just Sofia," I said when I finally reached him.

He tipped his cap. "Yes, ma'am. You can call me Charlie."

Unlike my solo arrival in Barcelona—navigating unfamiliar territory with nothing but Google Translate and a prayer—Charlie immediately put me at ease, commandeering my bags and leading me to a black limousine. I'd never been chauffeured anywhere fancier than a wedding, but settling into those buttery leather seats, I wondered why I'd spent decades treating myself as if I were on a permanent budget diet.

Despite the gray skies and chill in the air, my body buzzed with excitement when the car finally passed through the countryside and villages, then inched its way through traffic and into the pulsing city center. Though it was technically summer, the streets overflowed with people wrapped in sweaters and jackets, protected against the persistent drizzle that seemed to be London's signature accessory.

Interspersed among the tangle of buildings, towering green trees dotted the landscape near fountains and parks with dense foliage. In the distance, sleek, modern, high-rise buildings loomed high above medieval neighborhoods; the turrets barely visible, forming an odd juxtaposition against the skyline.

I was visualizing London in my mind, hazy memories from my younger days, when Charlie announced in a charming accent, "We're almost there, ma'am."

"Where are we now, exactly?"

"That would be Piccadilly Circus, ma'am."

"It's like a miniature Times Square." Well, if Times Square had been put through a shrinking machine and given a British makeover—one modest neon sign and queues where people stood waiting in orderly lines. Yet the number of people jamming the sidewalks, belching up from the metro stairs, and circling street performers rivaled the congestion in the Big Apple.

"Heart of the city. Covent Garden, Leicester Square, Regent Street—everything is at your disposal, if you fancy a little stroll." He held up a stubby finger and wagged it in each direction. "You'll have no trouble finding anything you want here."

Memories flooded back: twenty-four-year-old me bundled in a coat I'd bought on Oxford Street when my flimsy California jacket proved to be ridiculously insufficient for London weather—wandering until my feet screamed for mercy, wide-eyed and wonder-struck.

The guidebook had reminded me of all the places I longed to see again—to retrace my steps with a fresh perspective.

My head whipped from one side to the other as we inched through the clogged thoroughfare, taking in the iconic department stores, boutique shops, and pubs that sat between storefronts. Marquis displaying the latest Broadway shows blazed in bright lights, while the smaller productions appeared as modest signs atop dark, anonymous doorways.

"You can get in a fair bit of shopping here, and if you appreciate a good pint, there's no shortage of pubs nearby," he said, as if reading my mind. "And I know a guy who can get you right good seats at a theater show."

"Where's the best place to get fish and chips?"

He scoffed. "Most of the restaurants 'round here are for tourists. If you want real, tasty fish and chips, there's a little place over in Holborn I can show you. Mind you, it's not fancy, but Fryer's makes the best in town." He eyed me in the rear-view mirror as the car slowed at a traffic signal. "Mr.

Hunter uses my services quite a lot, so I expect I'll be seeing you again."

The limousine came to a stop on a curved driveway before what could only be described as a palace masquerading as a hotel. The facade stretched nearly a block in both directions, windows trimmed in stone, with a red carpet leading to gold-trimmed glass doors, where a doorman stood like a sentry in hotel livery.

Charlie sprinted around the car with surprising speed, opening the door for me. "Here we are, ma'am. Mind your step." He reached out a plump hand to steady me as I stepped onto the curb, and I couldn't help but notice the way his white shirt strained against the curve of his stomach, a loose button hanging at the broadest section around his middle.

My gaze lifted to sweep across the enormous hotel. "Wow." Charlie glanced at me, his eyes glinting with satisfaction. "Does Ryan usually stay here?"

"No, ma'am. I've only known him to book a hotel in the business district near his office, but he thought you might fancy a stay in the center, you being a tourist and all. He asked me where I might want to stay if I had a lovely woman visiting me." He chuckled then, his cheeks coloring. "I told him that if *me wife* didn't mind, I'd bring a nice lady to this fancy establishment."

"Well done, Charlie. It's a brilliant choice." I had to restrain myself from hugging him because, well, he was British. This wasn't Spain, where I had grown accustomed to the tradition of cheek-kissing everyone—their version of a handshake without personal space boundaries.

I thanked him again when he left me with the doorman, then rummaged in my purse and pulled out a
ten-pound note. He frowned and waved a hand in the
air. "Mr. Hunter takes care of everything, so don't you worry
yourself, ma'am."

"How long have you been working for him?"

"Oh, about three years, I suppose." He lifted the cap off
his head, running a hand over his thinning gray hair. "Mr.
Hunter is a right good man," he declared with authority, almost protectively.

"I have to agree with you." I smiled, and he gave me one
last nod before ambling back to the limo. Then I pivoted on
the tread of my sneakers and walked the red carpet, finally
shedding my nerves like an old coat that no longer fit.

Chapter Two

Ryan

"Charlie, did you receive the text I sent you with Sofia's flight information?" I placed my phone on the desk and switched on the speaker.

"Yes, sir. Don't you go worrying yourself. I have a sign with her name right here. Let me see now... Sofia Drake, right?"

"Right. And you'll be at Heathrow by two? Just before she's due to arrive?"

"Have I ever let you down, sir?"

I'd never worked with anyone as consistently dependable. "No, Charlie, you never have. It's just... I'm nervous. I want everything to go smoothly for her."

For a moment, there was silence on the line, but when he spoke, I swear I heard him chuckle, then cover it with a cough.

"I'll give her my special welcome tour of London and have her deposited at the hotel before you get there. Is that all, sir?"

"Yes, for now. Though I've told you before, you can drop the 'sir.'"

"Old dogs and all. I've been a chauffeur for the better part of my life, so you can't expect me to go changing now."

I let out a sigh, tilted back in my office chair, and looked out the window at fog-shrouded London. Sofia was used to the fog in San Francisco, but I wasn't sure she'd be happy with the weather here, especially after her month in sunny Barcelona. "I get it, Charlie, and thanks for taking care of Sofia. Seriously, though, my dad was the 'sir,' not me. But you do you, Charlie."

As I ended the call, I realized he wasn't unlike my father—old school. Except I liked Charlie a hell of a lot more than my dad. The last time I'd talked to him was during a phone call four years ago on my birthday. I was done with him.

"You disappoint me, son," he'd remarked in the same tone I'd heard for thirty-five years. "How do you expect to become successful in *banking*?" The way he'd said the word degraded my profession to the level of a street sweeper. There was no use in arguing the point, because in his eyes, investment banking didn't come close to running an entire company. I had been too pissed to have any kind of rational conversation. I'd hung up on him. He didn't call back.

Sometime in my twenties, I had finally registered that his approval was always just out of reach—like the brass ring I'd tried to grab when I rode the merry-go-round as a kid. I'd never managed to grasp that either.

So, screw it. I was done trying. And I *was* successful. He'd been wrong. But what did it matter? And why the hell was I thinking about him this morning?

Focus. The elevator bell chimed, echoing down the hall-way, which meant my private time was about to be invaded. I scrutinized the stack of files on my desk while footsteps echoed against the tiled floor, doors creaked open, and voic-es signaled that no one was wasting time with idle chit-chat. Hell, half the time, deals were being hammered out en route to the bathroom. Already, the chatter sounded frenetic. The pressure to hit the ground running was a daily occurrence, and I'd have to get my head in the game, but today I found myself resisting. My mind stubbornly refused to stop think-ing about Sofia and, for some strange reason, my family. Or rather, the remains of it.

There was some relief in knowing Sofia wouldn't have to meet my father. I would never subject her to his scrutiny. But my mother... If she could see me rolling my eyes right now... No doubt, she'd interfere, because that's what she al-ways did. Mothering at its best, in her opinion. "I only have your best interests in mind," she'd say. That was code for: *I know what's best for you, and I'm going to badger you until you see it my way.* She could badger all she wanted, but it wouldn't change my mind about Sofia.

At the sound of a text alert, I lunged for my phone, disappointed when George's name appeared on the screen. *I'm an idiot. Sofia is still in the air.*

The video conference still on for eight-fifteen?

Once I'd sent him a message to confirm, my thumb scrolled to the text Sofia had sent before she boarded the flight, reading it again for the tenth time.

> *Next stop, London. I plan to enjoy the flight, take full advantage of the champagne, and smother you in thank-you kisses for the biz class upgrade. The excitement has me nearly jumping out of my skin. They say home is where the heart is, and since you have my heart, I will indeed be coming home. XOXO*

That one text had made my whole morning. I'd had a stupid grin on my face up until I walked into the office and saw about a thousand emails waiting for me. Didn't matter, though. Staring at my computer screen, I tried to focus, but all I could think about was Sofia on that plane, somewhere over the Atlantic right now.

She seemed like home to me now, too. Still blew my mind how we'd found each other—pure luck or fate, whatever you wanted to call it. And in just a few hours, she'd be here. What Sofia was doing was huge: uprooting her whole life, flying halfway around the world to be with me to see if this relationship could work. She was braver than she gave herself credit for, that was for sure. I had seen her adventurous spirit the first time we met. It just took a vacation to Barcelona for her to realize it too.

I swiveled my chair toward the floor to ceiling windows overlooking London Bridge, watching the white clouds drift by. It wasn't often that I'd taken time to appreciate this city—all the history and stories packed into every corner—but I had a feeling I'd see it differently with Sofia here. I wanted her to be happy she'd made the jump, and I was going to do whatever it took to make these next two months count. There was no way in hell I was letting her go after sixty days.

"Did you get my email about your schedule today?"

I spun my seat around to see Cara's blond head popping through my half-opened door like a disembodied mannequin.

"I did, and you can reschedule my dinner meeting with the new tech client at seven," I said, glancing at my calendar on the screen. "And please don't schedule any evening meetings for the next week."

She pushed through the doorway and stopped in front of my desk, tiptoeing across the floor so her stiletto heels didn't make that clicking noise. During the two years she'd been assigned as assistant to James and me, I'd learned to be wary of her. She was the equivalent of a human megaphone, spreading gossip as fast as she could type, which was basically warp speed. So, when she looked at me with a coy, expectant expression, I prepared myself.

"Is it true? Global Allied Group's most eligible bachelor has snagged himself an American girlfriend?" She leaned in, placing her hands on the desktop, her blouse opened low enough to give me a view of her cleavage. I knew by now it was entirely intentional.

As much as I hated her knowing my business, I took advantage of the opportunity to set a boundary with her; one she'd implied she'd be happy to cross. "It's true, though I take issue with the 'most eligible bachelor' label. Sofia arrives today, so I'd like to keep my evenings free."

"Oh. I see." She straightened, brushing her hands against her too-tight skirt. "I thought it was just office gossip. I'll... um... see about rescheduling the new client."

"Wait," I said, and she pivoted in the doorway. "Hold up a minute until I talk to James. Maybe he can take Mr. Richardson to dinner. Is the prospectus complete?"

"I believe so, but I'll check."

After she left, I texted James and asked him to meet me in my office. We had just thirty minutes before our Zoom meeting with George. Luckily, he was a patient guy, because it hadn't been easy to negotiate the terms of his company's sale. I'd learned that conducting business in Dubai had its own set of complications. Omar. Jesus, what a nightmare—a hotshot Arabic magnate set on acquiring an American company. A wannabe king and a real pain in my ass.

"We may have a problem, Ryan." James bolted through the door a mere five seconds after I texted, a donut stuffed halfway in his mouth.

"Were you camped outside my office? I just texted you a second ago."

He stared at me blankly, then, with an "Oh" of recognition, he grabbed the donut with one hand and thrust the other in his pocket, reaching for his phone. "Didn't see it, mate. I was in the kitchen pouring a coffee."

"Take a seat," I said, "but I'm not in the mood for problems today. And grab a coaster for that coffee before it melts a ring on the wood."

James—arms too long for his thin frame and hands the size of dinner plates—might've seemed like a total goofball, except for his superpower with numbers. He reminded me of an adolescent still growing into his limbs after a growth spurt, except he was thirty-six and hadn't changed in the three years I'd worked with him. Sure, he knocked over coffee cups with the regularity of a one-man wrecking crew, but he kept spirits up, and some days, his humor was the only thing that saved me from short-circuiting when things went sideways.

"Oh, that's right! Sofia's arriving today. Bloody hell, you must be going batty. What's it been? Two weeks?"

"A very long two weeks, and after the time we spent together, withdrawal has been hell." She was my addiction. I needed to kiss her, to feel her body next to me. Heat rolled up my chest, familiar impulses rising, and I had to divert my attention to the lineup of meetings on my calendar to stop. "You, my friend, could have warned me that being hung up on a woman was *torture*."

"Ah, that totally fades when you've been with a bird for five years and have two kids killing the mood. I envy you. It's all shagging like bunnies in the first year. Take advantage, because after the babies, you'll be lucky if it happens once a fortnight." James leaned back in his chair and plopped his feet on my desk. I stared at his shoes. "Oh, sorry." His feet hit the floor with a thud.

"There won't be any babies. I thought I told you the last time I was in London. She can't have kids, so it will just be the two of us. It wasn't a difficult decision. I want to be with her, and these are the terms. But this will be a new experience for me—for us—living together."

When James started laughing, nearly falling out of his chair, I thought, this was the reason dudes didn't talk to each other about this stuff.

"What's so funny? Jerk. I don't see the humor here." I flicked a pencil at him.

"You're thirty-five and never *cohabitated* with a girl?" He made air quotes with his fingers. "You're in for some surprises. I can't remember when I've had a minute to myself. And just wait until she busts in on you in the loo. Say goodbye to freedom and privacy. This will be the true test—when you really get to know each other."

"I... um." No way was I going to confess these things had crossed my mind. Thoughts had been popping up at random, even in Zoom meetings, distracting me. *What if I screw things up? When life gets real, will she still be into me?* And of course my sadistic brain conjured the worst-case scenario: *What if she leaves me?* I honestly didn't know if I could survive that again. I took a gulp of my now cold coffee, pretending I had my shit together. "Don't put a negative spin on this. Everything is going to be fine, James. It has to be, because she's the *one*. Your gut tells you when it's the real deal, right? I mean, you're the one who's married."

"Yeah, mate. Trust your instincts." His face softened, his big eyes hitting me with a serious stare. "You're alright with the no kids thing?"

I shifted my gaze to a white ring on my desk, probably compliments of James. "To be honest, there's some lingering disappointment. She'd be a great mom, and, man, we'd have cute babies. But I'd never admit any of that to her. It would only make her feel guilty, or worse—she might unilaterally decide I'd be better off without her. We're good together, you know?"

He nodded. "Relax, then. Things have a way of working themselves out."

I went silent when Cara pushed the door open with her foot, carrying two cups of fresh coffee, which she deposited on the desk—no coasters.

"Your meeting with George is in five minutes," she announced, then sashayed her way out of the office, closing the door behind her.

I attempted to refocus, but it wasn't going to be easy keeping my mind on work today. Turning to James, I asked, "You mentioned a problem when you walked in?"

He nodded, his expression turning sober. "We need to discuss a certain situation before our meeting with George."

I leaned back in my chair, confident that whatever it was, James was probably blowing it out of proportion. "Okay." I breathed out the word with a sigh. "Give it to me."

"All the financial reports have been completed for the sale of George's company, and Omar's accountant has scrutinized the books."

"Is everything in order?"

James hesitated just enough to make me suspicious. "It appears to be, but there's a rumor circulating that George's primary IT distributor is going to pull out if Omar purchases the company."

"Rajit?" I pressed the heels of my hands to my eyes. "He can't. This sale must go through with all the contracts securely in place. Fuck. Does Omar know about this?"

"I don't think so; otherwise, he would have called here, bellowing his head off."

"James, please get George on the line."

I adjusted the position of my laptop so he could activate Zoom. Just as the video call connected, James swept his arm across the desk, knocking over his cup, sending milky brown liquid toward my lap like a river rushing downstream.

"James!" I growled and leaped out of my chair, my hand grabbing for the box of tissues.

"James? Ryan? What's going on there?" George's voice boomed through the speakers, but I couldn't stop to explain. I could only imagine his view: a blur of heads and flailing arms as we frantically mopped up the mess.

"Hold on a second, George. We'll be right with you," I called out.

"Ryan, I'm so sorry. I'm such a git."

"What's a 'git'?" George asked.

"Idiot," I replied and aimed my glare at James. Seeing the remorseful look on his face, I changed my tone. "No worries, James. It's all good."

"Now then, George," I said as we both settled into our seats and leaned toward the screen, "we had this meeting scheduled to give you a status update, but there's an issue that's just come to our attention, so I'm moving it to the top of the agenda." I gave James a nod.

"Have you spoken with Rajit lately?"

"About what? Can you be more specific?" George scratched his head, parting his thin gray hair. My stomach tensed. That was his tell whenever he got nervous.

"Rajit is reportedly sending out feelers in the industry, as if he's available to entertain the idea of contracting with another company to supply his distribution chain. We wondered if he's spoken with you about it?" James questioned.

George's eyes darted to the corner of the screen. "I've heard nothing about that. Why would he do such a thing? We've worked together for roughly ten years."

James shot me a look, his brows pinched together.

I turned my attention back to the screen and narrowed my eyes. "I hope your faith in him holds, because there would be serious implications for all of us if this deal proceeds and Omar discovers there's been deception. His lawyers would pounce on this."

George shifted in his chair. James side-eyed me, then jumped in. "All we're saying is this acquisition involves billions of dollars, and the sale is contingent upon full disclosure. Your company is worth a lot of money because you've established these contracts and cemented connections. So, I would suggest you get your bloody ducks in a row and make sure Rajit is on board."

"Of course. I'll get right on it," George sputtered. "Gentlemen, you have nothing to worry about. Now, can we move on to the timeline? I have some questions."

I nodded. After we'd addressed the remaining details and ended the call, I blew out a heavy breath. "He's lying. I've known George for years. He's basically a good guy and a fair businessman, but I'm aware of how desperately he needs this sale to go through."

James was beginning to sweat, fine beads forming a sheen on his forehead, and I suspected I looked about the same. "What are we going to do about it? If we let this go—"

"I know," I blurted out. "But for now, we don't know anything for sure."

"We could call Rajit, feel him out."

I flew out of my chair as if it had a hidden ejector button, then paced along the line of windows, weighing the options. As much as George needed to finalize the sale, so did I. My ability to navigate tricky negotiations and consistently close deals made me a valuable asset, and I needed to keep it that way.

"Let's not confront Rajit right now. It might spook him. Give George a chance to talk to him. Their existing relationship gives him a better shot at convincing Rajit to maintain the contract." Even as I made the decision, I realized the risk.

James stood, shoved his hands in his front pockets, and shook his head. "I hope you're right."

"Oh, there's something else I was going to mention. Can you cover for me tonight? The meeting with Mr. Richardson, I mean."

He elbowed me in the ribs with a goofy grin plastered on his face, one eye winking. "No worries, I'll handle the meeting. You go have fun. I'm sure you'll be *much* more relaxed tomorrow."

Despite his incredibly lame insinuation, I couldn't help breaking into a smile. No doubt I needed the relief tonight would bring. I was counting the minutes until she arrived.

Chapter Three

Sofia

"We've been expecting you, Ms. Drake. Henry will attend to your bags and show you to your room." The clerk slid my passport back to me across the marble counter. My eyes made a quick scan of the lobby—it conjured images of men in smoking jackets positioned in overstuffed, wingback chairs, puffing on their cigars. Walls paneled in mahogany, baroque drapes, polished banisters, and burgundy carpets lent a certain mystique to the place. An enormous arrangement of yellow and orange flowers provided the room's only splash of bright color.

Henry nodded, his fingers tipping the edge of his cap. I wondered if this was his first job, because he barely looked old enough to order a beer. The pubescent fuzz above his upper lip gave him away; a hopeful mustache that resembled a blond caterpillar. My son had to be older than this boy, and they couldn't have been more different. Ben—bearded, tattooed, and always wearing a leather jacket—strode through rooms full of strangers with confidence. Henry wore his hair clipped short, his shirt collar hanging loose on his long neck, and he walked with slumped shoulders. I'd lay odds he lived with his mother, while my boy had moved across the country to attend college when he turned eighteen. I'd tried to convince him to choose a local university and live at home. As a single mom, empty nesting felt like losing a limb. Both of us went through some growing pains that year.

Henry and I rode together to the top floor as he told me about the hotel's amenities. The five-star historic establishment had been built in the 1800s and had a staff that included a team of concierges, travel consultants, and even massage therapists in the spa. As I followed him down the carpeted hallway, the wheels of the luggage cart squeaking intermittently, he explained there were two restaurants, twenty-four-hour room service, and a bar that featured local musicians on weekends.

"Here we are, ma'am, room 802. If you need anything at all, just ring the desk." He hoisted my luggage onto the stands, handed me a set of keys, and stood at attention with his hands clasped behind his back. "Is there anything else I can do for you?"

"No, but thank you, Henry." I had the impulse to pat him on the head, but instead, I dug out my wallet and passed him a few unfamiliar coins.

After the door clicked shut behind him, I surveyed the suite and said to myself, "Not too shabby, Ryan." In stark contrast to the lobby, the suite was modern and bright. Floor-to-ceiling windows at the far end of the living room overlooked a bustling square, and a wet bar contained all the essentials, including a respectable wine selection that would satisfy Ryan. He was such a wine snob, but I had to admit he had good taste. But the bathroom? That was the crown jewel. I'd hit the bathtub jackpot: an antique clawfoot tub roughly the size of a small swimming pool. The only question now was whether room service delivered bubble bath, because this beauty deserved a proper christening.

Behind the wall-to-wall folding doors, I discovered the bedroom, which contained a four-poster king-size bed so high, I'd need a stepladder to get up there. I stood back a few feet, jumped and flung myself onto the bed, landing on my back, nearly swallowed by accent pillows. I stared at the embossed ceiling, seriously considering a nap. Unfamiliar sounds drifted from the streets below: the peculiar undulation of police sirens, the constant drone of engines, and horns beeping simultaneously in a misdirected symphony—fused together like a hypnotic sound machine. I nearly fell asleep, but that sweet tub was calling my name. Besides, *I'm in freaking London, for God's sake.*

I surveyed the mountain of suitcases—a taunting reminder of my habit to overpack, which may have bordered on a compulsive disorder. The unpacking might take days, but all I needed at the moment was some lingerie, toiletries, and that blue dress that Ryan loved. Finding them was the challenge.

When I hung my clothes next to his in the closet, the scent of him hit me—a mixture of oak and spice—followed by a rush of sensory memories, his pheromones giving me an instant high.

Although it was strange to see a wardrobe of his and hers again. I hadn't shared a closet with a man since I'd been married. Granted, having a closet all to myself happily fell in the plus column of the divorce. But counting on a relationship—becoming so accustomed to a man's presence that I couldn't sleep when he wasn't there—rallied my fears like ghosts coming back to haunt me. Before my mind could run with the what-ifs—*what if I lose this too*—I pulled the emergency brake. Sleep. I just needed some rest to reset my brain.

I padded into the bathroom and turned on the tap in the tub, pouring in a bottle of lavender-scented hotel shampoo, which would have to substitute for proper bath soap for now. The water erupted in mounds of bubbles.

My racing mind slowed as I slipped into the hot water, and my thoughts slid to Ryan. *What's he doing right now, and damn, why isn't he here in this nice bath?* I tried to imagine how he spent his days, picturing him in his office, the bands in his neck constricting when he was laser-focused on a task. God, he was so beautiful to look at, and I knew every nuance of his expressions, except I'd never seen his work persona—not really.

Our lives would be different now. Me with time on my hands, waiting for him to come home, him dealing with the pressures of his career. I should be ecstatic that I no longer had that pressure, but a kernel of uncertainty lodged in my stomach. I'd worked since I was a teenager, even through college, my entire identity wrapped up in my career as a psychologist.

Then I thought back to a conversation I'd had with my friend, Madison. She had no problem metaphorically slapping me upside the head. "*You should thank those adoles-*

cent executives responsible for downsizing you out of a job. If that hadn't happened, you wouldn't have gone to Barcelona, or met Ryan, and you certainly wouldn't be headed off to freaking London and who knows where on this adventure." I missed her already.

Thoughts began to slip away, the hypnotic sound of water dripping from the faucet echoing against the marble tile.... The world faded away, my body buoyed in silky warmth... until I melted into my dreams.

"Hi, Sleeping Beauty. Welcome home. I kinda like coming home and finding a naked woman in my bathroom."

Ryan. He nuzzled my nose with the tip of his before lowering his lips to mine, the sensation of his soft mouth devouring me... comforting, warm, easing me back to consciousness.

"Mm," I purred as my eyelids fluttered open to find him settling back in the tub, water heaving around me, his fine, naked body on display as he squeezed his legs around mine. Even though my eyes blurred from sleep and the circulated air of the plane, his beautiful face was still a gorgeous sight. I drank in the view of him—the way his muscles rippled with every movement, the smooth perfection of his skin, his full lips smiling at me. Most of all, I relished the way his blue eyes gleamed when he gazed at me, as if I was the center of his world. "I like waking up to find a naked man in my tub," I said, lacing my fingers with his.

I shivered under the water, now tepid, and Ryan reached for the faucet, steam billowing in the air. "You're too far away," I grumbled, stretching out my arms.

"Aren't you tired?"

I shot him a look. "I'm exhausted, but I haven't seen you in two weeks."

"Would you like me to do something to wake you up?"

He took hold of my foot, his thumbs massaging all along the bottom of my sole.

"I think that's relaxing me more than—" I bolted upright. His thumb pressed little circles into a point in the center of my arch. Heat rolled through my belly. "How did you do that?"

He shrugged, as if he'd innocently stumbled upon that move. I knew better than that. The water rolled and splashed at the shift of his body moving over mine. I wound my fingers in his thick, dark curls, bringing his face close.

"You seem happy to see me," I observed.

"Not at all." He shook his head, the tip of his nose grazing mine.

"Kiss me," I whispered, then moaned softly at the feel of his lips, the sweet taste of him.

"I've missed you," he breathed, cupping my breast in his palm. "Missed this..." Taking me in his mouth, my response came as a gasp—white, hot bolts of pleasure pulsing through me. Who needed words anyway? My brain short-circuited; my lips forgetting how to speak apart from whispering, "oh" and "yes" and "don't stop" while the water rolled and splashed around us, until finally, I screamed his name, the sound echoing against the tile walls. A roar rumbled from his chest—a perfect sound mingling with my voice—then the softest "I love you."

We lay pressed together as the tide receded, drifting in and out of sleep until the water turned cold again and my fingers looked like prunes. With our skin still damp, we tucked ourselves under the duvet, watching as the sun sank low, disappearing behind the cityscape and painting the sky in dusky rose streaks.

"Now that I'm here, should we talk about a plan?" I said, my voice raspy, though I had mixed feelings about returning to reality when I was floating on such a nice high.

"A plan?" His head lifted from my chest, his eyes searching mine.

"I mean, we didn't have much chance to talk about anything else except project Get Sofia to London."

"How about a plan to be spontaneous?" he suggested, his eyebrows bouncing. The mockery wasn't lost on me.

The tip of my finger traced circles at the center of his chest. "I can do spontaneous... except I still need a plan."

His laughter rumbled deep against my ear, his lips trailing kisses down my neck. "Okay, you win. I have to be at work for the next couple of weeks, and it looks like I'll need to go to Dubai to meet with clients. After that, how would you like to hit one of the dream places on your list?"

Pressing myself off his chest, I stared at him, trying to recall the lists we'd made of our top five travel destinations. "Where? Which one?"

"The Maldives."

"Seriously?" I felt the smile explode across my face. He'd listened and remembered. Was this normal? Possibly other couples did this all the time, but not in my experience. Ryan cared about making my dreams come true. The thought made my heart squeeze.

He tried to straighten his expression, but his eyes danced with the pleasure of surprising me. "Since you're the planner, why don't you take this one on? Two weeks. You and me on an island."

"Remember when I said you were spoiling me?"

He nodded, a smile threatening to twitch at the corners of his mouth.

"Yeah. It turns out I don't have a problem with that." He laughed, and I couldn't contain my excitement. Hurling my body on top of his, I heard a strangled growl as my knee barreled between his legs.

"Are you trying to sabotage our vacation?" He groaned, a pained, guttural sound.

"Oh God, I'm so sorry." Not to be insensitive, I added with a grin, "I can kiss it better."

He rolled to his side, his legs pressed together, half choking, half laughing. "Please don't make me laugh. It just hurts more. Give me a minute."

Curled around him, I rubbed circles on his back, cooing more apologies until his breathing returned to normal. When he insisted, "Let's give it a bit more time," I leapt out of bed, grabbed my laptop, then climbed in next to him.

"Oh, babe, look at this!" I gasped, clicking on idyllic images of islands in the Maldives. White sand beaches, palm trees, and crystal-clear waters. "It's going to be incredible."

He slid an arm around my waist, pulling me close. "I'm down with chasing our dreams if you are."

"Pinch me, because I'm still not sure this is real."

He shot me a look, his eyes flashing like a lion prepared to pounce. I squealed, and we ended up in an urgent tangle of arms and legs. Together again, all doubts and fears evaporated without a trace. I allowed myself to be engulfed in a bubble of happiness, aware that living in the moment meant appreciating the good ones, because they only ever lasted for just so long.

Chapter Four

Sofia

A sliver of light pierced through the parted floor-length curtains and took aim straight at my face. I threw an arm over my eyes while reaching for Ryan with the other. My hand skimmed over the cold sheets.

"Morning, babe." I blinked and saw him at the foot of the bed, fully dressed. He tugged the fabric of his tie through the knot he'd wrapped and straightened it to lie flat down the front of his shirt, then bent and kissed me on the cheek.

It took a moment to register my surroundings. Had it been two days ago that I left my home? The clock on the bedside table had numbers so small I had to squint to see it. "Seven?" I groaned and pulled the sheet over my face. "I don't do mornings, remember?"

"We're not on vacation yet. At least I'm not. You can go back to sleep for as long as you want."

I sighed at the injustice of it all, propped myself up on the pillow, and watched as he shrugged into a black suit jacket. "I do like the look of you in a suit, Mr. Hunter."

"If you get tickets to the ballet or theatre this week, I promise to wear it." He planted a quick kiss on my lips, then grabbed his briefcase and headed for the door. "Have fun today, babe. I'll leave Charlie's card here if you want to schedule him to take you on a tour of the city."

I'd barely called out "Bye," before the door closed behind him. The world suddenly seemed off kilter. Even the air in the room seemed to chill. In Barcelona, we'd spent almost every day together. I reminded myself that we'd discussed this before and Ryan had pointed out we were exiting the magical world of vacation and entering the real-life zone. I compared it to a trip to Disneyland. After a fifteen-hour day in the happiest place on earth, reality hit hard when you left and found yourself searching the vast parking lot for your car.

I reached for the guidebook, prepared to venture out and brave sightseeing alone—but only after I located some caffeine. As for the travel guide, it made my mind spin with far too many itinerary options. It made a lot more sense to set out on foot to discover the city, just as I'd done in Barcelona.

Several hours later, I was in the lobby and had pocketed the hotel's card before stepping through the revolving glass door. When you were directionally challenged, you learned tricks to keep track of where you were—snagging business cards from every location and photographing your parking space. It would be embarrassing if Ryan had to send out a search party to find me.

The tourist map inside the guidebook was useless. When I reached the end of the street, I rotated it in several directions in a feeble attempt to find my bearings.

Who was I kidding? Not only did I lack an internal compass, but reading a map was like algebra. I could look at it from a variety of angles, tell myself I was a smart, capable woman, but it still made no sense. Without taking the time to fold it properly, I stuffed it inside my bag and set out to let the city surprise me.

London splayed out before me in a clamor of noise and light—a steady stream of traffic and pedestrians rushing past me. I counted off the familiar sights, walking at a brisk pace as if I were on a mission. The boxy London black cabs still chased each other through the crowded streets, still driving on the wrong side of the road. And yet again, I failed to look to my right and nearly stepped off the curb into oncoming traffic.

I passed a shiny red telephone booth and flashed on a distant memory—feeding coins into the box, desperate to call home.

Stepping inside, I ran my fingers over the card reader, wondering how I'd traveled abroad for the first time without a cell phone (it had been useless for roaming in Europe), and no established credit. I'd had nothing but the cash in the money belt strapped to my body. Maybe youth made you fearless because you didn't know any better—didn't know the disastrous things that could happen. With age came wisdom gained from experiences that taught you to be cautious—maybe too cautious. Now, I was choosing to forget about being afraid. To live as if I didn't know any better.

With each block I walked, I couldn't help noticing that central London had become more international than I remembered. Aside from the hordes of foreign tourists, it seemed, in this part of town, the neighborhood's stores and restaurants reflected the diversity of cultures. Not that I didn't love a variety of ethnic foods, but I had to walk countless streets in search of an English breakfast experience, swept up in a sea of moving bodies like a living organism.

Finally, a tree-lined and cobblestoned alley caught my attention. Restaurants with bright awnings and terraces overflowing with greenery lined the block. The smell of sizzling sausages and pancakes drew me into a small cafe, the chimes on the door clanging as I swung it open. It was the sort of place that would be teeming with beer-drinking, sports-watching patrons by happy hour, but right now, the tables were full of diners. A server sped past me carrying a tray of plates, and my stomach responded with an audible grumble. She gestured with her chin, directing me to an empty table. "Have a seat over there, love. I'll be with you in a jiffy."

I settled onto the red vinyl cushion and scanned the menu for something resembling a proper English breakfast. What in the world was black pudding? And Scottish eggs? Were the chickens from Scotland? I chuckled to myself. The breakfast menu mostly read as I would expect: bacon, eggs, toast, and some kind of sausage. But the addition of baked beans to the mix was just weird. Scanning the lunch menu, my eyes caught sight of an item called *spotted dick*.

The server appeared at my side, and while she tucked a loose curl back into her bun, she asked, "Now, what will you have, love?" Her hands slid down her apron, retrieving a notebook and pen from a pocket. According to the badge pinned on her shirt, her name was *Maggie*.

I wanted to say, *Anything but the spotted dick.* "Um... the traditional English breakfast, please, Maggie." I pointed to the menu. "But hold the beans, if you don't mind."

"Got it. Anything else?"

"Oh, what is black pudding?"

"That would be blood sausage."

I made a face. "You can leave that off too, please."

She laughed. "Are ya sure you don't want the American breakfast?"

"I think I've pretty much narrowed it down to American, haven't I? But I will have the English breakfast tea and one of those delicious-looking buns."

The way her smile lit up her cheeks in rose-colored patches reminded me of my mother. Maggie was considerably younger but just as warm. I made a mental note to call home and let her know I'd arrived safely.

"I'll have this ready for ya in a jiffy."

'Jiffy' seemed to be the word of the day here, and I hoped it would arrive in a 'jiffy,' because I was salivating from the scent of bacon at the next table.

Amazingly, it did. I stared out the windows, fogged with moisture, while I forked bites of the American breakfast and watched the steady stream of people passing by. Mothers strolled with reticent teenage daughters trailing several feet behind, their arms loaded with department store bags, and couples pushed oversized prams, babies protesting in loud cries. But mostly I observed tourists, distinguished by their meandering gait, a tourist map clutched in their hands, and eyes that glazed with exhaustion. I sympathized, because that would be me by the end of the day—minus the map.

After I'd cleaned my plate, I eyed the bun. *Come to mama!* One bite, and I was in heaven. It was as delicious as it looked, fresh out of the oven, warm and sweet with little bits of fruit. I tore off small bites and let the flavor linger on my tongue, taking a sip of tea between each one as I committed my first day in London to memory.

Despite the jet lag and an impulse to return to the hotel for a nap, I trudged out again into the streets of London, my jacket zipped for protection against the elements. Dark clouds passed overhead, and the wind whipped through my hair. I spent a few hours ducking in and out of shops for cover when the clouds burst open with rain showers. Yet most people—probably locals—weren't even carrying umbrellas, so I wasn't about to act like a tourist afraid of getting a little wet.

I strolled past small boutiques with historic facades wedged between large department stores, and gazed through the windows of chocolatiers, getting a sugar rush from the smell alone.

But when I wandered into Leicester Square, I felt a pang of disappointment as reality crashed into memory. *Had there always been this many tacky souvenir shops?* It was like trying to swim upstream as I pushed through the crowds toward the small park in the center, dodging tourists wielding selfie sticks like weapons. The grass I remembered as lush had been trampled into a balding patch of dirt with a few stubborn weeds still trying to make a go of it. Only the statues seemed unchanged, but then, stone tended to weather time pretty well.

I sank onto a bench canopied by lacy tree branches, while the wind rustled the leaves, scattering green castaways like confetti. My mind drifted back twenty-five years. *Twenty-five?* How was that possible? Nostalgia settled over me, and random memories flickered through my head like the jittery film of an old home movie. Like when my best friend, Anne, and I splurged on cheap theater tickets to see A *Midsummer Night's Dream*, then climbed what felt like a million stairs to seats so high the ballet dancers looked like tiny, graceful dots.

It was hard to believe so many years had slipped by since that trip because I'd always planned to come back, but life sent me in another direction. Marriage, career, and motherhood had a way of filing away dreams like important papers you swear you'll need someday but never actually dig out of the drawer. Now, here I was at forty-nine, trying to pick up where my twenty-four-year-old self had left off. I was trying my best to channel her, yet the whole "living adventurously" thing felt a bit blurry around the edges, like looking through a camera that couldn't quite find its focus.

Would I change anything if I could? Honestly, I didn't think so. I'd been lucky enough to raise a kid, and now, somehow, I'd gotten a second chance at love. But thinking about Ryan and all the choices ahead of us made me queasy. Would he look back someday and wonder if he'd gone in the right direction by giving up on having a family? I rubbed my face, refusing to fall down that rabbit hole, then pushed off the bench. *I will remain optimistic.*

Before I left the park, my cell rang from one of the pockets in my bag. When I managed to locate it and saw my son's photo appear, my heart squeezed. I was even more surprised when the video call connected and his face filled the screen. "Ben!"

"Mom?"

"Yes. I can hear you. Can you hear me?" I asked, because it still seemed weird that we could be three thousand miles apart, yet talking on the phone as if we were next-door neighbors.

"Yes, *Mother.*" He let out an exasperated sigh. "Why haven't you checked in? You said you'd call when you got to London."

"Hi Sofia." Callie's head replaced Ben's on the screen. "Don't let him get to you. He's such a worrywart."

Ben pressed his cheek against Callie's and shot me a look. "I wonder where I got that from?"

I walked towards a group of trees where it was quieter, away from the main walkway. "Sorry about that, but if it helps, I'm really trying to change that trait."

"I'm not sure if that's a good thing. I liked it better when you worried because then I knew you were taking precautions. You're tripping around the world with that guy, and

I don't even know his number in case I can't reach you." Callie whispered something in his ear. "Ryan, okay? Does that help?" He directed that last part to Callie.

Keeping my voice calm, I said, "I'll text you his contact as soon as this call ends, and make sure he has your number. You're absolutely right and I'm glad you're checking in. I'm going to be fine, but just in case, I have a card in my wallet that lists my emergency numbers."

The edge in his voice was gone when he said, "You know I fully support what you're doing—I mean, traveling—but I don't know this guy."

"But I know him very well, and you're just going to have to trust my judgement. It will help when you meet him, but you're in New York, so logistically, it's complicated."

Callie kissed his cheek, her eyes soft with love. I was grateful that he had such a wonderful partner. "Ben will be fine. You do you and have fun. This is an opportunity of a lifetime for you."

"Keep in touch, Mom. Let us know how you're doing."

I smiled at him because despite his irritation, it was sweet of him to be concerned about me. "Of course, and I'll send photos too."

After we ended the call, I forwarded Ryan's contact. They were going to have to meet at some point for Ben to realize that Ryan was one of the good guys.

"Can I help you find anything?" said a young woman in her twenties, with pin-straight brown hair that hung down her back like a curtain.

I was staring at the stacks of new releases. I'd found this bookstore while strolling down a quaint street in Notting Hill. Outside the storefront, baskets of flowers hung on each side of the door, bursting with color, and a wooden plank swayed on rusted chains bearing the name *Green's Books*. As soon as I'd stepped inside, I felt like I'd discovered someone's secret hideaway. The place had that perfect bookstore smell—paper and ink mixed with something spicy. High ceilings made it feel almost grand, and in one corner, a few people sat reading in wingback chairs around a fireplace, looking like they'd stepped out of a cozy British movie.

"I'm not sure," I replied, then paused. "Do you have any fictional stories based on, say... sixteenth-century England? I remember reading about kings and lords when I was young. Last time I was in London, those stories inspired me to visit real historical places, like the Tower of London."

Her face brightened. "Oh yes, historical fiction. That was a favorite of mine too when I was at uni. Let me show you a section in the back."

I followed her to a corner where a wooden ladder rested against shelves loaded with books stacked almost to the ceiling. She climbed a few rungs and retrieved several dusty paperbacks, then flashed me the covers.

"This one is the story of Anne Boleyn. Do you know it?"

"I have a vague recollection. Wasn't she imprisoned in the Tower?"

"Yes, and beheaded by King Henry VIII. But she stood out as a beacon of determination, personifying a strong, passionate woman. Unfortunately, in her time, even being queen couldn't save her from ruthless Henry."

She chose several versions of the story of Anne and passed them to me. In the end, I picked the one with the most striking cover; the beautiful queen in a seductive pose—deliberately scandalous considering the era.

"You seem to know every inch of this store. How long have you been working here?"

She climbed carefully down the ladder and tucked a strand of hair behind her ear. "I've grown up in this bookshop. My parents own it. Well, until my mum passed away. Now it's just my dad and me keeping this place going."

"My condolences about your mom. I'm sure you miss her. I do love your shop; you've created a lovely ambiance," I said, letting my gaze travel to the fireplace in the corner; the glow of the gas logs bathing the alcove in a cozy hue. "It has more warmth than the big, commercial bookstores. I would imagine you've developed a loyal clientele?"

She nodded, and following my gaze, gestured to the group seated in overstuffed chairs in a semicircle by the fireplace. "Josie over there comes every day just to have some company and a spot of tea. She lives alone, and

I don't think she has many friends. John lost his wife last year. Cancer, it was. We delivered him his supper for a week, plus meals he could keep in the freezer, because everyone knows John hadn't as much as boiled water in thirty years." She shook her head, but it wasn't in disapproval—her smile conveyed a gentle understanding that he was from a different era. "Since then, he's been a regular. Then, one day, he brought his mate, Arthur, with him. Although mates might be overstating their relationship. I hear them having a row every now and again. Arthur's wife left him six months ago. Rumor has it she ran off with a burly Scottish fella. Poor Arthur, he's been so melancholy. Twenty years they were married."

I looked at each one as she discreetly pointed—three unlikely friends sitting in companionable silence. A lonely hearts club of sorts. *Isolation*, I thought, *is an insidious destroyer of lives.* These three had found refuge here.

"May I ask your name?" I said.

"Of course. It's Victoria."

"Pleased to meet you. I'm Sofia. I think it's wonderful that you've created a space where people feel welcome to come and hang out. Everyone needs companionship."

Her face beamed. "Let me introduce you to my dad," she said, as a middle-aged man emerged from a door tucked in the rear of the shop, his arms straining with the weight of a large box.

"The new shipment finally arrived from the publisher." He dropped the box onto the table with a thud.

"Dad, I want you to meet Sofia. She's interested in English history. Sofia, this is Oliver."

I wasn't certain, but his eyes seemed to widen when his gaze landed on me. A tall man with broad shoulders, his features struck me as strong and rugged. His salt and pepper hair had that bed-head vibe—rumpled and still flat on one side.

"Lovely to meet you, Sofia." He held out his hand, grasping mine in a delicate handshake. "Are you visiting London?"

"You mean I don't look like a local?" My attempt at humor fell flat. I regrouped. "This is actually my first day. Your shop has been my favorite discovery."

"I'm so glad you like it."

Victoria poked an elbow into his ribs. He glanced at her, his brows knitted together. She responded by darting her eyes to the kettle on a table.

"Oh, right," he sputtered, "would you like a cuppa tea?"

I followed his glance to a round table covered with a white lace cloth, tins of tea bags and biscuits neatly arranged on the surface. "That's very nice of you, thanks, but no. I've got to get back to the hotel, but I would like to look around a bit more before I go." Honestly, I didn't get the concept of afternoon tea. In Barcelona, the afternoon drink of choice was beer or sangria on a terrace.

He nodded. "Very well, I'll leave you to it." British politeness—I wasn't sure I'd get used to it.

I wandered the aisles, browsing the new releases, and a stack of leather-bound journals caught my attention. Running my finger down a blank page, I flew back in time. A sullen teenager, splayed out on the bed, scribbling diary entries about my latest heartbreak. Composing melancholy poems, of course, because I had a heavy case of adolescent angst.

Then, during my marriage, I had begun writing again. It was both documentation of more angst and a cathartic release of all the feelings I couldn't share with my husband. The words spanned several journals. Later, when I opened those journals—the Pandora's box—it was slightly disturbing to review the unhappiness I'd endured.

Maybe it was time to start a fresh journal, chronicling my new beginning, my new travels, my new life.

I selected one in smooth brown leather and took my purchases to the counter, where Oliver rang up the items. He placed them neatly in a forest green paper bag, which matched the store's color theme. "I hope you'll come back and see us again. You're welcome to browse whenever you like. Are you staying long?"

I hesitated. "I'm not sure, but certainly for a few weeks, so I'll be back when I finish this book."

As I turned to leave, I checked my phone and found Ryan had texted. *He's already back at the hotel?* I looked at my watch and realized it was five o'clock. The day had flown by. Shooting off a quick text response, I darted to a taxi stand and handed the hotel address to the driver.

"Only one bag? You're not exactly a shopping queen, are you?"

I pulled out my treasures and laid them on the dining table.

"Books?" He slid in behind me, one arm wrapped around my waist, the other reaching to examine my purchases.

"I thought I would immerse myself in the spirit of the Tudor Era of England while I'm here. And..." I fanned the empty pages in front of him. "I plan to keep track of my journey. By the way, when did the clock start ticking on our contract?"

"Good point." A hot shiver ran through me, his lips nibbling down the curve of my neck. "Let's say it was yesterday, the day of your arrival."

"Got a pen?" I asked.

He reached into his jacket pocket, then slipped the pen between my fingers. Balancing the journal in one hand, I wrote, *Day One. Got shagged in the bathtub by my handsome lover.*

"One day and you're already speaking like a local. I like the sound of that."

I swiveled to face him, locking my arms around his neck. "Speaking of..."

"Shagging?"

"No, silly. I was thinking about being a local. Charlie told me where to get an authentic fish and chips meal. You up for a cafeteria-style dining experience?"

"Sure. Let me change into jeans."

I positioned myself on the bed to take in the show, watching him undress with the kind of pleasure one experiences when staring at a beautiful sunset. Propped on one elbow, I asked, "How was your day at work?"

"Not as enjoyable as your day."

"Problems?"

He slipped on his sneakers, his footsteps heavy as he moved to the wet bar. "Wine?" he offered, uncorking a bottle of white. I nodded, noticing the muscles along his jawline becoming tense. He joined me, handing me a glass while he perched on the edge of the bed.

"Nothing I can't fix." The slump of his shoulders made me think otherwise. I reached a hand to stroke his back. The tendons below his neck were like iron bands.

"You want to talk about it?"

He swirled the wine with a twist of his wrist while fixing his gaze on the glass.

"It's just... There's a multi-billion-dollar deal resting on the portfolio I'm putting together for the company I'm representing. The owner is an old friend, and George is counting on me to make this sale happen." When he paused, tiny lines creased between his brows. "George's competitor, Omar, is a very powerful businessman, maybe the richest in Dubai. He's proposing a buyout, and I've been forewarned that he's not easily satisfied. I expect this deal will be a pain in the ass to complete."

"That sounds like a tremendous amount of pressure." If this were the reality of Ryan's job, I couldn't imagine coping with that stress on a daily basis.

Easing himself onto the bed, his expression relaxed. "I'm glad you're here." His gaze slid sideways at me, and I leaned in to kiss his forehead.

"Me too. Maybe some fish 'n chips will help?"

He shot me a look I understood all too well.

"Fine. I think some shagging is in order later," I said in my best British accent.

Finally, the lines on his forehead disappeared. He grinned. "Like I said, I'm so glad you're here."

I tried hard to remember his words over the next week, as the high I felt at my arrival in London was slowly replaced by... homesickness? Anxiety? I couldn't understand why my emotions were flopping up and down faster than a roller coaster.

Worst of all, I felt selfish for wanting more time with Ryan. Sure, I visited all the sights in my guidebook and kept myself busy. But each evening, when Ryan came home dead tired, I slightly wanted to poke him like a little kid who had been waiting all day for someone to play with.

Then it hit me. This wasn't like our time in Barcelona, when we were equals—both of us having nothing but time for each other. In London, I was folding myself into and around his life.

Ryan had been looking wearier than I'd ever seen him, barely able to keep his eyes from closing while we lay in bed watching movies at night. Despite what he'd said, I began to wonder if my being here was creating an even bigger burden on him.

Chapter Five

Ryan

"Do you think we'll have time to take a drive in the countryside before we leave?" she asked, stepping out of the shower and into the white hotel bathrobe, then knotting a towel around her wet hair. Steam instantly fogged the bathroom mirror. After I toweled it off, our eyes met in the reflection, the buzz of my electric razor echoing off the tile walls.

I paused, feeling a slight pulse of irritation rise in my chest like a pressure valve edging up a notch. Didn't she realize I couldn't talk and shave at the same time? "That sounds like a great idea, but I'm not sure if I'll have time before our flight."

"Oh. Sure, that's fine," she said, but between her clipped tone and the frown on her face, she didn't seem like it was fine. "Can you move over so I can get my brush?" Our morning routine resembled a badly choreographed dance in this cramped space, and I flashed back to James' warning.

I reminded myself that it had only been a week and we were still getting used to *cohabitating*, finding our rhythm. Granted, we hadn't seen very much of each other, since I had a backlog of paperwork to get through, but we'd gone out every evening for dinner at least. Things were good. So why was there tension this morning? For my part, I guess I needed some privacy. Not like a whole evening, but I wasn't used to sharing a bathroom. Yeah, well, I couldn't just blurt out, *could you get out of here so I can shave in peace?* No, this would require some diplomacy.

"Just a second, I have to be near the plug. My razor is out of charge."

"Unfortunately, there's only one plug near the mirror." Her clipped tone told me she wasn't feeling this situation either.

I didn't answer her this time and ignored her fingernails tapping against the top of the counter. What was the point? There was a spot I'd missed on my chin, so I ran the razor over my face again without rushing. She could take all morning to get herself ready, but I had to go to work. When I'd finished, I slid sideways, and she let out a huff as she grabbed her brush from the drawer.

"What's wrong?" I finally asked, then realized it was a stupid question, because I knew how she'd answer.

"Nothing."

"Okay." I had to stop myself from rolling my eyes. "Let me back up and rephrase. You seem annoyed this morning. What's bothering you?"

"I could ask you the same question."

I put down the razor. We were face to face, staring each other down, both of us waiting for the other to come clean. "Okay, fine," I said. "I have a lot on my mind, and I might be a little impatient this morning. I'm sorry. It's not your fault. Now, it's your turn. What's wrong?"

She plopped down onto the toilet lid with a heavy sigh. "There's no point in laying my stuff on you when your mind is preoccupied. It's fine. I'm fine."

Oh, boy. I knew better than to accept that answer. I squatted down by the toilet so we'd be at eye level with each other. "Tell me. I really want to know what's bothering you." I could sense her frustration building; it was obvious from the way her brows drew together.

"That's the problem. I don't really know. It feels like there's a ten-car pileup inside my brain, but I'm not sure what caused the accident."

I could have asked her if it was my fault, because wasn't it always the man's fault? But did I really want to go down that slope? Instead, I waited for her to sort out her feelings. After all, she was the psychologist. I was just a guy who was good with numbers and making deals. Not that I wasn't concerned, but this was a little outside my wheelhouse. I also knew I'd be late for work, so even though I'd learned it was best to just listen when she was upset, I went straight for the fix.

"Besides the fact that I'm in your way and the bathroom is cramped, can you pull a few cars out and describe them? Can I do anything to help?"

She opened her mouth to speak but stopped. I waited again. And waited.

"Look, this isn't about you; it's all me. I'm untethered. This isn't like our vacation, and I know that you have a job to do. But I've always worked—have been focused on my job too.

I can keep myself busy for a while here playing the tourist, but I'm afraid I'm becoming too needy. Afraid that I'm in your way and it would be easier for you to do your job if you didn't have to worry about spending time with me."

"Whoa. Where is this coming from? You know I'm glad to have you here."

She pushed off the toilet lid, barreling past me to find the brush. Silent for a moment, she ran the bristles through her hair, wearing that look on her face when she was searching for words. At least Sofia wasn't impulsive when it came to revealing what was on her mind. I'd experienced women who blurted out their feelings, no filter. Explosions usually followed.

"I don't know, maybe I'm being too sensitive. It's just... I've been disoriented, missing my friends, especially Madison, and my son is so far away. Not to mention that this stupid menopause phase is fucking with my hormones. I thought having PMS was bad, but at least that was only once a month. Menopause is my little visitor all the damn time."

She growled a sound of frustration, and I ran through the list of possible fixes in my mind. Nothing. If this was hormonally induced, there wasn't much I could do, and anything I said might make it worse. It was like walking through a minefield, not knowing where to step.

"What if I'm not cut out to be a nomad, a world traveler, an adventure seeker? Am I losing precious time when I should be looking for my next job?"

"C'mere." I wrapped her in my arms, my hand stroking circles on her back. Holding her seemed like the best, if not the only, solution, and I was right. She folded into me and snuggled her face against my chest. "You're going to be fine. This is just an adjustment period, and you'll get your bearings. As for a job, taking a break won't hurt your career. It will give you time to reassess, and who knows, you might discover a direction you never considered before."

I pulled back, tipping her chin with my finger. "Look at me." She slowly raised her face until our eyes met. "This is what you're going to do—you're going to call Madison today and have a heart-to-heart with your bestie. I know she always grounds you more than I ever could. Then get on a video call with your son and his girlfriend. I'm sure Ben and Callie would love to hear what you've been up to in London."

She nodded, raising her eyes to meet mine. This wasn't how things were supposed to go. She'd uprooted her whole life to be with me, but would she turn and run again? Self-ishly, I needed her to stay, but she was right; we weren't spending as much time together—not the way we did on vacation. And with the pressure at work, I was dead by the evening. So, yeah, I hadn't been paying enough attention to her needs, and this was the result. Her emotional state shouldn't come as a surprise.

"I have an idea," I blurted, as a fix popped into my head. "Why don't you meet me at my office today for lunch? You can see where I work and meet my colleagues. I speak from experience when I say that James is very good at cheering people up."

"Okay. I like that plan." Her lips quivered into a smile. "You're pretty good at this. Thank you for listening to me ramble."

I planted a kiss on her forehead. "Hey, it's like I said before; good days, bad days—it doesn't matter, because I'm always going to be in your corner. Even when you're grouchy."

"Yeah, well, I'm sorry about that. I'll be in your corner too, but now I'm making you late for work." She grabbed my ass, then gave it a slap, which made me consider calling in to postpone my meeting. "Get going. I'll be fine."

The corners of her mouth ticked up, and my shoulders dropped a few inches in relief. While her fingers worked the buttons on my shirt all the way to my neck, I pressed my lips against hers. God, she made me want to stay in this room all day with her. I told myself that we'd find our routine, some balance in our lives. She broke away first, admonished me with a look, and said, "Don't start something you can't finish. Out the door with you."

"I could—"

"No." Her mouth tightened into a line, but her cheeks flushed red, and I detected that crinkle at the corners of her eyes when she was trying to keep a straight face.

"Fine. I'll see you around noon. Give Charlie a call for a ride."

At least I'd made her smile. Before I stepped out the door, I kissed her goodbye, and my satisfaction came when she melted into me. For the moment, she was staying; she was okay.

When I saw Sofia talking to my assistant at the desk outside my office, I couldn't believe the transformation. Her face lit up with a smile, no trace of the worried look she'd had this morning. And damn, she looked drop-dead gorgeous, wearing a dress that clung to all her curves—my favorite parts. Seeing her happy made me realize I should have invited her to visit me sooner, but my life had always been divided into compartments: work in one box and girlfriends in the other. My job demanded intense focus, and I could already tell Sofia was going to derail me in an instant.

Cara popped open my door, saying, "I believe you've been expecting this visitor." I stood and reached Sofia before she was halfway across the room, whispering low in her ear as I pulled her into an embrace. "You look so damn fuckable."

She smiled as if that was exactly her intention. "Maybe I can oblige, but first, show me around."

I glanced over her shoulder to see that Cara was backing out of the office, closing the door behind her. It was good she'd seen us together, I thought. "Come look at the view."

Sofia followed me to the window and blew out a breath through pursed lips that vaguely resembled a whistle. "Wow. You can see the Tower of London from here. I don't think I could get any work done in this office. I'd just stare out the window at the city all day."

"Believe me, I would, except that I never have time. Come with me. I'll take you to meet James."

We linked our fingers as I led her down a hallway and found him typing at his computer, deep in concentration. "Hey, mate."

Without looking up, he said, "Could you fuck off for a minute 'til I finish this email?"

Sofia giggled, and his head shot up. "Oh shite. Sorry, I didn't know you had someone with you." He popped out of his chair so fast, it shot back, ramming into a shelf and upending a stack of books that tumbled to the carpet—so on brand for James. He ignored the clatter as he strode across the office and reached to shake her hand, assuming she was a client.

"Relax, James. This is Sofia. I just wanted to introduce you two."

"It's good to meet you," she said, accepting his hand-shake.

"*The* Sofia?" James, never subtle, ran his gaze over Sofia from top to bottom, then back up again to her face. "Ryan mentioned you were pretty, but I gotta say, you are way above his pay grade."

"You may have a point, but stop checking out my girl." I flicked him on the head.

James turned to Sofia. "See what I have to put up with? This bloke can be so abusive sometimes."

The sound of her laughter made me glad I had asked her to come. This was just the beginning of blending our lives outside our private world. And now, during the time we were apart, she could picture where I was stuck all day.

"Ryan mentioned you're great at cheering people up, and I see why."

"We should go out some night," James suggested. "A double date. Me and the wife can ditch the kids—I mean find a babysitter—and go out on the town. It would be good craic!"

Before Sofia could ask, I said, "He means it would be fun."

"Huh. There are so many gems in the language that didn't make it across the pond to America."

"That sounds good, James," I answered, shooting a glance at Sofia. "Let's see if we can find a free night before we leave on vacation."

"Mate, weren't you just on holiday?"

I shrugged. "My schedule is open after we close the deal with George, and besides, this one is for Sofia. She's dreamed of going to the Maldives."

"You ruddy bastard. Don't you dare mention that to my wife or I'll never hear the end of it."

"Oh, now I'll be sure to tell her all about our vacation."

He pretended to scratch the top of his head—with his middle finger. "Real mature, James." I headed towards the door with Sofia. "I'll leave you to it. Hold down the fort while I take Sofia to lunch."

"Righto, mate." Then he mumbled something as we left his office that sounded like, "And I'll be sure to leave tacks on your chair."

With my hand resting on the small of her back, we made our way to the elevator. I thanked the office gods when I saw it was empty, which gave me the chance to pin Sofia's back to the metal wall and kiss her as the elevator descended ten floors. She responded by grabbing my ass again, pressing herself against me—moaning into our kiss. When the elevator pinged and came to a stop, we broke apart just in time to see two dudes in suits as the doors opened.

"You're so bad," she whispered.

"I'm just getting warmed up."

She cocked an eyebrow at me in mock protest, but she'd already proven how much she enjoyed those spontaneous moments. Sex with her was mind-blowing—the best in my life—and I needed to up my game to keep it going. I already had a few ideas for later.

The restaurant was within walking distance of my office, but I picked it because we could have a view of the river from our table. She chose the fish and chips, and I ordered a steak with fries. As my body relaxed, feeling the warmth of the sun on my face, I realized I needed this as much as she did. Just getting out of the office for lunch was a luxury. More often than not, this job was intense, and I wondered how long I could keep this up while being in a committed relationship. In the past, I never took relationships that seriously, and since my job had me bouncing around the globe, potential girlfriends lost patience pretty quickly. I'd have to work out this balancing act because this time I was taking it very seriously.

"You look like your mind is a million miles away," she said.

We sat at a table with a view, just staring out at the river. The sun was shining, making the water sparkle. "I'm just taking it all in. I don't often stop to appreciate the beautiful sights in this city, and I know I've said it before, but I'm glad you're here with me." Her hand reached across the table, lacing her fingers in mine. The sun reflected in her eyes, revealing the shades of gold and green in her irises. The way she looked at me with so much love... God, it wrecked me. It was weird that I could read all her emotions just by looking into those eyes. I'd never been so tuned in to another human like this. But then, she read me better than anyone else, too. "Please give me a little time to get a grip on my work/life balance. I promise I'll improve."

"I'm sorry for freaking you out this morning. It's my is-sue, not yours, but I really appreciate spending time with you today." She paused, and I could tell her mind was churning, picking out those cars and examining them one by one.

Practically all my life, I've been focused on my work. Be-sides motherhood, my identity has been wrapped up in being a psychologist. When I lost my job, it opened up possibilities, but it feels odd to be in limbo. I've always known exactly where my career was headed, and now?" She huffed out a laugh. "Here I am in London, living out my dream to travel the world, and I'm complaining. I really am being a git."

"A *git*? How did you manage to pick up the lingo so fast?"

She shrugged it off. "It's a thing I do when I travel."

I leaned forward in my seat and scooped her into my arms, burying my nose in her hair and breathing in the fa-miliar lavender scent. "Just live in the moment, remember? You had the carpe diem thing down in Barcelona, and you can do it again. The answers about the future will come to you when the time is right."

I felt her smile rise against my neck when she said, "You were wrong about one thing this morning."

Frowning, I pulled back so I could see her face. "What's that?"

"You said Madison could ground me more than you ever could. It's not true. You're my rock... my person.... You make me feel safe and loved and heard. It's one of my favorite things about you."

God, her love was the best aphrodisiac. In that second, I wanted her so badly—needed to strip her naked and feel myself inside her. I was already hardening against my pants. I couldn't let our relationship slip, and after this morning, I knew we both needed sex—needed that intimacy to anchor us.

"Come with me back to the office. I want to show you something."

She eyed me with curiosity. "Let's go."

I picked up the pace as we practically sprinted down the crowded sidewalks, weaving around meandering tourists and street merchants selling overpriced souvenirs. Once we reached my floor and walked past the reception desk, I was relieved to see that Cara wasn't there. Then I recalled she had a dentist appointment, so she wouldn't be back for a while. *Thank God. Perfect timing.*

Sofia was out of breath from our sprint, and her brows arched when I flipped a switch to darken the glass, then locked the door. Her expression changed in an instant. Eyes locking on mine, her gaze turned molten as I strode toward her, removing my belt before I pressed my body against hers, my fingers threading in her hair, kissing her hard. Her lips parted, tongue exploring mine as her breathing became ragged. I could feel her heartbeat against my chest, and I didn't have to wonder if she'd be into this.

I walked her backward until her ass hit my desk, then hoisted her up on the edge. "I've been neglecting you." Unbuttoning the top of her dress, I planted kisses down her neck, then to the swell of her breasts. "Should I remedy that now?"

"Oh, yes... Please." Her voice, resonating from deep in her throat, was like catnip, making me even harder.

With one hand, I cupped her breast, while I made quick work of unzipping my pants with the other. Her chest heaved against my mouth, her breaths coming faster and faster. When I slid my hand up her thigh and ran a finger against the fabric of her panties, she made those soft keening sounds I loved, but when she cried out, my other hand covered her mouth.

"Shush. We'll get caught."

She nodded and pressed her lips together, her head lolling back as she climbed higher.

"Sofia," I said into her ear, "tell me what you want."

"I want... you. All of you."

"You have all of me."

Her eyes darkened, peering at me like she wanted to devour me. "No. I mean *all* of you."

"I know what you mean, but I want you ready." She responded to my touch with a guttural moan. I freed myself from my boxer briefs and stepped between her legs. She watched while I pressed into her, a hiss of "Yes... yes... yes..." escaping her lips, and I thought I might come undone too soon as the warmth of her enveloped me.

"My God, you feel so good. I'd stay here all day if I could."

"This is your home," she breathed. "You belong right here. Stay as long as you like." That grin—so sexy—it made me want to bite her bottom lip.

My hands cupped her jaw, my lips crashing into hers; a hungry kiss that grew more fevered as we rocked together. The words "I love you" burst out of me.

She whispered the words back between gasps, and there it was—that deep connection I hadn't ever felt with anyone else. I gripped the sides of her hips, pulling her into me until I felt her tremble and stifle a scream, then I let go. The explosion racked through my body, my brain, and damn near burst through the top of my head while I forced back the growl climbing in my throat.

We were still gasping for breath when I collapsed onto her, our arms wrapped around each other, holding on tight as if we weren't ready to separate. Her belly bounced against mine as she giggled. "I really should take more interest in your work. Can I visit your office again sometime?"

I burst out laughing, and with impeccable timing, we heard James' voice penetrating the door. The insistent knocking had us scrambling off the desk.

"Mate, are you in there? Why are the windows dark?"

I almost said *keep your pants on, James*, but instead called out, "I'm on a call. I'll come to your office when I'm done." Sofia straightened her dress and fixed the buttons, while I zipped up and found my belt, both of us swallowing our laughter. Her flushed cheeks were round with a giddy smile, and I couldn't help feeling pleased I was responsible for putting that look on her face.

Sofia threw the purse strap over her shoulder, then wrapped her arms around my waist. "Thank you for making my day. I hope you'll be able to concentrate this afternoon."

"You've made my workday much more pleasurable. I'm not sure I'll be able to think of anything else today, but James is waiting for me."

"I'll see myself out and wait for you at the hotel tonight. I'm going to call Madison and Ben as well. It will be good to touch base with them. Is takeout okay for dinner?"

"It's perfect." I kissed her softly, then watched her walk down the hallway and disappear into the elevator, thinking I was the luckiest guy in the world.

When I turned, I saw James watching me, a shit-eating grin on his face. *Here we go*, I thought, and prepared to be heckled for the rest of the afternoon.

Chapter Six
Sofia

Dear Ryan - Day 14

I had this brilliant idea to begin my journal by writing to you, and maybe someday I'll share my entries with you when we're growing old together. In my imagination, we'll be sprawled out on a glorious beach, watching the seagulls dip and dive in the air, looking back over our lives together. We'll travel back through time, marveling at our experiences since we first met. At least, for me, the journal will serve as a reminder of these early days. For you, it may prove interesting to know what I was thinking and feeling as we embarked on this adventure together.

So, here goes. I plan to cherish each day of our contract, because there's no predicting the future, as much as I want to see us on that beach someday. This is quickly becoming the most exciting time of my life. London is growing on me, despite the changeable weather and some questionable food. I hope you're not ruddy tired of the way the flippin' accent here has rubbed off on me.

Though Barcelona captured my heart, here, I sense a deep, ancestral connection. I may not have mentioned it, but I have *family roots in England, too, and there is almost an eerie familiarity about the medieval parts of the city. Maybe I had a past life as a maiden, or a mistress to a duke. It's fun to think about, until I reflect on the lack of indoor bathrooms.*

This week, I took my book and sat on a bench where I could view the Tower of London, pondering both the life of Anne Boleyn in that castle as well as my own journey since I was last in that very spot. You should have seen me then, just a girl of twenty-four. Anything seemed possible. My whole life stretched out before me. Strangely, though, until I met you, I don't think I've ever lived it so fully.

Fourteen days and counting. The adjustment period hasn't always been easy, but you've kept the promise you made before we left the States—to communicate and work things out, day by day. You continue to amaze me with your love and commitment. You are the guiding star helping me navigate through uncharted waters, and no matter the outcome, I'll be forever grateful you found me... cherished me... and held on tight.

Like most mornings since arriving in London, I had breakfast at my favorite pub, where Maggie now greeted me with familiarity, calling out an enthusiastic "Mornin', love." Without my asking, she preemptively delivered a fresh, hot bun to my table. It had been a week since my minor meltdown in the bathroom, and I couldn't stop thinking about that morning, or the lunch with Ryan—or that desk. Check one more fantasy off my list.

I still didn't understand my raging emotions, but letting them spill out was cathartic, at least for me. I wondered if, subconsciously, I was testing our relationship to see if it could withstand conflict (and my menopausal flares). Performing postmortems on my own hiccups in life came with the business of being a shrink. If I were writing session notes for that encounter, I would report that the couple handled emotional tension fairly well. Their communication style was healthy (no blaming or name-calling); they resolved conflict in a positive manner, and Ryan's solution was effective at re-establishing intimacy. Very effective.

I took a sip of coffee, reliving the sensory memories from yesterday. The effect of Ryan's solution was going to reverberate through me for the next few days. But equally important was the way he'd put me at ease by listening to my problems without judgment. Something had shifted in me—I felt more sure that we could make this work, more patient with myself, more tolerant of the ambiguities. In part, I owed the change to Ryan and his reassurance. Again, I reflected on my marriage—how emotionally charged conversations had become ugly, destructive arguments, the residual resentment poisoning every aspect of the relationship. Whatever challenges Ryan and I might face, I would still choose him. He was worth it—my second chance to get it right.

"Are you alright, love?" I startled at finding Maggie hovering over me. "You've barely touched your breakfast. Is it boyfriend trouble? A fella will either make you lose your appetite altogether or have you eating everything in sight." She chuckled like she'd had some experience with said 'boyfriend trouble.'

"You've got that right. But no, everything's fine with my guy. I'll finish up while you get my bill."

Maggie eyed me suspiciously, as if she didn't trust my answer, but returned with the check and her usual smile.

When I returned to the hotel, Charlie was waiting for me. "Lovely to see you again, ma'am. Where to today?"

I rummaged in my bag and retrieved the paper bookmark with the address of the bookshop. "Could you drop me off at Green's bookstore? In Notting Hill?"

"Certainly, ma'am."

Victoria looked up from the table where she was organizing the display and smiled when she saw me. "Hi, Sofia. Nice to see you again."

"Oh, you'll be seeing a lot of me while I'm here. It's my favorite shop in town, and since I've finished the book on Anne Boleyn, I need to pick up a few more."

"I'm pleased to hear that. What are you looking for now?"

"Do you have any travel guides for the Maldives?"

"The Maldives?" She exhaled a whistle. "That's where you'll be going?"

"Believe me, I was just as surprised when my boyfriend told me. I'm in charge of planning, so I need information."

Her brow furrowed. "Oh. You're going with your boyfriend?"

"Yes, he works here in London, and since he has to be in Dubai on business, we'll leave from there."

She leaned over, straightening the stacks of books on the table—books which looked like they were already in neat piles. "Isn't that grand. I'm sure you'll have a lovely time. Now, let me show you to the travel section."

Oliver glanced up as I passed the counter, his eyes beaming. "Sofia, good day. Are you well?" At once, I noticed something different about him. His cheeks were smooth, without a shadow of a beard, and his hair was perfectly trimmed. No bedhead today.

"I'm doing fine, enjoying your lovely city. Nice haircut," I said, flashing a friendly smile. He dropped his gaze to the floor, his fingers brushing through his freshly trimmed hair; embarrassment splashed across his face.

"Sorry. Americans can be very direct. We just get up in people's business without permission." My cheeks started to burn. "I just meant it as a compliment."

"Ah, no worries. Victoria's been after me for weeks to get cleaned up." He smiled shyly, as if unaccustomed to receiving compliments, yet I found that hard to believe. He had a rugged, handsome quality women usually loved. "Thank you," he said finally. He picked up a pen, then twirled it between his fingers. An awkward silence hung in the air.

"Well, I'd better see what Victoria has found for me," I said.

"Oh. Yes, of course," he stammered, then glanced toward his daughter.

As I walked in her direction, I thought I felt his gaze skimming across my back but didn't turn around. Instead, I kept my focus on the colorful sign marking the travel section.

My online research had led me in circles, leaving me overwhelmed by too many options. Which island, which resort? They all promised luxurious accommodations. Normally, I took budget vacations, or at most booked three-star hotels, so planning a luxury vacation was as foreign to me as trying to read a wine list written in French.

I flipped through at least five books before choosing a comprehensive travel guide that must have contained five hundred pages. Sorting through all the options was going to take forever.

As I approached the counter, I glanced at the reading lounge in the corner. "I think I'll sit for a while, if you don't mind," I said after Victoria rang up my purchase.

"Of course. You can join Josie and the lads."

Three pairs of eyes looked up when I lowered myself into a brown leather wingback chair in the circle.

"Hello," I said tentatively.

After a moment, Josie leaned forward and said, "I heard you talking, love. So, you're American, are you?" Her voice lilted sweetly, her eyes inquisitive and warm.

"Yes, from California." I scanned the three faces. "And you're all from London?"

"I'm originally from Sussex." The stocky man leaned in closer, his broad shoulders casting a shadow over me as he extended his hand. His grip was firm and confident, the calluses on his palm giving me the impression he wasn't the kind of guy who sat at a desk all day. "I'm John."

"Nice to meet you. I'm Sofia."

He continued, "I moved to London when my wife passed away. My kids are here. Well, they're not kids anymore. They're married and all now, raising families of their own. They don't pay me much mind, but that's how it is nowadays. For the better part of my life, the house rumbled with noise, and now it's as quiet as a church." He shook his head, then pointed to the man next to him. "This is my mate, Arthur."

Arthur waved, slumping in his chair, his neck disappearing into his tightly buttoned shirt collar. Unlike John, whose shirt was stretched precariously over a bulging stomach, Arthur's clothes hung loose, as if he'd once been several sizes larger.

I nodded. Josie shot out a hand to shake mine. She had a surprisingly forceful grip. "And I'm Josie, originally from a little village on the border next to Scotland." She had to be in her mid-fifties, but her porcelain skin was smooth, pale against a mane of dark, curly hair.

Arthur stiffened in his chair and harrumphed, "Ruddy Scotland." He made a noise as if spitting on 'ruddy Scotland.'

Josie tilted her head toward me and remarked, "He's still sore about that Scottish fella running off with his wife." Then she glared at him. "Now, Arthur," she said, bristling, "don't go blaming the whole bloomin' country just because Eleanor couldn't keep her knickers on."

Arthur whipped around toward Josie. "Would you like to post it in the ruddy papers? Honestly, you're like the bloody town crier the way you go 'round telling every Tom, Dick, and Harry my business."

John interrupted—and by the look on Josie's face, she was about to lay into Arthur with a vengeance. "Sofia, what brings you to London?"

Josie and Arthur retreated, still eyeing each other as if the battle was far from over.

"It's a long story, but in a nutshell, I lost my job, and now I have the chance to begin a new life. My boyfriend is American, but he also works in London. I followed him here. We're sort of trying things out for two months and traveling together."

The three of them gaped at me.

"You just up and left your home to follow this bloke all the way across the pond?" John asked.

"What did I have to lose? I've been divorced for a long time, and my son's living with his girlfriend, so I was rattling around my house alone." I thought John might relate, but he looked unconvinced.

"Still, how long have you known this boyfriend?" John persisted.

Josie interjected, "So, now you're Sofia's father? Jesus, Mary, and Joseph, she's a grown woman."

"Quite grown, I'm afraid. Actually, John, it all happened rather fast."

"Well, I think it's bloody brilliant," Josie remarked. "When I moved to London, everyone back home thought I might as well have taken off for Australia, when here I am, just 'round the corner. But look at you! What a grand adventure."

Arthur appeared to come out of his daze. "What happens at the end of two months? Will you both be heading back to California?"

"That's a hard question to answer. Yes, I'll have to go back because my house is there, but we've only made a two-month commitment. After that, we'll reevaluate."

Arthur stared at his shoes for several moments, the fight dissipating from his face. "Maybe that's a brilliant way to do things—two months at a time, I mean. Keeps you on your toes, it does. In truth, I probably took Eleanor for granted after all those years. I didn't think to ask if she was happy, but she never said anything. One day, she just ran off."

John dropped his gaze to his lap. "I think my Tillie was happy. She always had a smile for me when I walked through the door after work. We got on pretty well, considering how long we were married. But you never really appreciate someone until you realize they might just up and disappear from your life."

Josie looked from one man to the other. "C'mon now, cheer up. Sofia didn't come 'round to drown in a pool of pity."

I shook my head. "No worries, it's fine. I know something about loss. You're reminding me not to take a moment for granted, especially with the one you love." I swiveled to face Josie. "What about you, Josie—do you live alone?"

A fleeting shadow of sadness clouded her features, casting a veil over her bright demeanor, but in a flash, it was gone, replaced by the smile that appeared to be her default expression. "My children moved on years ago, but I look on the bright side. I don't have to cook if I don't want to, and I can live anywhere it pleases me. It's freedom, it is, not having to answer to anyone." Her gaze dropped to the floor, then with a burst of enthusiasm, she blurted, "So, tell us—what's your fella like? I'm betting he's a handsome bloke."

I felt a smile creep across my face, along with a flush of pink at the thought of Ryan.

Josie caught my expression. "Ha! He is."

"He's pretty fine, Josie. And he's smart, and cultured, and perfect at pretty much everything he does."

"Bloody hell." She blew out a long breath. "You won the lottery on that one. I don't think I could handle the pressure to keep up."

I raised an eyebrow at the thought of the pressure I was under, then found myself telling complete strangers the story of our relationship. I shared how we met at a job networking event after I lost my job due to a company-wide restructuring that only affected employees over forty. How I ran from Ryan because of the fourteen-year age difference and my fear of another heartbreak, but that he inspired me to travel, and then how fate threw us together on the flight to Barcelona. She laughed when I explained that the first agreement we made was just for vacation fun, Ryan acting as my tour guide.

Meanwhile, the men stayed silent as I rambled, listening to this crazy story with rapt attention. Josie rested her hand over her heart, looking almost misty-eyed when I recounted how it had ended after I learned he wanted children but that he persevered, convincing me he would willingly give that up to spend his life with me.

"And that's how we ended up with this sixty-day con-tract—a trial run to test the relationship. He wants to con-vince me he's fine with remaining a couple, just the two of us, but I hate the position we're in. The pressure is enormous, especially because I keep thinking about how he deserves to be with a younger woman."

"Oh, love." Josie leaned in and gave my back a quick pat. I wondered if that was the British equivalent of a hug. "Don't go torturing yourself like that. I'll bet he's thanking his lucky stars that he found a fine woman like you. Age doesn't matter when you meet your true love."

John popped halfway out of his seat with his hand shoot-ing up in the air like a kid in a classroom waiting to be called on.

"Yes, John?" I said.

"My sister—she's always been the rebel in the fami-ly—she took up with a bloke ten years her junior after her divorce. She's having the time of her life, she is. Says men her age can't keep up with her. Now, she and her bloke are always traveling. Mind you, she gets a fair amount of stick from some folks, but she just tells them to sod off."

My head snapped back. I did not expect that from John. "Good for her."

"Sofia," Josie said, "have you considered that there may be other ways to have a child with Ryan? That is, if you fancy starting a family."

"What? Like a surrogate mother or something? I'm not sure I could handle that scenario."

"There's also adoption. There are lots of babies in the world who need a good home instead of living in an orphanage or bouncing around foster homes. My aunt couldn't bear children, so they adopted a baby from China back in the day."

It wasn't as if adoption hadn't occurred to me, but I didn't want to introduce the idea to Ryan just yet. Maybe I wanted to keep him all to myself for a while, and maybe I wasn't sure if I wanted to start over again raising children. But hearing Josie's suggestion, the idea bubbled to the surface again. "You're absolutely right, Josie. There are all sorts of ways to create a family. I'll consider the options."

"But don't do it only for Ryan. You have to want it as much as he does, or you might muck up the relationship, and then it'll all be for nothing."

At once, it struck me how strange this was. Moments ago, they were strangers; now they supported me without judgment. Their life experience, their triumph over tragedy and loneliness, had given them perspective on what was truly important in the end. "Thanks for the advice. You're a very wise woman." Josie waved me off with a *pishah*, but I continued, "If I could trouble you all with another question—have any of you been to the Maldives?" I held up my book. "I have to plan our trip there, and I'm not sure which island to choose."

They stared at me blankly, then John said, "Tillie always dreamed of going, but we never made it. She even picked up those travel magazines. It's paradise there, it is. There's a travel agency down the high street. Why don't you pop in? I'm sure they'll sort you right out."

"Brilliant idea, John." I checked the time on my phone. "I'd better hurry because I have to be back at the hotel soon."

I stood to leave, the men rising with me. "It was lovely to meet you, Sofia," John said, while Arthur nodded in agreement.

"Pop by the next time you're in town and let us know how your trip went, all right?" Josie added.

"Will do," I replied, and I meant it. As I turned to leave, Oliver caught my eye and gave me a nod. I waved in return, and as I pushed open the door, I wondered what his life had been like since his wife died. Was he just the same as John and Arthur?

On my way back, I did as Josie instructed, locating the travel agency on the next block. A middle-aged woman dressed in a pencil skirt and blazer greeted me. After listening to my questions, she rummaged through a file drawer, then handed me an envelope stuffed with brochures. "I'd be happy to help you, dear, but we're about to close. Maybe tomorrow?"

I let out a sigh of relief, promising to return, then hailed a taxi. But if I had known what was waiting for me when I arrived back at the hotel, I would have rushed back to the bookstore and offered to work the night shift stocking shelves, just for the fun of it.

Chapter Seven

Sofia

While the taxi weaved through traffic, I wondered if Ryan's meeting would keep him out all evening. I was prepared to wrap myself in a chenille blanket and study the guidebook alone, when what I really wanted was to plan the trip together. The half hour it took to push through London's clogged arteries at rush hour gave me time to reflect, then stew as my thoughts simmered to a boil. Should I talk to him about adoption?

I was mulling over conversation starters when the taxi arrived at the hotel. The middle-aged doorman—whose name I still couldn't remember despite his daily kindness—greeted me by opening the car door.

"Good evening, ma'am." He extended his arm, gesturing toward the hotel entrance with the same slight bow and warm smile he offered every time I arrived. I wondered if his job ever got tiresome, if he was counting down another ten years until retirement. If he was bored, he never let it show. Just ordinary people doing their jobs well.

That had been me just a few months ago until I discovered I'd buried my dreams so deep I'd forgotten they existed. Who knew? Maybe this doorman had his sights set on becoming the next great author, stories penned during long winter nights. A few million people lived in this city, each holding secret desires close, protecting them from disapproving spouses or judgmental parents.

As I retrieved my keys and reached for the door handle, I heard voices coming from inside our suite. One was definitely Ryan's; the other was female. My stomach tightened reflexively. Ryan had a woman in our room? Of course, my next move was perfectly reasonable—I pressed my ear to the door, straining to hear the conversation, until the couple from down the hall stepped off the elevator with their little dog, Toto. Yes, really. The tiny terror usually ran loose down the hallway while his owners called after him, probably in desperate search of anything resembling grass. As they passed, I nodded and pretended to dig through my cavernous purse for keys. I could swear Toto eyed me suspiciously.

When the coast was clear, I tried again but could only hear muffled sounds. Finally, I decided there was no choice but to open the door and face whatever awaited me.

Two heads whipped in my direction. Ryan practically launched himself out of his chair, while the woman lounging on the sofa let her gaze settle on me with the slow, methodical precision of a jeweler appraising a questionable diamond.

She was probably in her sixties, with features unmistakably related to Ryan's—the same oval face structure, though hers was framed by a sleek black bob that fell to her shoulders with the kind of precision that suggested regular appointments with someone who charged by the minute. Her olive skin was flawless, her lips full, and her bright blue eyes currently fixed on me as if my presence was an intrusion on a private conversation.

The Queen of England couldn't have looked more out of place in our modest suite. Her dress was pure couture—expensive silk in a bold geometric print that cascaded over her legs like liquid money, just skimming the floor. That kind of casual elegance probably cost more than everything in our shared closet combined. This woman had elevated haughty to an art form.

In the stretched seconds before Ryan spoke, her eyes remained fixed on me with the kind of blank stare that somehow managed to size me up and dismiss me simultaneously.

"Sofia, come join us." Ryan's voice had that overly bright quality of someone trying to convince himself (and me) everything was fine. He motioned me into the living room, and I shot him my best *what-the-actual-hell* look, but his face was locked in one of those dinner party smiles—the kind you wore when the person next to you was insufferable but you kept grinning while shooting inconspicuous daggers at the hostess for her seating choices. "I'd like you to meet my mother, Clara. She flew in from Boston to surprise us."

Surprise seemed like a generous word for what felt more like an ambush.

My head whipped toward Clara, then back to Ryan, trying to wrap my mind around the fact that his mother was sitting in our living room and I'd had absolutely no time to prepare. Whose mother just popped in from across an ocean with no notice? *Is this how your family operates? She's trying to mess with me, right?* These were the questions I flashed at

Ryan with my eyes in the time it took to navigate toward the sofa.

He read me—our nonverbal communication was nearly telepathic—but just shrugged, that smile still securely fastened to his face. Resigned to my fate, I pulled my spine straight and faced Clara, extending my hand.

"I'm pleased to meet you. Did you have a good flight?"

This wasn't how I'd thought this day would end. My stomach twisted into a knot. Ryan had mentioned telling his mother about our relationship, but he'd been evasive about specifics. His grimace had conveyed more than his words ever could. I'd dreaded this moment and never imagined it would come so soon, let alone without warning.

"Pleased to meet you too, dear." We all knew *that* was a lie. She shook my hand with just the tips of her manicured fingers, as if barely conceding to the obligatory greeting. "The flight was tolerable but tedious, and the food in first class was subpar. But it was worth it to see my son again." The way her eyes narrowed when she glanced at Ryan told me everything about their relationship. *Manipulative* was the word that came to mind. "Heaven knows, he rarely comes to see me in Boston."

And there it was. The dig. This wasn't a social call—it was going to be a trip down guilt lane.

Bracing myself, I obeyed as Ryan patted the seat cushion. "Come sit with us." Unsure of the etiquette when meeting a disapproving mother, I positioned myself at least a foot away from Ryan, crossed my legs, promptly uncrossed them, then folded my hands in my lap. I'd learned a thing or two from tense work meetings—to stay completely still, not fidget, and not speak unless absolutely necessary, to dodge the live wire like your life depended on it, and whatever you did, don't appear defensive.

"We were just talking about Mom's recent retirement," Ryan announced with forced cheer.

"Oh, what line of work were you in?" An innocent question I'd soon regret.

Ryan interjected before she could answer, his voice pitched unnaturally high. "Mom was in fashion, holding top positions over the years for companies like Saks Fifth Avenue and Neiman Marcus."

"I've been in love with fashion since I was a child. I learned to make my own clothes as a teenager. Of course, I never imagined I could build a career from my passion, but I've enjoyed my years as a buyer and fashion consultant."

My eyes dropped to my lap to assess my outfit: jeans from Ross, a T-shirt, and a blue V-neck sweater, probably from Target. Would I have chosen these clothes if I'd known she was here? Hell no. In my defense, my well-worn sneakers were necessary, given the excessive walking I'd been doing. I snuck a glance at Clara's shoes—stiletto heels with red soles—and shrank in my seat, wishing I could disappear.

"That sounds exciting," I offered in a small voice. "Quite a glamorous career."

"It had its moments." Her arm stretched across the sofa back, fingers tipped with red polish drumming against the gray fabric, her eyes cast toward the ceiling as she considered this. Abruptly, her gaze shifted to me. "But, honestly,

I'm relieved to retire from the rat race. Ryan mentioned your unfortunate unemployment. Will you be taking early retirement? It must be difficult to find another position at your age." She reached a long, slender arm to the coffee table and raised her wineglass to her lips.

At *my age*? A hot flash burned up my chest, setting my head on fire. Ryan placed a hand over my clenched fist, and while his face remained neutral, the muscles in his neck twitched. Obviously, he'd had plenty of practice dealing with his mother's calculated jabs.

"Ryan, could you please get me a glass of water?" I asked, the inside of my mouth as dry as cotton. His eyes darted between his mother and me, probably questioning the wisdom of leaving us alone, but after a beat, he pushed off the couch and headed for the kitchenette.

Following his lead, I fixed my expression to a neutral position and pretended there was absolutely nothing to be nervous about. Then I practiced the technique used for public speaking, attempting to picture her in her underwear. Okay, never mind. That was just gross. So, I trained my voice to sound oh-so-casual. "To your point, Clara, my severance package has afforded me time to travel, but I still have my license to practice psychotherapy and haven't decided whether I'll go into private practice or what direction my career will take. I'm certainly not ready to retire—that's still years down the road." *Checkmate.*

Her smile, when it appeared, was pure saccharine—sweet enough at first glance, but it left something bitter lingering in the air. "And for now, you're taking an extended vacation? How does your son feel about his mother being so far from home? He's what, twenty-two? You must miss him. I know I've missed Ryan."

Wow, she's good. She'd just captured my king. There was so much packed into that round, I didn't know where to start. She seemed to know everything about me, while what I'd gleaned about her from Ryan's stories wouldn't be appropriate to bring up. She hadn't been the model parent she obviously thought she was. But did she have any limits? What else would she throw at me?

"Here you go, Sofia." Ryan handed me the water with an apologetic—or maybe desperate—look in his eyes. After all, he needed saving as much as I did. He reclaimed his seat and offered to refill his mother's wine glass. We were going to need several bottles to get through this evening. "Sofia has a wonderful relationship with her son, and he's very support- ive of her trip to Europe with me," Ryan answered belatedly, but at least he was in the game now. It didn't matter that, in reality, my son was skeptical about my running off to Europe with Ryan, but I hadn't told him about that conversation.

"My son has a girlfriend, and they're living together. He has a life of his own now and really doesn't need me hovering over him." *Hint.* I paused, taking gulps of water, though I really needed to dunk my fiery head in a bucket of ice. "You must be so proud of Ryan. He's built such a successful career."

"I am very proud of him. He's quite the businessman, just like his father."

Heat radiated off Ryan like a furnace. Even from a foot away, I felt ten degrees warmer. But he stayed silent. I knew he wanted to be nothing like his father. How could she be so clueless as to compare him to a man accused of embezzlement? It was only a matter of when, not if, he exploded.

Adding gasoline to the fire, she dropped the bomb I'd been expecting. "But when his father was Ryan's age, he was married with a child on the way. I'd been hoping to entertain grandchildren during my retirement years, dear." She was leaning forward now, the saccharine sweetness gone, her sad eyes pointed directly at Ryan.

"That's enough, Mother," he growled, slamming his wine glass down so hard that red spray peppered the mahogany table. "We've already discussed this, and it's really none of your business what I decide to do with my life. Frankly, giving you grandchildren is not my top priority. Sofia is my priority, and if you want to be in my—*our*—lives, you damn well need to respect that. So far, I've seen little respect from you tonight."

Kaboom.

I was flooded with love for Ryan but also guilt that he was at war with his mother over me. It was enough that he was at war with his own desires. We were only several weeks into our arrangement, barely learning to be a couple, and despite his insistence, her objections might cause him to question his decision. I couldn't blame him if he did. The brewing conflict sent me back to the day he first told me he wanted children of his own, reliving that crushing disappointment.

The roaring in my ears and blood pumping furiously through my veins obscured their conversation as voices rose in anger. Clara might have said something about respecting your mother, and then she was on her feet.

"I'm tired from the long journey. I think I'll retire to my hotel." She waved a hand with a backward glance at Ryan as she glided toward the door, her dress billowing behind her like a designer cape.

He rose from the couch and stepped toward her, but before he could respond, she announced, "I'll have the porter call me a taxi—don't worry about me." *Was she channeling Scarlett O'Hara? Bravo.*

"Goodnight, Mother."

Seconds after he closed the door behind her, his forehead hit the wood frame. Once, twice, three times.

Chapter Eight
Sofia

"Well, that was fun. Should we invite your mother for dinner? Better yet, maybe Jerry Springer could join us as mediator."

It worked. Maybe it was the sudden release of tension, but Ryan started to laugh. Then I was laughing, and he slumped down onto the sofa next to me, his forefingers pressed against his temples.

"That was one hell of a shitshow," he said. "I'm sorry about the surprise, but she blindsided me too. I don't know what possessed her to show up like that. She called to confirm I'd be at the hotel only minutes before she arrived—probably from the lobby."

"Maybe she figured catching you off guard was the only way to find the truth."

"The truth about what?"

"Me. She must have been curious about this new woman in your life." I refrained from adding a reference to Mrs. Robinson. "And I suspect her ultimate motive is to change your mind about continuing our relationship."

"You think?"

I withered under his sarcastic glance. He only used that tone when he was fuming. "Yes, I suppose she made that crystal clear."

"Sofia, I'm sorry. I didn't mean to snap at you. I'm furious with her for bringing that up in front of you—though it's so on brand for her. That was fucking rude."

"But you were aware of her disapproval, right?"

Ryan hesitated, reached for his glass, and downed the contents. Matching the mood inside, I could hear a storm brewing, wind whistling through a crack in the window. "She did make a few, um, remarks during our previous phone conversation, and I told her in no uncertain terms to butt the hell out."

"Did you mention the sixty-day contract? That this is a trial run and you have time to make decisions?"

"No, Sofia." His voice softened as he pivoted, drawing me close and threading his fingers through mine. "Because I told you—I'm not changing my mind."

I wanted to relax, to err on the side of optimism, but I still wondered if he was simply stubbornly holding his course—or if, faced with our new day-to-day reality, the slightest doubts weren't creeping in. His mother had extremely strong opinions. Could she influence him? Or was he staying the course deliberately to spite her?

"Hon, I never wanted you to give up your dream of having a family, but selfishly, I don't want to let go of you either." I waved a palm in the air to stop Ryan from interrupting, keeping my voice gentle. "One thing is clear—there's a chance both you and your mother could end up disappointed down the road if you stay with me. Your mother may never forgive me for standing in the way."

He shook his head adamantly, his lips forming a sharp line. "Dammit, Sofia, you're not hearing me. If my mother can't accept our relationship, that's her problem—not yours, not mine. Second, how can I prove to you I'm serious? How can I make you believe you're my priority? Do you think I'm going to give up the woman I love on the off chance that down the road I might find just the right person who wants to give me children?"

A confluence of emotions swirled in my chest and stung the back of my eyes. I couldn't name them all if I tried. The contrast between Ryan and the men who'd come before him struck me with such force it took several moments before I could speak. "No one has ever prioritized me. Not ever. No one has ever fought to hang on to me or valued me the way you do." The look in his eyes stunned me—compassion, maybe? A sincere expression that conveyed more than his words, and I believed him.

I gripped his hand as if it were a lifeline out of a dark place. "Babe, what you're giving up for me is huge. Let's both acknowledge that. It makes me feel sad, and happy, and so grateful. Honestly, I'm trying to let it sink in, to make sense of all these feelings." I swiped a hand across the moisture on my cheek, willing myself not to cry.

"It's unbelievable to me that those assholes before me didn't see your worth, didn't show you the love you deserve." The tip of his finger was on my chin, lifting my gaze to his. He saw my raw vulnerability—he saw *me*,and his gentle look nearly broke me apart. His voice soft, he said, "But in the end, it worked out for me because I got the prize."

I let him wrap me in his arms, his warm body like a blanket of safety and security—soothing me, blocking out all the noise and things that didn't matter. We stayed locked together in silence for so long I lost track of time. The room darkened, rain spat ferociously at the window, and trees whistled against the wind. But inside, we were safe—just the two of us, a team against the elements.

Finally, I broke the silence, muttering into the soft fabric of his sweater. "Are you going to spend time with your mother while she's here?"

His chest rose and fell with a heavy sigh. "I suppose so. Maybe I'll have lunch with her tomorrow." He groaned, his head tilted back, staring at the ceiling. "Oh God, she is such a pain in my ass, but she's my mother. She's all the family I have left."

"Do you want me to join you?"

"No, I think we need some mother-son time to work things out. Besides, I don't want to risk her offending you again."

"I appreciate your protection, but whether or not we like each other, if you and I are a couple, we'll have to work out how to be on good terms."

He dropped a kiss on my forehead and made a weak attempt at a smile. "Thank you, Sofia, but let me work out how to be on good terms with her first."

"Ryan?"

"Yes?"

"I never asked you—why do you want children?"

"Why do I want children?" He repeated the question, then fell silent. I raised my head from his chest and sat up to face him. This was too important—I needed to see his expression, gauge his response.

His words, when he finally spoke, came in starts and stops, sputtering like a car engine with a faulty ignition. "I'm not... Why does anyone... I just always thought..." He ran a hand through his hair. "Jesus, it's hard to put into words."

I waited as he struggled. This question was at the crux of everything, and despite the anxiety mounting at the thought of confronting the issue head-on, I had to know.

"When I think about it, I realize it has something to do with my family and how I was raised. My father wasn't exactly a model parent, as I've mentioned," Ryan began slowly, his voice so low I had to lean in to hear him. "I paid a high price for his insistence on perfection. But what it did to me didn't compare to the impact it had on my sister—it literally killed her."

Seeing the sadness in his eyes was like a punch to the gut. He paused, staring at the rain-spattered window as if he were a million miles away. "As far back as I can remember, I've always thought about what a family could be like. I've thought about how I could be a better father than my dad—more loving, more caring, how I'd be there for my child in a way he never was."

Something in me sagged under the weight of his hopes and dreams. There was no possibility of countering this, of hoping this was a whim. I understood now, and there was at least some peace in knowing.

"What about you?" he asked. "Did you always want to have children?"

"What? Oh." Dragging myself from my thoughts, I said, "I wasn't the kind of girl who dreamed of her wedding day and already had baby names picked out before her first date. But when I finished college, I knew. It became a biological imperative, I suppose."

"And your ex-husband?"

"He had to be convinced, but once Ben was born, he was all in. Ben was the pearl that emerged from the marriage, and though I don't have regrets, I wonder sometimes if staying with a man I no longer had feelings for was the right choice." My words reverberated back at me: *Ben was the pearl.* I couldn't imagine my life without him.

"I'm not sure I could have stayed if I were in your position," he admitted.

Silence fell over the room again. It had been a long day, and he looked exhausted in the pale light of the streetlamps pouring through the windows. But now, with this topic looming so large it was like the proverbial elephant in the room, it was the right time to reveal what I'd been wrestling with all afternoon.

Leaning back to reach the side table, I turned on a lamp. "There, that's better. Now I can see you." I straightened my spine and took the leap. "I have a possible solution to our problem—or rather, your perfectly reasonable desire to raise a family. What if we adopted a child?" I said it brightly, boldly, as if I didn't have a million reservations.

"Adoption?" His head shot back a few inches.

"It might be possible. Earlier in my career, I worked for a private adoption agency—foreign adoptions, mostly. It's a long, arduous process, but there's a chance a birth mother might accept us, or you, as a single father."

He looked blindsided; his eyebrows had risen somewhere near his hairline. I waited for them to settle. "I never would have imagined you'd suggest... You'd be willing to adopt a child with me?"

We'd reached the tricky part. Would I really be willing to start all over again? Lose my newfound freedom? I inhaled a deep, cleansing breath before answering. "I'm willing to consider the option. There was a point sometime after the divorce when I thought of adoption as a single parent. I always wanted another child, but it didn't seem right since my marriage was in so much turmoil. Then I realized it would be a monumental undertaking to raise a kid on my own—between my job and caring for Ben." His forehead relaxed as I cupped his cheeks in my hands. "I love you. I've never felt as happy as I am with you."

He didn't look convinced, so I forced my voice to sound more sure than I felt. "Hey, if you had a time machine that could make me young and fertile again, I'd take it. No doubt we'd make good parents, and I'd like nothing more than to give you the kind of family you've wished for."

"But this is quite different, isn't it? You'd be going back in time, losing the gains you've made."

This man could see right through the plot holes in this story, I'd give him that. I decided it was time to spin us toward the positive. "Second chances don't come around very often—rarely, in fact. In a perfect world, I'd be younger, you'd be a few years older, and we'd meet in the middle. But sometimes second chances are worth compromising. You are worth a million compromises." I leaned into him, kissing him gently.

"Wow, I never dreamed..." Excitement spread across his features, and he lunged, capturing me in his arms, both of us tumbling back on the sofa. "This is a lot for one day. My mother, adoption... I don't know what to say, except I love you now, in this moment, more than ever. Thank you."

Emotions flashed across his expression so fast I couldn't keep up—elation, relief, worry, and finally confusion. Folding my arms around him, I said, "The idea is on the table, but it's a lot to digest. We can take our time to consider all the options. For now, you have your mother to deal with, as well as work tomorrow."

He shifted, looking straight at me with a new emotion: a calm clarity. "Let's postpone making a decision until the end of the sixty days. I'd like to have this time to focus on us—to build a solid foundation."

"Wow." It came out louder than I'd intended.

"What?" He studied me.

"It's a good wow. I mean, you blow me away with your maturity. You really are an old soul, aren't you?"

A grin teased the corners of his lips. "So, we're in agreement?"

"Again, I agree with the terms, Mr. Hunter." He barked out a laugh, which became a yawn, his hand moving to cover his mouth. "Okay, I get the hint—no more talking. Let's call for room service, then get some sleep," I said.

He curled his body around mine, cocooning me against his tall frame, saying sleepily, "Perfect. Just as long as we don't have to move."

I did make a move, my arm stretching to reach the phone on the side table, but his arm grasped me even tighter. The next sound I heard was his soft snores.

Chapter Nine

Ryan

"I took the liberty of ordering martinis. Dry, two olives, just the way you like it," my mother announced as I pulled out a chair and positioned myself across the table. She'd picked the restaurant, because I couldn't be trusted to choose an establishment that met her standards.

"Looks like you've started without me." I eyed her half-empty martini glass.

"Since you were supposed to be here fifteen minutes ago, I didn't have much choice, did I?"

"Always the timekeeper, Mother." I raised my glass to her, then took a hefty swig. The vodka burned a path down my throat. Of course she'd ordered the expensive stuff. I was going to need another round to get through this lunch. "Sorry, but my meeting at work ran late. How long are you planning on staying in London?"

"I'm not sure yet," she answered evasively, her eyes fixed on the ceiling.

Five minutes in, and I was already losing patience. "Is there a reason you decided to show up now, without warning?"

Her brow furrowed—well, as far as the injections would allow. It was easy to read her expression, which said, "*I'm shocked and offended that you'd say such a thing.*" My attention shifted to the server as he deposited appetizers on the table. "You already ordered food, too?"

"Well, as I said—"

"Yes, I know."

She waited until the man filled the water glasses, then retreated, before resuming our conversation. "Can't a mother drop in to see her son?"

I had only to cock an eyebrow at her for her to get the message I wasn't buying it.

"Oh alright. I needed to see for myself how you're doing. After our last phone conversation, I became concerned." She evaded my probing stare by sliding some of the caprese salad onto her plate.

Here we go, I thought, and took a deep breath before diving in. "And your concern revolved around my relationship with Sofia?"

"Ryan, you haven't touched the food. Aren't you going to eat before you go back to work?"

I wanted to say that she'd made me lose my appetite, or that I wasn't in second grade anymore, but instead I took a bite of the green salad. Today, I'd choose my battles.

"Your father and I have discussed it, and we're both concerned about your... life choices."

"Wait a minute," I said, my fork clattering onto the plate. "Why would you discuss my life with Dad? You've been divorced for years, and I haven't communicated with him since my birthday four years ago."

"Dear, we're both still your parents."

I ran a hand over my hair and attempted to clear my head, then my eyes locked on hers. "Let me be crystal clear. You have nothing to be concerned about, and my 'life choices' are just that: mine alone. And I'm choosing to be with Sofia." She opened her mouth to interject, but I stopped her with a raised hand. "You judged her before you even met. Sofia is a phenomenal woman, and I'm in love with her, so you'd better get used to the idea."

My mother shot back in her chair as if I'd slapped her. In all my life, I'd never talked to her this forcefully. It occurred to me that, given all the turmoil and grief in our family, I'd retreated rather than risk confrontation. Oh, I'd acted out and even got myself arrested, but in their presence, I'd remained silent.

A few moments went by while we sat in silence, the elevator music blending into the background against the noise of clattering dishes and the buzz of conversations. I drained my glass with sheer determination, caught the server's eye, and motioned for another martini, then watched as my mother collected herself, her face fixed in a neutral expression before she spoke.

"Well, if that's the way you feel, son. You certainly are a grown adult and can make your own decisions." Just when the bands on my shoulders dared to release, she added, "Though I wonder about your choice to abandon the prospect of having a family. You may regret that decision someday."

I should have known that was coming, that she wouldn't let me off that easily. There was no perfect answer to her implied question. Hell, Sofia and I were still discussing this very topic. It was risky to share our idea with her, so I chose my words carefully.

"Before building a family, the most important aspect is a healthy and loving relationship. I have that with Sofia. And there are no guarantees in life. People get married and expect to pump out kids, then they can't conceive. So, given the odds of finding the right person, I'm just happy I found Sofia. That said... we're exploring options for someday bringing a child into our lives."

My mother huffed out a laugh. That wasn't the response I expected. "IVF would hardly be successful for a woman of her age, especially if you plan to wait a few years."

"I know," I agreed. I had no intention of admitting that I'd already researched that option, not when I hadn't even told Sofia. Her eggs wouldn't likely be viable, so we'd need an egg donor, plus she'd have to endure hormone shots. In the end, a *geriatric pregnancy*—a term only a male doctor would come up with—could be risky. There was no world in which I'd subject Sofia to all that, or risk losing her. I had pushed the thought from my mind until she brought up the idea of adoption. Still, she'd be doing it for me, and I wasn't convinced it was fair to ask her to make such a sacrifice. I decided to run the idea by my mother. If nothing else, it might get her off my back.

"Actually, Sofia suggested we look into adoption."

Her mouth formed a perfect O, and I took some satisfaction in her surprised silence; her lack of a derisive comeback. Striking her mute? That never happened. Her special power was the quick comeback. I waited while she digested the idea, turning the word over in her mouth.

"Well..." she began in an unusually soft tone, "that's an interesting idea. You know, my brother—your uncle Mark—was adopted."

"What?! Why have I never heard about that before?" I nearly knocked over my glass as I leaned halfway across the table.

"It was different back then. People didn't talk about it openly. There were no open adoptions, and Mark was dropped into the family as if he had been born naturally. My parents never told him until he was an adult and had become suspicious. One day, he asked them directly."

It took a few minutes for this to sink into my brain. "Huh. I always wondered why he didn't resemble Grandma or Grandpa, but I assumed he must have inherited the genes from a more distant relative." Somehow, knowing there was an adoption in my own family made the idea seem more... acceptable?

"Of course, nowadays, they do things differently, discussing birth parents and adoptive parents right from the start. I think it's a healthier approach." She paused, and her eyes grew soft when she looked at me. Maybe the grandchild thing really was important to her, not just an excuse to reject Sofia. "You and Sofia are seriously considering this option?"

Fuck. Now, I hated to get her hopes up only to disappoint her later if it didn't work out. "It just came up last night, and we're giving ourselves a couple of months to consider it. I mean, it's pretty early in the relationship. We just started living together."

At the look of hope on her face, I let go of my anger. She was all the family I had left. My sister was gone, and I couldn't stand the sight of my dad. As abrasive as she could be, she was still my mom.

I reached across the table and squeezed her hand, daring a smile. "We'll definitely keep you posted. But, Mom, please be nice to Sofia. It would mean a lot to me."

She pursed her lips, but conceding a fraction, her hand squeezed mine in return. "You always were headstrong; had to do things your way. But, my dear boy, all I want is for you to be happy. If you become a parent, you'll understand."

"Mom," I said, drawing out the word until it formed a question, cocking an eyebrow at her.

"What? Haven't I been perfectly nice to Sofia?" The corner of her lips drew up in a wry grin, and while she wasn't going to admit bad behavior, she received the message.

"Just so long as we have an understanding, because if you want me to be happy, I need you two to get along."

As she released my hand, she scanned the restaurant. "Where has that server gone? He hasn't brought your martini, and I want to order lunch." She made a *tsking* sound. "I'll have to tell the manager the service here has gone downhill."

By the time we finished lunch and said our goodbyes, she admitted that she'd be going back to Boston in a few days, staying long enough to catch up with some friends in London. All things considered, it had gone better than expected, but then I'd been prepared for a catastrophe, so it wasn't a high bar.

While I walked back to my office, I left Sofia a voice message, reassuring her that my mom would not present a problem for us. I might have made it sound like I had set her straight, like I was some macho guy. But hey, it didn't hurt to be the hero in Sofia's eyes. I only hoped my mother would stick to her word.

Chapter Ten

Sofia

Retail therapy seemed like the best solution for dealing with my anxiety while Ryan had lunch with his mother. Since the weather was colder than this California girl expected, I was in the dressing room trying on sweaters—or jumpers, as they called them in England—when I missed Ryan's call. My face broke into a smile when I played his message. I wouldn't have imagined he could change her mind, but I knew firsthand how persuasive he could be. For now, at least, the tension was gone from his voice, and I felt a little more hopeful.

There was another reason for my shopping expedition. Before he'd left for work this morning, Ryan had announced, "We're going out for dinner tonight with some of the guys from the office at seven."

"Just guys?" I asked tentatively.

"One or two of the women may join us, but there are mostly guys in my department."

I stayed quiet.

"Sofia?"

"Um, remember the sports bar in San Francisco?"

"What? We had fun. Except for that little problem with Johnnie."

"Right. A *little* problem. You almost decked him, and because of me, your friendship is done. Having a root canal would be preferable to going through that again."

"Johnnie was a drunk and an asshole. The guys I'm working with are pretty decent. There's not going to be a problem, and we're a couple now. I'd feel weird leaving you out."

Yes, he could be incredibly persuasive. I agreed, but having a new outfit to wear tonight wasn't negotiable.

After he'd left for work, I'd texted Charlie, and in a flash, he had been waiting for me in front of the hotel. "Lovely to see you again, ma'am. Where to today?"

"Can you take me to Harrods?"

"Of course, but my wife tells me that store can be mighty pricey. She only goes when they have the big sales, and then the women fight over stuff like a pack of dogs with one bone."

He wasn't wrong. It took several hours of wandering aimlessly through seven crowded floors before I found the sale racks, finally scoring a leather skirt and blouse suitable for London weather, as well as some summer clothes for our upcoming trip to Dubai, then the Maldives. It was hard to believe that in just a few days, I'd be lounging in a bikini instead of bundling up in a coat.

Just before I reached the checkout counter, I caught sight of a slinky evening dress with a low, draped back, and detoured to the changing room. The fabric poured over my curves like it was made for me. It was one of those *wow* dresses that said *buy me*. It didn't have to ask twice—until I checked the price tag, and the frugal voice in my brain screamed, *what the actual hell?* In the end, I won the internal battle, justifying the price, as it was my one big splurge—a special souvenir from my London trip.

I texted Charlie when I was done, and right on cue, he pulled the car around.

"Only one bag, ma'am?"

"What can I say? That place made me dizzy. They have everything from wine and chocolate to designer gowns. I got a bit lost."

He shook his head. "My wife could give you a tour. She knows every nook and cranny of that store. Unfortunately."

Back at the hotel, Ryan's text arrived a few hours later.

> Hi, babe, I'm at the pub. Can you meet me here? I'll send you the location.

I sent off a quick reply, then padded over to the closet. Despite Ryan's reassurance, a sense of foreboding twisted my stomach in knots. This wasn't much different from preparing for a job interview when you already knew they'd probably send you a form letter stating it just wasn't a good fit.

The evening would be so much easier if James were going to be there. I liked him, and he seemed supportive of Ryan. He'd been invited, but Ryan reported that he'd replied, "If I don't get home to the wife and kids for dinner tonight, my wife won't have sex with me for a month. Mind you, she's pretty much cut me off anyway, but a bloke can hope."

A flash of light briefly illuminated the room, followed by a loud clap of thunder. I looked out the window and groaned when I saw the sky rolling with angry, dark clouds. The only thing certain about tonight was that my sleek waves would transform into a frizzball, and I'd look like a poodle within an hour of absorbing the humidity.

I had to admit my new leather skirt and black lace blouse pumped up my confidence as I inspected my reflection in the mirror. Thunder boomed again as I applied a coat of fresh lipstick and curled my hair while cursing uselessly at the rain. After slipping into a pair of high-heeled boots, I grabbed an overcoat and ventured one last glance in the mirror, telling myself it didn't matter what anyone else thought. I looked good. As long as I didn't let doubt creep in, nothing and no one could derail me.

Thankfully, the doorman hailed a taxi for me, because by the time I exited the hotel, rain spat down in windy gusts, soaking the red carpet under the awning. The taxi dropped me off in front of the bar in the historic part of town. With the Tower of London looming against the dark sky, it appeared ominous in the storm. Preparing for the downpour, I tented my coat over my head and made a dash for the door. Even though it took only seconds to enter, the fabric was soaked, water pooling on the tiled floor as I peered through the sea of heads, taking in the dark wood walls and stained-glass windows, the smell of lager hanging thick in the air. The tables were jammed with an after-work crowd of men in suits and a smattering of women. I wedged my coat on a hook between the others by the front door and reached for my phone, typing out an SOS to Ryan.

I'm here by the door. Rescue me!

In moments, he emerged from the crowd, his tall frame striding toward me, freed from the jacket and tie he'd worn when he left that morning. He nuzzled his face near my ear, kissing his way down my jawline until reaching my lips. He tasted of beer and salty chips. I kissed him back, trying not to worry about who was watching.

"I see you've started without me," I said.

"What will you have? A stout? Or maybe a pilsner?"

"Definitely a lighter beer." As soon as he signaled to the server, my hand tightened on his forearm. When he looked back at me, my mouth went dry, and something in me clenched.

"What's wrong?"

"Are you sure you want me to meet your work friends?"

"Why wouldn't I?"

I gave him a look. He shook his head.

"Stop worrying, Sofia. There isn't a problem, except the one you're conjuring in your head."

"Actually, I have experience to back up the worry."

His voice soft, he said, "I couldn't care less what anyone else thinks. I want you here by my side. Anyway, let's relax and have some fun." He reached a finger to my chin, tipping my head up to meet his gaze. "Just be you. There's no need to be anyone else."

I nodded, and he laced his fingers through mine, leading me toward a table in the back. Reflexively, I took a deep breath.

A female server with terrifyingly large biceps careened around a corner, balancing a tray the size of a satellite dish. Ryan raised his hand in the air again. "When you can, will you bring the lady a pilsner?"

She nodded. "You got it, love."

After she sped off, Ryan lowered himself into a chair, then patted the seat next to him, motioning me to sit.

For several moments, my arrival went unnoticed in the din of noise—dishes clanging, wait staff scurrying, and overwhelming chatter filling the room. My head swiveled back and forth across the table at the three thirty-something men dressed in almost identical blue, pinstriped suits, and to the lone woman at the end. I listened as they lobbed banter like tennis balls, already in the middle of a conversation.

"There's a rumour going around that they're going to be making redundancies," said one guy, his haircut shaped like a bowl had been used as a template.

A man with a shock of red hair puffed out his chest. "Ah, mate, I'm not at risk. Don't you know the company can't afford to lose me?"

The other two threw peanuts at him; one ricocheted off his cheek and landed in his beer.

Bowlhead was insistent. "Well, did you know an assistant got sacked today?"

"Marc? He probably deserved it. What a wanker. Not much between the ears on that one," Red responded.

"Rumour has it he was shagging his boss's best friend," a hairy guy chimed in. He had an overgrown beard that covered his neck, reminding me of the Scottish Terrier that had lived next door to my childhood home.

"No, really? That cheeky bastard. Having a little bit on the side with Mrs. Robinson, was he?" *Could you be more cliche, Bowlhead?*

"You mean Marjorie? Didn't know he fancied the cougars." Hairy dude was getting on my nerves.

"You're just jealous you didn't get in her knickers first." Bowlhead lobbed the jab.

Hairy retorted, "I'm sorry, you must be mistaking me for some other desperate bloke."

"That's a bit ironic, don't you think? Since your last girlfriend was in nappies when Winston Churchill became prime minister," Red said. I rolled my eyes.

"Piss off." Hairy's cheeks reddened just above the muff of facial hair.

"All of you can piss off," the woman chimed in. She wore a soft red blazer over a white blouse, a striking contrast with the men in blue, and her hair was styled in a sleek bob. "Not one of you could get a woman in the sack, let alone a looker like Marjorie."

Ryan cleared his throat and coughed unnecessarily.

"Here you go, love," the server said, setting a beer on the table in front of me.

Suddenly, all eyes turned toward me. Nobody said a word.

Ryan spoke first. "Everybody, this is Sofia." His voice boomed through the din as he pointed to each person. "This is Thom, Samuel, William, and last but not least, Laura."

I didn't mention to Ryan that names weren't necessary. Red, Bowlhead, and Hairy would do just fine.

I nodded at each one and forced my spine straight. My heart pounded against my ribcage as fury rolled up my chest, boiling to the surface until I was an active volcano poised to erupt.

Laura's eyes brightened, looking at me from across the table. I liked her immediately. There was something in her soft expression that let me know she could be a friend, or at least an ally tonight. She'd already put the guys in their place.

"Lovely to meet you, Sofia. Ryan has told us about you coming all the way from California," she said.

I could see by the slack-jawed look on the men's faces that they hadn't received that memo.

"Yes, Ryan and I are both from California—San Francisco, to be precise. Have you ever been there?" I scanned the men's blank faces, their heads shaking. Straightening in my seat, I fought to keep my voice steady as I prepared to level a blow. "There's a bit of a cultural divide between London and San Francisco. The term 'cougar' is so... 2000 where I live. And definitely not politically correct."

William shrugged, looking sheepish. "We didn't mean anything by it."

Samuel dismissed me with a wave of his hand. "Don't go making a storm in a teacup. It's just the way we blokes talk."

I swallowed hard, sensing Ryan's gaze on me. He swung his arm around my shoulders, the muscles pulled so taut, they rose somewhere around my ears.

"And how do blokes talk about dating women half their age?" I swung my gaze from one man to the next, pinning them to their seats with a glare. "If that bloke, Marc, was shagging his twenty-year-old assistant, would you be calling him desperate?" One by one, their eyes darted away from mine. "No, I bet not. You'd be calling him lucky. It's just fine for a man to be twenty years older than his girlfriend. That's perfectly acceptable, right? But if the woman is even five years older than a man, it's scandalous. She's a cougar robbing the cradle, or worse... desperate and pathetic."

My eyes must have looked like a wild animal on the hunt as I scanned the table. Only Laura was smiling. The men avoided my gaze, their lips pressed together in tight lines. "Well, I'm sick of the status quo and the way men perpetuate the stereotype. It's demeaning to all women. It's demeaning to me." I huffed out an angry breath and glanced toward Ryan, but I wasn't done yet. "And if you guys had any sense, you'd know that Marc was damn lucky to be dating a woman with maturity instead of some Barbie doll."

My body trembled, but even Ryan's grip on my shoulder wasn't going to distract me. In the middle of my tirade, I considered that maybe I was projecting my own issues and probably shouldn't have picked this moment to get on my soapbox, but they'd hit my hot button. And maybe I was playing offense instead of defense, anticipating their appraisal of me and, worse—how they'd voice this to Ryan.

To my relief, I caught him nodding in agreement, then we both jolted at the sound of glass breaking. Two tables to the left, a server was bent over, his tray empty. Beer glasses lay in a shattered heap on the floor. Suddenly, the pub erupted with loud cries of what sounded like, "Waaaey." I glanced at Laura. She instantly clocked my unspoken question.

"That's just something we do here, a bit of pub fun. It embarrasses the hell out of whoever smashes the glass, but it's all in good jest."

It gave the guys a reprieve, their laughter breaking the tension, until Laura continued, picking up where I'd left off. "But to your point, Sofia, you're dead on. This kind of double standard has been going on for donkey's years. It's not fair. The men get to do whatever they please and they just get a pat on the back and a 'Well done, mate.' The middle-aged men 'round here are stuck in front of the telly with a pint in hand while their belly gets as round as a beach ball. Why should we put up with that while we still have a lot more life in us? Besides, the younger men are still up to the task, if you know what I mean."

I had to stifle a laugh when she winked at me. No question, I definitely liked her. She appeared a few years younger than me but old enough to know exactly what I meant.

I raised my glass to her. "I couldn't have said it better, Laura. Culturally speaking, there's no difference between our countries on that note."

The men turned their attention to Ryan, looking for backup from the only other man at the table. He threw his palms up. "Don't look at me. I agree with the ladies. I love a strong, feisty, grown woman. Especially this one."

I swiveled my head toward him, and seeing his smile—the pride in his eyes—the storm in my belly ebbed. When I turned back, the guys were draining the last of their beer, poised to make an exit.

"Well now, look at the time," Samuel said.

"Yes, right." The others nodded. "We'll just be showing ourselves out."

They kept their heads ducked as they passed me, and I heard their mutterings in staggered phrases. "Lovely to meet you," and "Right then, we're off."

Laura chuckled after they were out of earshot. "What a bunch of sodding wankers. Now that we have that sorted, who's got the next round?"

Ryan raised his hand, waving to the server. I turned to him and lowered my voice. "You're not mad that I chased off your buddies?"

"Hell no. It was fun to watch them squirm. I would have put them in their place if you hadn't jumped in. Honestly, it was fucking awesome watching you in action. You went all badass on them. However, I am making a mental note to stay out of your way when you're angry."

I shrugged. "Well, you did tell me to be myself."

"I wouldn't want it any other way."

"Aww, you two are the cutest." Laura rested her chin on her hand, observing us.

"Okay, Laura, teach me some of your pub games," I said.

Just then, a glass toppled from the table onto the floor with a crash. Ryan struck the palm of his hand against his forehead and cringed. Heads swiveled in his direction, and then the cry bellowed through the pub. "Waaaey."

Chapter Eleven
Sofia

Monumental skyscrapers glittered in the sun's light, rising from the obscurity of a desert surrounded by water. The oasis looked as if it sprang from the imaginative mind of a science fiction writer. The plane circled toward the runway, my nose pressed against the glass, my hand laced in Ryan's.

"Is that a sandstorm?" I asked. Wind whipped thick dust into whirling clouds below.

He leaned across my lap to peer out the window. "Looks like it. Nothing a dip in the pool won't fix. Be prepared for heat like you've probably never experienced."

"I'm more of a tropical heat kind of girl, not desert heat," I said as a voice boomed over the loudspeaker from the cockpit.

We'll be landing in Dubai soon. The temperature is ninety-eight degrees Fahrenheit.

"Another thing," Ryan said, talking over the captain, "this is a Muslim country, so you're going to need a crash course on cultural norms." He glanced down at my skirt.

"I know, dress conservatively here. When I stand up, my skirt will cover my knees."

"Good girl. It's an exciting city, actually, but there are rules. I'll fill you in as we go along, but the first is important." He made a serious face and said, "No PDAs. We can't hug and kiss in public."

"Seriously?" I frowned. "I guess we'll just have to make up for it in private."

"I intend to hold you to it." The way his eyebrow cocked and the glint in his eyes was enough to make my panties melt. I wondered if I'd ever become immune.

He wasn't kidding about the heat. Stepping out of the airport was like entering a walk-in oven. "How do people live in this weather? Sweat is already trickling down my back," I said, climbing into the relief of the air-conditioned limo.

"Air conditioning, pools, and the ocean. And only go out in the evening, when it's slightly cooler." He took the opportunity to pull me into a kiss while we were secluded behind the tinted glass windows.

"How do you always taste so sweet?"

He reached for the container of breath mints in his pocket, shaking the pellets with a self-satisfied grin.

"Smartass." I snatched the mints from his grip. "So, what am I going to do while you're in meetings?"

"Probably work on your tan at the pool. Anyway, we'll only be here for a couple of days."

Examining my arms, it was evident I'd lost the bronze since returning from Barcelona. "I'll have to be careful. Don't want to scorch myself before we hit our island paradise."

The limo's engine whined as it accelerated and made its way through the city center, snaking through pristine streets shadowed by the impenetrable wall of impressively sleek buildings.

"How did you make out with the travel plans?" he asked.

"Two weeks on a private island in our own villa, and hopefully, a private beach. Robinson Crusoe style, except with luxury amenities. That's all you need to know for now."

"I'm prepared to be naked and thoroughly impressed, I'm sure," he said.

"If you're naked, I believe I'll be the one impressed."

He tucked a strand of hair behind my ear and smiled. "How did I get so lucky?"

"Good karma?" I shrugged and secretly thought about how I was the lucky one. If I hadn't chosen to join him, I'd be missing out on one hell of an adventure.

When we reached the hotel desk, the adventure took an unexpected turn.

"The reservation is under the name of Ryan Hunter. My wife is joining me. It was a last-minute decision." He took the passport from my hand and gave it to the clerk, who then eyed me suspiciously. Ryan kept his gaze straight ahead, as if daring the man to challenge him.

My eyes darted toward his profile, then slid to the window of the lobby, remarking casually, "What a beautiful fountain you have here." I was never good at holding a poker face, but I knew Ryan had his reasons. My hands remained glued to my sides, out of sight. Would they notice I wasn't wearing a ring? Of course, at that precise moment, my nose started to itch. Oh God. My palms went clammy, and sweat congealed under my arms. I tried sniffing, then twitching my nose. The clerk shot a furtive glance at me. "Allergies," I muttered.

"Very well, sir," the clerk finally said to Ryan. "The porter will see you and your luggage to the room."

As soon as the porter was out of earshot, I whispered to Ryan, "You could have given me a heads up on that one. A ring would've helped, too."

"Don't worry, you did fine. It's illegal for unmarried couples to get a room together, but the large hotels usually just look the other way."

"And you know this because...?"

We entered the elevator along with the porter. He still couldn't touch me, but the look in his eyes gave me reassurance.

"Because I have many clients in Dubai. It's important I know the rules." My shoulders sagged with relief.

"Wow. They really know how to do first-class elegance here," I said, marveling at our ultra-modern hotel suite with a view of the Persian Gulf waters and white sand beaches through immense, floor-to-ceiling windows. The expansive panorama stretched seemingly forever from this vantage point on the highest floor in the hotel.

I felt his arms wrap around me from behind and his chin rest atop my head as I opened the sliding window, letting in a fiery blast of desert wind. "It's spectacular, isn't it?" he commented. "This city oozes money. It lends new meaning to the saying, *if you build it, they will come.* They built a luxury city on land created from the rocks of the seabed. Now it's both a tourist destination and a business hub. Go figure."

"How's the shopping here?"

He laughed, his chest rumbling against my back. "World class."

"Maybe I should find an evening dress, something fitting for Dubai. I'm thinking gold to match the obscene amount of bling here." I was only half joking. "That is, if we're going out tonight." I cocked my head to the side, my eyebrows twitching.

"Of course! But nothing too daring."

"Got it."

He released me, planted a quick kiss on my lips, and headed for his suitcase, saying apologetically, "It sucks to leave you, but I have to get ready for my meeting."

I pouted for a second, then rummaged through my suitcase until I found my swimsuit and cover-up dress. By the time he left, he was eyeing me from the doorway, and now *he* had a pouty face.

"Damn. You look too good, babe. Stay covered until you get to the pool. Enjoy."

I did a pretty good job of not feeling guilty while I enjoyed the day, knowing he was locked up in an office. I wondered what he was grappling with while I floated in an infinity pool, my arms resting on the edge, letting my gaze wander across the expansive azure sea. Nope. Not even a little guilty.

When the limo took me to an enormous, air-conditioned mall and the effusive staff of an opulent boutique waited on me graciously, I considered how, just a few months ago, I had been stuck in an office all day. It seemed like a lifetime ago.

I slipped a cream-colored, elegantly beaded dress over my head and looked in the mirror. *This is the one*, I thought, and slid the band from atop my head, allowing the mass of dark curls to cascade over my shoulders. The dress flowed gently over my curves, clinging in all the right places, but it was modest enough to walk down the streets of Dubai.

Dubai. A few months ago, it would never have occurred to me I'd visit such a foreign place, let alone explore a shopping mall on my own. An unfamiliar woman stared back at me in the mirror. I almost didn't recognize her in my reflection, but I liked what I saw: her eyes confident, her face radiant; she personified the woman I'd somehow always known was buried in the shadows.

After choosing a pair of glittery high-heeled sandals, I zig-zagged through the crowded mall until I reached the entrance, then texted the driver. Within twenty minutes, I burst through the door of our hotel room, still glowing with the rush of a shopping-induced high.

"Ryan?" No response. Silence filled the room. I found him sitting at the dining table, holding a glass of wine. Slowly, his glance slid to mine, and I knew in an instant that something had gone terribly wrong today.

"Hey," he muttered, his eyes dull and fixed, like he barely registered my presence.

"Hey yourself." My mood plummeted. I dropped my bag on the chair and stroked my hands over his slumped shoulders, then began kneading the tense muscles with my fingers. "Are you going to tell me what's wrong? And don't say 'nothing.'"

"That feels so good. Don't stop, please." He rolled his neck, stretching from side to side.

"I won't stop if you just talk to me."

After a long pause, he began. "I'm dealing in the big leagues, Sofia. Multi-billion-dollar conglomerates. It's just... well, there's been a lot of pressure."

"Did you close the sale today?"

"It appears we've struck a deal. Nothing left to do but sign the paperwork." His head dropped, and he ran his fingers through his hair.

"Really? Then why aren't we celebrating?"

"You're right." He tilted his gaze up to meet mine, flashing me a smile that didn't quite reach his eyes. "Did you find a dress?"

I picked up the bag and clutched it to my chest. "Oh yes. But you don't get to see it yet. I'm going for the *wow* response, so you'll have to wait until I'm all put together. Do you want to shower first?"

"I think the shower is big enough for both of us. You know, I'll wash your back, you wash mine?" A sly smile replaced the frown he wore a few minutes ago. Was sex a cure-all for guys?

"I think you've used that line on me before."

"Did it work?" he asked. When his lips pressed against mine, there wasn't a trace of worry.

"Yes, always. But I doubt it will be my back you'll be washing," I said in an accent which had been stuck in my head since London. My clothes came off, leaving a trail on the floor on my way to the shower.

Sometime later, when I finally emerged from the bathroom after another hour spent in a private flurry of make-up and curling irons, my skin glowed with an iridescent blush and my hair hung over my shoulders in perfect curls. I made a dramatic entrance, my stiletto heels ticking across the floor until I was standing in front of Ryan as he sat on the couch, already dressed in a black jacket and slacks. He lowered the newspaper until his eyes met mine, then scanned me from head to toe.

"Definitely WOW. You look stunning."

I grabbed his hand and pulled him into my arms. "You look pretty stunning yourself, hon." I breathed in his masculine scent, instantly stirring all my senses. When he pressed against me, it was like my body went rogue. I was no longer the captain of this ship. A visceral sound rose in my throat, a low moan of pleasure escaping my lips.

He echoed my response, his voice rumbling against my ear. "We could just stay in, you know."

"We could... but then you'd miss showing me off in this new dress." I felt his arousal pressing hard against me. "Hold that thought, babe. Call it... extended foreplay."

"I can live with that," he said, stroking his thumb across the line of my jaw just before he tipped my chin and pressed a kiss on my lips. "Alright then, I'll call for the car."

"Where're we going?"

He opened the door for me, and as we left the room, he answered, "To be seduced by Dubai."

The lavish restaurant, set in the middle of the waters surrounding the Dubai Fountain like a floating island, was the perfect setting for an intimate, celebratory dinner. Our table perched at the edge of the bank, giving us a view of the water shimmering in hues of... yes, you guessed it, gold—since the color was literally everywhere. As darkness fell, the city sprang to life, sparkling like a jewel illuminated from every angle. We drank signature cocktails from martini glasses and indulged in beautifully presented fusion cuisine. I felt like a princess on a Disney movie set.

"Would you like dessert?" Ryan asked. My eyes darted to the young male server hovering nearby, then back to him. Surreptitiously, Ryan leaned toward the server. "I'd like a little privacy, please. We'll let you know if we need anything."

The overzealous server reluctantly edged over to another table. "Do they always refill the water glasses every two seconds?" I asked.

"Maybe he's just fascinated with you."

I pulled a face. Then I felt his leg stroking mine under the table. "I'm about to undress you with my eyes, because that's all I can do under the circumstances." I let out a frustrated growl.

"Extended foreplay, babe." He winked at me, and I slid my bare toes against his thigh. He laughed and shifted in his chair. "Now you aren't playing fair."

I watched his face dissolve into a look of pleasure, set against the surreal backdrop resembling a sultan's palace. White drapes billowed in the breeze of the open terrace, and candlelight glowed atop tables. "I hope you're enjoying this as much as I am."

He coughed out a laugh. "I'm enjoying this even more than you are right now."

Lowering my foot to the floor, I slipped back into my heels. "So, are we going home now?" After that tease, I fully expected him to agree, but he had other plans.

I assumed dinner would be the highlight of the evening, until the limo whisked us to a chic lounge set on the edge of the Arabian Sea. A DJ spun sounds of world music; golden chandeliers cast a dim light, and the scene reeked of money, as if membership in the elite upper class was a prerequisite for entry. This was the place to be seen in Dubai, the bar overflowing with smartly dressed men and elegant women dripping with jewels, which sparkled against glittering dresses. So much bling! The reflections were almost blinding. I straightened my spine and held onto Ryan's hand as we edged our way to the bar, trying to fend off the observation that I was old enough to be the mother of most of the youngsters there.

"You seem like you're in a better mood now," I said as he handed me a pink cocktail, which tasted as delicious as it looked—probably deceptively potent, too. I'd have to be careful because drunk me would forget all about the rules.

"Thanks to you." He smiled and took my hand again. "I see some seats on the patio. Let's go enjoy the view."

I nestled my cheek against his shoulder as we sat side by side on a bench, checking to make sure no one was close enough to see us. The city lights danced across the water in a dazzling spectacle, set against a landscape of gleaming skyscrapers and modern art sculptures.

"I think I *am* being seduced by this city. It's stunning."

"I knew you'd—" He stopped, the look on his face suddenly stone cold. A man was striding across the patio, headed right for us, his eyes glaring at Ryan.

"Ryan. I didn't expect to see you again today." A short, stout man with a sharply receding hairline stood directly in front of Ryan, his jaw clenched so tight that his cheeks rose into round pillows.

"Brian," he said with a chill in his voice I'd never heard.

The man squared his shoulders just before his voice bellowed. "What the hell do you think you're playing at?"

"Excuse me?"

"I did some digging, and the company you're representing in the buyout is not as solvent as you make it out to be. If this sale is finalized, what do you think Omar is going to do when he discovers that you've lied?"

Ryan's voice emerged through gritted teeth. "I believe you read my detailed report, and you've had access to my client's records as Omar's accountant. So, tell me, why are you objecting now?" Ryan leveled a steeled gaze at him.

"Oh, the figures look good on paper. I don't have conclusive proof, but you're hiding something. There's a weakness you haven't disclosed. Rumors are flying, and if they're true, George's company is about to lose a major contract, which will cost my client millions. If this happens, don't think you won't be liable in court."

I watched Ryan; his expression a mask, revealing nothing. Maybe only I noticed the bands on his neck pulsing as his jaw clenched. His hands pressed against the arms of the chair, pushing himself to his feet. As he towered over Brian, the man stumbled back a few feet. I'd seen Ryan become enraged at a guy before, and given the culture here, I worried he was about to get into some serious trouble.

"I don't think you're in a position to threaten me. After all, it was your job to do a thorough investigation before we prepared the purchase agreement for signature—due diligence and all. I think your neck would be on the chopping block. I know nothing of these rumors, but if you did and didn't come forward... well, that might be a career-ending move."

"We'll just see who's going to take the fall here. The truth has a way of being discovered." Brian's voice was even, but there was no mistaking the threat in his tone. He squared his shoulders, then turned away, his footsteps heavy as he stormed into the lounge.

"Ryan?" I waited for him to turn around. His hands went to his head, slowly running his fingers through his hair, his body locked in a rigid stance.

"Let's get out of here," he said flatly.

During the twenty-minute ride back to the hotel, we sat in agonized silence. It wasn't until we were back in the room that I dared to speak.

"Things are not okay, are they?"

He paced the length of the living room, and sighing heavily said, "I did know about the contract, the one they might lose. It was a risk versus loss decision. If I didn't make this deal, my reputation as a closer would be in question. Sellers count on me to make it happen. *George* is counting on me."

"But if this comes out, your reputation will also be in jeopardy."

"More than that, I could be held liable. I just have to hope that the acquisition goes through without a disaster."

I felt helpless, seeing the worried look on his face, the way his shoulders slumped with the weight of the entire merger on his back.

"I know there's nothing I can do," I said. Moving toward him, I reached out and took his hand. "But whatever happens, I'm here for you."

The corners of his mouth twitched, a meager attempt at a smile. "Thanks, Sofia, but it's my responsibility, and I'm going to have to make this right tomorrow. I'll be tied up all morning, at least. When is our flight?"

"Late afternoon. Do you think we'll have to postpone?"

He pulled me in close, wrapping his arms around me. "Not if I can help it."

I buried my face in his chest and tried to conceal any trace of disappointment, telling myself that Ryan's obligation to his client took priority for the moment. We'd make it to the Maldives, sooner or later. "I don't want you worrying about our trip. We can reschedule if necessary. Right now, just focus on resolving this problem and getting the deal signed. Okay?"

When I lifted my chin, the look in his eyes nearly melted me. "I love you, in case I haven't said it enough recently."

I pressed my lips to his, rocking my hips against his body. He kissed me, his fingers lacing through my hair, then pushed away, leaving me breathless.

"I can't, not tonight." He let out a frustrated groan and slid his palms down his face. "I have to make a few calls to organize meetings for the morning, then formulate a strategy. You go on to bed, and I'll try not to wake you when I climb in later."

It took several seconds for me to realize I was pouting, then I quickly straightened my face. While I was in the bathroom, peeling off my beautiful new gown, I heard Ryan's voice on the phone, each word enunciated with sharp intensity, and agonized at the sound. It was impossible to imagine what he might face in the morning.

Even after I climbed into bed, my thoughts raced for what seemed like hours. I wondered why he needed to win at any cost, why he hadn't disclosed the information sooner. Was he at all like his father? I shuddered at the thought. No, he couldn't be. Ryan at his core was honest. This was the way business was done, after all. I convinced myself that everything would be fine, and slowly my thoughts settled into a low hum.

Ryan sat silently at the desk, the faint light of the computer screen illuminating his weary face.

Sometime after listening to noises passing in the hall-way—girls giggling, parents tugging cranky toddlers into their rooms, and doors closing as guests turned in for the night—I drifted off to sleep in the silence. When I woke up the next morning, Ryan was already gone.

Chapter Twelve

Ryan

"Mr. Hunter, how are you?"

George's receptionist raised a smile when she looked up from her computer screen and saw me standing at her desk. "Very well, thank you," I lied, then peered around her shoulder at the glass-enclosed corner office where George was hunched over his desk, the receiver of a phone pressed against his ear. His balding head reflected the light bouncing off a sea of gleaming skyscrapers beyond the plate-glass windows. "Is George ready for me?"

"It will be just a moment." She raised a finger tipped with bright red nail polish.

"This can't wait." With long, determined strides, I crossed to his door and turned the handle.

"Mr. Hunter—" Her voice, an indignant protest, disappeared as I shut the door behind me. George saw the look on my face, his eyes flashing something like fear. I didn't back off; instead, leaning in, I pressed my palms on his desk to get his attention.

"Can I call you back? I have a pressing matter to attend to." He lowered the receiver, and his eyes met mine, his gray, bushy eyebrows arching. "Ryan, what's going on?"

"Someone leaked information. The accountant who reviewed your books knows that one of your distributors plans to pull out. George, this will affect the entire United States IT distribution chain. We can't close the deal, not with this threat hanging over us." I slammed my palm on the desk, hating myself for letting things get this far, then paced the length of the carpeted floor. My mind churned through solutions to this mess.

"Ryan, please. I need this." He shot out of the chair and moved toward me but halted when he spotted men in suits striding down the hallway. George looked like he could jump right out of his skin. The guy was hiding something, no doubt. When he turned back to me, his eyes were pleading. "Look, you and I have been in business together for a long time. You know I'm not a dishonest man, but my back is up against the wall. It's time for me to retire and get back to the States. My health won't hold up much longer."

"Don't you think I know that? But dammit, my reputation is on the line here. No client will trust me if I let you sign the deal under these circumstances. We need to fix this now, or I'll be forced to disclose that the sale is compromised. Get Rajit on a video call."

George pulled up his desk chair and reached for the computer, his hands trembling on the keyboard. "What time is it in San Francisco?"

"I don't care. Just get him on the line." My voice reverberated against the glass window, and George cringed. I took a breath, forcing myself to lower the volume. We'd all be screwed if George keeled over with a heart attack.

Five agonizing minutes went by before Rajit's video screen flickered to life. He didn't look happy to see us. "Do you guys know it's the middle of the fucking night?"

"Hello, Rajit." I kept my tone even. The last thing I needed was to piss him off even more. "Sorry to bother you, but we have an urgent matter here. We're about to close the deal on the sale, but there's one problem. We need you on board."

"I already told George that I'm not working with Omar. If he's your buyer, then no deal. He's a ruthless son of a bitch, and everyone knows he'll step all over his distributors. Money is his bottom line; he doesn't care about business relationships."

"So, you'd rather screw over George?" I wrapped my arm around George's slumped shoulders. "Your contract is with George. You've been loyal to him for over ten years, and he's always been a fair business partner. If you pull out, several things will happen. George won't be able to retire, and you know his health is failing. Do you want to be responsible for his death here in Dubai?"

Okay, maybe I was being overdramatic, but I was betting on their relationship to swing things in our direction.

There was a long pause. Rajit's eyes grew wide, and I knew I had his attention. "And the second thing that's going to happen is that your reputation will be ruined. You'll be known for reneging on contracts. In the IT world, word gets

around fast, and the competition is fierce. Do you think anyone will want to do business with you again? Not to mention
what it would do to your stock value."

As his face fell, I seized the opportunity to play my high
card. "I hope you're aware of the legal consequences you'll
be facing. The contract doesn't have a clause exempting
disruptions because of the sale."

Rajit was shifting in his chair, running his hands through
his spiky dark hair. I sensed my opening. Time to shift tactics.
"Look, no one wants to see you get trampled. Your company
is absolutely vital to the success of the entire team. I give you
my word, I'll make Omar understand that."

Rajit leaned into the camera so that his scowling face
filled the screen. "And how are you going to manage that?
Omar doesn't listen to anyone," he said, enunciating every
syllable for emphasis.

"Let's add an addendum to the contract, stipulating your
terms. Omar will listen, because he has a vested interest
in this deal going through. Trust me to act in your best
interest." When he relaxed back into the chair, I ducked out
of the screen just long enough to release the breath I'd been
holding. "Put something together and send it within the
hour, because I've called a management meeting with the
heads of both companies. I'll present your terms and get this
done—for George."

He nodded, and I felt George's shoulders lower a few
inches under my arm. "Thanks, Rajit. I really appreciate your
help," George said, a fake smile plastered on his face until

the screen went dark. Then he sank his head into his hands. "God, I hope this works."

"You should have come clean about this before, George, instead of waiting until the bottom of the ninth." He had the grace to look embarrassed. I straightened my spine and headed for the door. No choice but to appear confident and stay in control. Omar would smell weakness from a mile away. "Wait for Rajit's email, run it by me, and then have it printed. I want four copies."

Pausing at the door, I turned back. "George, fix your tie and get a cup of coffee. I need you to keep a poker face. Under no circumstances are you to show any reaction. You are prepared and ready to sign the deal today, right?"

He nodded. Christ, he looked like hell—weariness and gravity tugging down the corners of his mouth. Part of me wanted to let him off the hook, but in the end, I had to stay tough. For his own good.

I headed for the men's room and splashed cold water on my face. My reflection stared back at me in the mirror, and I could almost see my father's image. Had I noticed that before? That I resembled him? I wiped my face with a paper towel. *I am nothing like my father.* I couldn't lose Sofia's respect, the way my father had lost mine, though I wondered if I'd already skated too close to that line.

George and I were already seated in the plush, white, leather chairs when the receptionist swung open the door of the conference room and Omar strode in, his advisor following behind. I stood and extended my arm. Omar pinned me with his gaze as his hand gripped mine with so much force I rocked forward a step. He was as tall as I was, maybe five years older, with jet-black hair and a fiery look in his deep brown eyes. He'd earned his reputation as an obscenely wealthy, powerful man, known for his questionable business tactics, but most of that wealth was not self-made. As a member of one of the elite Arab families, he controlled a good deal of the business in this region.

I didn't want to think about the consequences if this deal was aborted, but I also knew he needed George's company if he wanted to dominate the U.S. market. It was a gamble, and I'd bluff if I had to, but I believed we had the edge.

"Omar, thank you for coming on such short notice." While he positioned himself at the head of the table, I shifted my attention to his advisor. "Saeed, I trust you brought the purchase agreement?"

Saeed regarded me for a few seconds before reaching into his briefcase, then placed the papers in a neat pile on the mahogany table. Saeed had always treated me with disdain—or at least mistrust. While he'd been in banking longer than me, I had more experience handling multi-billion-dollar clients. His insecurity manifested itself every time he tried and failed to prove me wrong, which made the stakes of this meeting even higher. I couldn't afford to fail.

"Gentlemen," I said, relaxing back in the chair opposite Omar, my hands pressed together while steepling my fingers—a clear signal that I was in control here. "We received your letter of intent stating the terms for purchase, and due diligence has been performed. Your accountant studied our company's records and found everything to be in order, but he called my attention to a matter that needs to be resolved before proceeding."

Omar looked at me suspiciously as he leaned forward, his broad chest cresting over the polished wood. "I don't understand. Haven't we discussed this deal at great length? I thought we came to a firm agreement at the last meeting. What could have emerged since yesterday?"

Bile rose in my throat, and I glanced sideways at George. His expression was unreadable, but I caught sight of the droplets of sweat emerging at his hairline. "Omar, I know you value honesty, and I want to honor you with transparency. George has spent his life building this business, and his reputation is impeccable. That's why we want to bring this matter to your attention. With the sale nearly completed, George learned that a contract with his major distributor was at risk."

"What contract? The distribution in the U.S.?" Omar interrupted, raising his hands in protest, then slamming his fists on the table—his eyes bulging nearly out of their sockets.

Keeping my voice level, I continued. "I said it was at risk. We spoke with the head of distribution this morning and resolved the issue. When a company undergoes this kind of transition, fears and concerns are inevitable. It's my job to make sure everyone's interests are protected, and as a successful entrepreneur yourself, you know compromises are sometimes necessary."

I noticed the slightest acknowledgment in Omar's expression.

George swiveled his chair in my direction, and I nodded. He passed me the printouts. With a confident stride, I moved around the room to deliver copies to Omar and Saeed.

"With your approval, I'll add this addendum to our agreement. It will secure the contract with the distributor and ensure that your target for the U.S. market is fully realized."

"But, sir, I'm not convinced this addendum is in my client's best interests," Saeed said, his eyes scanning the page. Then, turning to Omar, he added, "This will limit your ability to exert control or change the financial structure of the arrangement."

Sweat trickled down my back, and I wished I'd brought an extra shirt. Silence descended on the vacuum-sealed room while Omar studied the document. When he finally met my gaze, he no longer looked like he wanted my head on a stick.

"I am a fair man, Ryan, despite what you may have heard about me. I understand this Rajit seeks to maintain security for himself and his workers. As you said, business sometimes requires compromise. I accept this addendum."

I glanced around the table. Saeed's lips were set in a firm line. George couldn't conceal a noticeable sigh of relief. I dipped my head in a nod to Omar, took a deep breath, and turned to Saeed with a smile positioned on my face. "I believe it's time to sign the agreement." The steel bands constricting my shoulders didn't release until Omar signed the documents, then Saeed reluctantly placed them in my hands. Still, I couldn't help suspecting that Omar was already concocting a plan to find a loophole.

When we returned to George's office, he nearly bowled me over with a bear hug, tears welling in his eyes. "Thank you, Ryan, for everything," he choked out. "You were right. I wouldn't have wanted to leave this business under a cloud of deceit, especially after putting so many years into it—sacrificing so much for the sake of the company."

"George, my friend, it's time to go enjoy the rest of your life." I broke from his grasp and gripped his shoulders. "You deserve to take a vacation and relax for a change. Too much work does a person in."

His chest heaved with a deep breath. "I'm getting out of here as soon as I tie up loose ends. I'll take the wife on a nice trip, maybe a cruise around the world. Who knows?" He scratched his head, parting the thin wisps of gray hair with his fingertips, his brows drawing together. "It's hard to imagine what life will be like without work."

"It's a new beginning, George. You'll figure it out."

"So, are you heading back to London or San Francisco?"

For the first time all day, I allowed a wave of relief to sweep over me. I was going to be on an island naked with Sofia. I couldn't help grinning. "Neither. I'm going to the Maldives with a beautiful woman."

"Jesus. You're my hero!" He laughed, a deep sound that made his belly shake.

As I raced to the elevator, all I could think about was leaving Dubai behind and boarding the plane with Sofia. I couldn't wait to see the look on her face when I told her our vacation was back on track.

Chapter Thirteen

Sofia

As we circled over the Male Hulhule airport, I gazed out the window at the turquoise sea, which from this height looked like a vivid watercolor painting. Countless islands stretched in the distance, appearing as tiny patches of sand topped with a garnish of parsley. I glanced at Ryan, fast asleep in the seat next to me, softly snoring. He'd begun to fill me in on the morning's events but, in the middle of a sentence, he'd drifted off. I would spare him the details of how his mouth fell open and a little drool escaped as he snored. I couldn't blame him, since he'd barely slept at all last night. When he'd finished his meeting, he had rushed back and whisked me to the airport so we could make our flight, saying, "Let's get the hell out of Dubai."

When I'd returned to the travel agency in London, Helena had presented me with so many options it had made my head spin.

"You can stay on just one of the approximately one-hundred-fifty tiny islands, or you can island hop if you fancy that." She had gestured to the pile of brochures I'd gone through. "Let's narrow this down. Are you interested in a five-star resort? A private villa and beach? A spa? Or loads of activities and things to do?"

I stared blankly at the photos of countless resorts, which boasted villas that were perched directly atop the calm ocean waters, while others sat within the lush tropical forests like treehouses. Each one looked like paradise.

I nodded yes to each question. "Can we have it all?"

She smiled. "Well now, let's see what we can do." Then she swiveled her chair toward a filing cabinet, her polished pink nails flicking through the folders. "I think this resort would work quite nicely. It's incredibly romantic, has the privacy you're looking for, and they offer excursions to other islands as well as dive spots. I think you'll find the coral reefs just divine for snorkeling."

She slipped the brochures across the desk, and I pored through each page, in awe of the natural beauty of the pristine beaches lined with coconut palm trees and luxurious villas set on top of the powdery sand. Most resorts were all-inclusive. The photos of the buffets—the endless rows of exotic fruits I'd never seen before, and the freshly caught seafood—made me salivate. For Ryan, ever the foodie, this spread might be more tempting than seeing me half-naked.

Then I saw the price, and my jaw dropped several inches. I could never have imagined spending that much on a vacation. On my salary, which wasn't too shabby, it would have taken me years to save enough money. But Ryan had insisted I use his credit card and stop worrying about the expense. His travel style couldn't have been more different from mine. I stayed in apartment rentals instead of hotels, partly because I could cook meals rather than eat out. Hotels were expensive and cramped even for a family of three, and when my son was older, he appreciated having the privacy of his own room.

But this was the mother of all romantic holidays, deserving a resort-style splurge. Finally, I shoved aside my deeply rooted instinct to pinch every penny, handed over Ryan's credit card, and allowed Helena to book our dream vacation.

I had never been so excited about a trip. Even as we'd boarded the plane in London, I'd felt like a little kid, giddy with anticipation—*Are we there yet? Are we there yet?*

"Hey, sleepyhead," I said, dropping a kiss on Ryan's forehead as his eyelids blinked open.

He straightened in his seat, pulled off his sunglasses, and rubbed his eyes. "How long have I been out?"

"You fell asleep as soon as the plane reached altitude. We're about to land now."

"Damn. I was going to meet you in the bathroom," he said, a grin playing on his lips, "you know, for old times' sake."

"Hah. Next time we find ourselves in the bathroom together, it had better be more fun than tending to my bloody nose."

He squeezed my hand and softly kissed my knuckles. "Remember when we were stuck, your body pressed against mine, and my hand accidentally grabbed your boob?"

I nodded. "I was mortified."

"It might not have been such an accident," he admitted, the corner of his mouth breaking into a mischievous grin. "You gave me such a hard-on."

I lowered my voice to a whisper. "In my fantasies, I've replayed that scene with you taking me from behind, and—"

"Please prepare for landing. Seatbacks up, tray tables secured," the flight attendant commanded, rudely interrupting. We complied, Ryan alert now, his eyes wide and full of want as he swiveled to face me. "Oh... you are *so* going to finish that thought later."

When we boarded the seaplane from the international airport to our island destination, I secretly crossed my fingers, praying Ryan would be delighted with the resort I had chosen—hoping he could leave all his worries back in Dubai and relax. I'd never seen him so stressed, but he'd returned from his meeting acting more like himself. Yet, the weary look in his eyes told me the battle had taken more of a toll than he'd been willing to admit.

To: Madison555@gmail.com
From: SofiaDrake01@gmail.com
It does feel weird that we're writing emails instead of hopping on the phone every day, right? I'm relieved that Kevin—or, as I like to call him, the asshole ex—hasn't bothered you again, and it sounds like you and Roger had an honest heart-to-heart talk. It seems promising. Roger is a great guy, and I'm rooting for you guys.

Try not to hate me, but I'm writing to you from my private deck (with a pool), looking out at the crystal-clear waters of the Indian Ocean. It's like I've been photoshopped into a picture postcard, with palm trees in the background and the whitest sand beaches you've ever seen. In my wildest dreams, I never could have imagined actually vacationing on a Maldivian island, let alone with a man who loves me. I think this takes carpe diem to a whole new level!

You probably wouldn't recognize me—I don't even recognize myself. Who would have thought I'd become a world traveler, an American with a peculiar British accent? I can't seem to shake it, but maybe it suits me. My old life seems a million miles away and so long ago. Time is speeding by. I want to take the battery out of the clock and make this last forever. Reality is never too far from my awareness, but for now, this is as real as it gets. Did I mention I'm sitting here naked in the shade of an umbrella? I will send pics... of the scenery. Xo

Ryan's shadow arrived in front of me before he did. I closed my laptop and tipped my chin, drinking in the sight of him. His skin had already become deep bronze from the sun, his hair a mass of tousled waves, glistening from a swim in the ocean.

"I thought we had agreed to go off the grid—cell and computer off." He leaned over me, his broad chest rising with heavy breaths, as if he'd sprinted back from the beach.

"I know, but I had to touch base with Madison."

His brow furrowed. "Is she okay? No problem with Kevin, I hope. That dude was crazy."

"She's good, and yes, I'm happy Kevin is out of her life. It looks like she and Roger are doing just fine—more than fine, I think." I reached out to touch him, the tips of my fingers stroking lines on his chest and the cut of his abdomen where droplets of water carved paths across his muscles. It was almost obscene—his body was so gorgeous, and entirely my playground.

"Good to know. Let's hang out with them again when we get back." He dipped his head and shook the water off his hair like a dog, spraying droplets across my belly.

"Hey!" I cried, but he showed no remorse. Laughing, he dove for the cushions of the sunbed, landing with his leg slung over mine, his cheeks dimpled with the widest grin. It had only taken a few days in paradise for him to put work out of his mind. My playful Ryan had returned; his happiness an infectious force making me giddy.

"I think I may have just found a new girlfriend."

I lowered my sunglasses and narrowed my eyes.

"Well, I think it was a girl. I'm not sure how you determine the gender of a sea turtle, but she was following me in the water."

"Could have been a gay sea turtle, you never know."

"Or gender fluid. Either way, babe, it was incredible to be that close to such an amazing creature."

I leaned over and picked up two slices of pineapple from the breakfast plate delivered by the staff, placed one between his front teeth, then popped the other in my mouth, the sweet juice bursting against my tongue.

"I can't wait to swim with them. The concierge said they can arrange to take us out where there are loads of turtles."

I shifted on the sunbed so I could wrap my arms around his neck. The feel of his naked skin on mine had become something I craved, as if my body needed him as much as food or water. All of my senses were magnified a hundred times stronger thanks to this lush setting—the humid, warm breeze caressing my bare skin—the warm salt water that had flowed around my body like liquid silk. The air was tinged with sweet frangipani, the perfume a heady aphrodisiac that seemed to pulse through my veins. The sensual experience and all the nakedness made me constantly ache for him. He hadn't complained. The feeling appeared to be wonderfully mutual.

We were becoming something more, the bond deepening between us, tucked away in our own private world—exactly as I'd promised him. "You look happy." I traced the line where worry had once etched itself on his face just a few days ago.

"I'm in paradise with my girl. I don't think I could possibly be any happier." He pressed his body tight against mine. "Plus, I have unrestricted access to this..." His hand reached for my breast, cupping it possessively. "And this..." My skin tingled as he ran a finger down my belly, then between my legs, and then he was inside me.

My back arched in one swift motion, reflexively rising at his touch. My eyes fell shut as I felt his tongue sweep across my breast, my breath becoming shallow, until all I heard was the wind rustling through palm leaves above and the faint cawing of an unfamiliar bird. Then, the raw, primal sounds he made melded with nature's symphony, just as he melded into me.

At this moment, the world was perfect. We moved together in harmony with the familiarity that comes from knowing your partner so well, you read each other's signals intuitively. Naked, breeze on our skin... it was as if we were part of something bigger than just the two of us—surrounded by nature's grand plan embodied in the constant ebb and flow of the tides, in the rhythm of the life force teeming all around us. My soul vibrated with the need to absorb him through my skin, to melt into him until we were one being. My arms wrapped around his back, clinging to him, tethering myself to his heart.

The look on his face told me he felt it too, his eyes penetrating mine with pure awe. He paused, poised above me, the strength of his arms supporting his weight while he gazed at me, and his voice emerged, laced with emotion.

"I love you." He shook his head, and this time, he repeated the words slowly, his eyes widening as if those words held an even deeper meaning now. "I... love... you."

I reached up and stroked his cheek with my fingertip, whispering, "I know." I did know. Never in my life had I felt someone's love with such certainty, the power of that knowledge splitting me wide open—leaving me vulnerable and exposed, yet completely safe with him. We were in this together, each risking in equal measure.

Amidst a sudden frenzy of desperate kisses, I held the sides of his face, my eyes boring into his, my heart nearly bursting.

"And I love you." I rocked my hips upward, and he pressed deeper into me, barely breathing.

We stilled, a moment of calm before a storm enveloped us, our bodies crashing and tumbling with fierce intensity, driven by a force we were powerless to control.

Our villa, double the size of my house, was covered with a palm-thatched roof and came with a sundeck, pool, outdoor shower, and its own private beach. Over the course of the first week, we made love in every location, including the beach. We both learned that while incredibly romantic, sex on the beach was far less enjoyable than Hollywood's version. I had sand in places it should never venture, and the chafing to prove it. And, oh my God, the itching. I wondered if the sand fleas had made a feast of my delicate tissues. Gross. Lining up for the buffet while scratching my crotch was definitely not my finest moment. Since I always traveled more prepared than a Girl Scout, I rummaged through my luggage for the cortisone cream, thinking, *See, Madison, I told you not to judge me for overpacking.*

Since recovery time was necessary, we booked excursions at the front desk, which promised boat trips to nearby islands, including swimming with turtles and an underwater experience with silver-tipped sharks. The tour guide assured me that there had never been shark attacks on humans at this dive spot. Apparently, they dined only on the small fish inhabiting these waters, but I wasn't convinced. I'd committed to discovering my adventurous spirit on this trip but reserved the right not to be served up as dinner.

Each day, I pushed my own boundaries. Snorkeling in the coral reefs? Not a big challenge since I'd done that before. But I'd never seen such vibrant coral; the colors splayed out as if they'd absorbed a package of Skittles. The fish darting in and out of the coral or moving as one in tiny groups appeared to be neon-coated as the sun pierced through the crystal-clear water. The lagoon hosted colonies of unusual varieties I'd never seen before—all visible just by ducking my head in the knee-deep water.

Then Ryan got the bright idea to plan something more exciting for our next excursion.

"Oh no, not for me," I said, shaking my head emphatically. "Look over there. Have you noticed that unusual bird?"

He turned toward the lagoon, its water encircling the open-air restaurant where we lined up at the sumptuous brunch buffet. "Where?"

I snatched a banana pancake from his plate.

He pulled a face. "I saw that. And don't think you can distract me."

Out of nowhere, our usual server appeared as if he'd been waiting for precisely the right moment to interrupt. "Madam, sir... when you are ready, I will escort you to your table."

"Thanks, Imad, we'll be right behind you." Ryan grabbed the tongs and lifted another pancake onto his plate.

We followed Imad to our favorite table at the edge of the thatched roof. On the first morning, we had claimed this spot for its spectacular view of the tropical garden and beyond to the palm-fringed beach. We watched as birds dipped and chased each other against the azure sky that stretched deeper and deeper into infinity.

"You look beautiful, babe. You've bronzed up nicely." I was wearing a flowery sarong tied around my neck, my hair hanging in loose, natural curls, albeit frizzy. With the humidity, there wasn't much to be done with my hair, but I appreciated the way my skin plumped up in the warm, moist air.

"Sorry." I took a sip of the mango juice and narrowed my eyes at him over the rim. "Flattery isn't getting you anywhere."

"What are you afraid of? I'll be right by your side."

"Yes, down at the bottom of the ocean floor with your own tank of air. I'll be flailing and gasping and panicking. Is that really how you want to see me?"

"The instructor will be there, too. C'mon, he won't let you drown." His hand reached across the white tablecloth and clasped mine. "You can do this, Sofia. I know you can. You'll regret missing out on the experience, I guarantee it."

Maybe it was his confidence in me or the way he looked at me with those glossy puppy-dog eyes. I could never resist that look. By that afternoon, we were gliding over the waves on a small boat, setting out for a coral reef far from shore. Along the way, my excitement at seeing giant manta rays gliding through the water overshadowed my fears as I peered over the side, the tips of their fins almost brushing against the boat.

"It's not often we see manta rays; they're usually skimming the bottom. But keep your eyes peeled for dolphins. They're pretty common here." The captain's weathered hands gestured toward the horizon.

We scanned the water's surface, and it wasn't long before we spotted a pod of dolphins jumping and diving across the waves in the distance. I caught Ryan watching me, amusement dancing across his features when I squealed like an excited toddler.

The engine sputtered to a stop, the boat rocking with the tide as the captain anchored at the dive spot. The instructor helped me squeeze into the rubber suit, rattled off instructions, then jumped in the water to give me a diving lesson. As I'd feared, I couldn't go more than a few feet under the surface before I shot up for air—ignoring the fact I had a tank full of air strapped to my back which, in theory, would enable me to breathe. My brain couldn't wrap itself around the concept, my natural instincts defying the very idea of breathing underwater.

Finally, Ryan wrapped his arm around my waist, both of us kicking our flippers. He motioned for me to breathe through the mouthpiece, then pointed below. I could already see brightly colored fish darting around the reef through water clear as glass. The impulse to see more overrode my fear. I gave him a thumbs-up, then dove beneath the surface, headfirst.

This time, I didn't turn back. Instead, I focused on a target toward the lower section of the reef where a school of black and yellow striped fish floated on the current, then changed direction in perfect unison.

The goal of swimming to that precise spot led me deeper into the silent underworld, hearing only the rhythmic *gwoosh, gwoosh* sound in my ears as a reminder that I was indeed breathing. Occasionally, Ryan swam to my side and wagged an excited finger toward a gargantuan fish, or at the miniature sharks that barely noticed our presence. But mostly, I explored on my own, careful not to nick my skin on the sharp coral—a veritable village teeming with life tucked deep underwater. More than once, I reached out my hand and came so close to touching those creatures, I could feel the swish of their tails.

It was as if I were observing another planet, an unseen world hidden deep within the sea, its inhabitants holding only mild curiosity at my invasion. Having forgotten my panic, I felt only the serenity created by this silent world as I navigated through the depths. With each new discovery of a species I'd never seen before, I wagged my finger to get Ryan's attention, my squeals muffled by the mouthpiece.

So absorbed in exploring, I barely noticed time passing, until Ryan and the instructor appeared at my side, shooting their thumbs upward.

Climbing back into the boat was even less graceful than getting out, because maneuvering with flippered feet was impossible. I fell into the boat with a *thunk*, kicked off my flippers, and sputtered as I removed the mouthpiece. "That was amazing!" I threw my arms around his neck, nearly tumbling both of us over as the boat tilted to one side. "You were right. I wouldn't have wanted to miss a minute of that experience."

"You were pretty badass. I saw you swimming straight through that school of sharks."

"But you said they were safe."

He laughed and threw his palms in the air. "You really never know where sharks are concerned."

My jaw dropped, then I slapped his arm. "Thanks."

After that experience, it wasn't difficult for him to convince me to go parasailing the next day—another first to tick off my list.

"If you think the view is spectacular from the rooftop of the resort, the scene you'll witness while flying over this ocean will knock your proverbial socks off."

It did. Ryan insisted we go individually rather than in tandem, and at first, I was apprehensive. But the thrill of the boat's powerful surge upward, lifting me high above the waves, transformed my apprehension into pure joy. Flying solo, speeding against the azure sky, yielded not only a breathtaking view but also an overwhelming sense of freedom. Tethered on ropes, I flew through the air, braving the skies all on my own, the wind capturing my screams of delight. The combination of terrifying and exhilarating gave me an adrenaline-infused high.

A flock of birds passed me in flight. Although I was invading their airspace, they didn't seem to notice me. How I envied them. They could go anywhere their wingspan would carry them, liberated from limits, boundaries, or borders.

Another boat pulled ahead, and there was Ryan, waving his arms, suspended high in the air. I let go of the ropes long enough to shoot him a thumbs-up, then brush away the strands of hair whipping across my face. Beaming at me, his face grew farther away—higher now—as his boat curved in another direction. *Daredevil*, I thought as he all but disappeared into the horizon.

A sudden updraft captured my sail, and I looked down at the vast sea—at the sheer miracle of life. Sometime during those thirty minutes, a craving for freedom filled me with excitement, as if a dam had burst and the bubbles were tickling my insides. What if I could go sailing on the wind's current, metaphorically speaking? After all, did I really have borders anymore?

If I had any remaining doubts, by the time my boat chugged into the dock and Ryan whisked me into his arms, they'd been obliterated. I was all in—no reservations. Tugging off my helmet, I beamed at him. "You win."

"It wasn't a competition. Well... maybe." He shrugged, a boyish grin spreading across his face.

"Not that. I mean, you've succeeded. My adventurous side is officially unleashed."

He shook his head, then lifted his eyes to mine. "Babe, you did that all on your own. Maybe you hid that part from yourself, but I could always see it was there. You're just catching up."

"I... really?" Standing there on the dock, it took several seconds for his words to sift through me like sand through fingers.

I was still processing this when he took hold of my hand. "Let's hit the lunch buffet."

Initially, it had seemed like two weeks on an island together would be more than sufficient. I had wondered if we'd get bored with one another, but I couldn't have been more wrong. Besides the lovemaking, which neither of us ever tired of, we settled into our own rhythm, finding a balance between togetherness and taking time for ourselves. When torrential rains poured down for two days straight, we stayed confined in our villa, only occasionally competing for the remote that controlled which Netflix series we'd watch.

There were moments of companionable silence while we read our books side by side on a hammock dangling over the ocean, our toes skimming the warm water. And times when we lost ourselves in the incomprehensible beauty of the surrounding nature, walking for hours along the shore or watching the sunset from our terrace while listening to the cacophony of birds signaling the end of another day.

Our conversation flowed easily, maybe because we both felt so at peace here. It was in one of those tranquil moments that Ryan confided how much he had loved his sister and how he'd been buried in grief, then anger, when she died.

"I was her big brother. I was supposed to protect her."

Long, curly strands of his dark hair splayed across my breast. His languid blue eyes turned toward mine for a second, then shot into the distance over the vast, turquoise sea. My arms wrapped around his chest, and my palm rested on his heart.

"What was she like? Tell me about the good times you remember."

He paused, letting out a heavy sigh. I held my breath, hoping my question would help, not make him feel worse. His cheek rose against my skin with a smile.

"She loved horses from the time she was little. One summer when she was about twelve, Dad arranged for us to take care of a couple of horses. He probably figured it would build character or instill a sense of responsibility in Jennifer. By his standards, she was a total slacker. Anyway, we rode every day. We fed them, brushed them, and cleaned out their stalls. She was different—happier. I think that's when we grew closest." His voice trailed off into a whisper. "That was a great summer."

I laid my cheek on his head, watching a flock of birds dip and dive into the crimson horizon. His hand caressed lightly along my thigh as he added, "I wish you could have met her."

"Me too, baby. Me too."

For the rest of the day, Ryan was distant, taking time for himself. He went for a swim in the sea while I stayed by the pool at our villa. I tried not to worry and resisted playing the *what-if* game—as in, *what if he's pulling away from me?* It was tempting to expect the worst and slip into old habits. Past wounds surfaced at times like these, sort of like a jack-in-the-box springing to life, its wonky arms signaling, *danger, danger!*

Yet the rational part of my brain knew his distance had nothing to do with me. He was wrestling with the ghosts of his grief.

When evening rolled around, he snuggled next to me in bed, and though he was quiet, nothing between us had changed. In fact, his body relaxed against mine as if all the tension was slipping away.

The final days of our trip were shadowed by the looming return to reality. Though we'd almost never missed a sunset on the beach, on the last night, the swirl of colors at dusk was like the grand finale in a fireworks display—vibrant pinks and yellows painted the deep blue sky with sweeping brush strokes, the hues deepening as the sun dipped below the clouds, then the horizon.

I'd tamed my hair into perfect curls and slipped on a flowy white dress, which by this point didn't make me look like a ghost, since my skin had tinted a deep, coppery brown. Kicking off my flip-flops when I reached the sand, I captured a candid photo of Ryan, already seated at our table at the edge of the water, his profile silhouetted against the sky's canvas. Our last night. A wave of melancholy crashed over me at the thought of leaving paradise, our private cocoon, protected from the pressures and expectations that lay just outside this island.

"Hey, gorgeous. Come here." He reached for my hand, pulling me onto his lap. I wrapped my arms around his neck and rested my head against his, taking comfort in his embrace. He smelled of the island's flowers, thanks to the hotel shampoo and body wash. I'd grown to love his new scent, the crisp linen shirts he wore when he wasn't bare-chested, and the way his buttery skin glowed with a deep tan.

Everything will be fine. We've grown stronger together, and nothing can break us apart, I thought, trying to convince myself that happy-ever-after stories did exist. I knew what he would say if I told him my worries. *You're overthinking things again. Just relax.* Sometimes, he was right.

For a long while, we sat in silence, gazing out at the tropical sky until the colors melted into darkness. Unlike me, Ryan exuded a sense of calm. Being in the moment was never easy for me, but now I clung to the sensations, the images becoming snapshots in my mind's eye, imprinting the memories so I'd never forget how to feel this way.

Imad trudged toward us through the sand and lit the lanterns strung high on poles around our table, greeting us warmly with a smile.

"Sir, madam." He nodded as he lit the candle on our table. "Have you enjoyed the island?"

Ryan and I looked at each other first, then at Imad, mirroring his smile. "Very much, Imad. Thank you for everything."

"I hope you will come back and see us again. Shall I bring you the first course now?"

We nodded, and my eyes began to brim unexpectedly. After Imad turned and made his way back to the restaurant, Ryan tipped my chin with his finger until our eyes met.

"Hey. We can come back here, you know. Just because I have to go back to work in London for a while, it doesn't mean we're losing what we've had here. Out of all my travels, being here with you has been the best two weeks of my life."

I swiped a hand across my cheek as a tear fell. "For me too. I love being in a bubble, just the two of us, but it's back to real life tomorrow."

He raised his brows at me and gave me that penetrating look. "We both know feelings are running deeper than ever. Nothing is going to take that away. Life isn't always paradise, but I love you. So, we'll ride whatever wave is yet to come. Together."

"Together. I like the sound of that," I whispered, then promptly pushed aside my worries as his delicious lips devoured mine in a long, deep kiss.

Day 31

Dear Ryan,

While you are peacefully sleeping, unaware I've slipped out of bed, I sit out on our deck for the last time and gaze up at the inky sky, where I can see a million stars winking back at me.

I hear the gentle sound of the surf, a tide that rises and falls as it has for centuries, and I feel so small in the grand scheme of this planet. Some force in the universe brought us together, and sometimes I wonder about the wisdom of fate. But I am amazed at the miracle of it all—of you and me, and how, out of the millions of people in the world, we found each other.

Soulmates? I never really believed that there was one person who could complete me, understand me, and make me whole through a deep, profound connection. But you've made a believer out of me. I may be leaving the Maldives, but I'm keeping this island—and you—in my soul. After all, it certainly won't fit in my suitcase.

Chapter Fourteen

Sofia

"Charlie!" I exclaimed. He tossed my suitcase in the boot, then I leaned in to hug him. His body stiffened, and his arms shot out to the side like a police officer directing traffic.

"Ma'am."

I couldn't help it. The two weeks on an island had put me in the best mood, and besides, the sun was shining. Coming back to London when it wasn't cold and dreary was like winning the lottery. My glass was more than half full.

"I trust you two had a jolly good time?" he asked.

Ryan and I grinned at each other—the kind of grin that could have meant anything, except Charlie got the message.

"Right." He cleared his throat, and his voice went up an octave. "Well, we'd best be getting on the road. Traffic and all, you know."

I whispered in Ryan's ear when we got into the backseat. "I think we made him nervous."

"I think *you* made him nervous."

I slid my hand along his thigh, over the fabric of his jeans until it came to rest between his legs. "We could really make him nervous if you don't raise the privacy screen."

"Here?"

"Uh-huh. I miss being naked with you already."

He pushed a button, and the opaque screen rose, obscuring Charlie's view to the backseat. In one fluid move, his arms lifted me by the waist and I swung my leg over so that I was straddling his lap. He lunged, and his mouth found mine—hungry, needy kisses that arrowed heat low in my core. *God, can I ever get enough of this man?* Like a potent drug, it was as if he'd infiltrated my blood and pure euphoria traveled to every nerve ending.

I glanced sideways at the tinted windows as I raised my skirt with one hand, the other wrapped around his neck.

"Hold on, babe. This is going to be fast and hard."

I steadied my hands on his shoulders while his fingers made quick work of the buttons on his pants, letting out a moan at the first thrilling sensation of him. His breath was on my neck now, coming in sharp bursts. I didn't care about anything except that I needed to feel him inside me, to feel our connection before the real world swallowed us up again.

I was distantly aware of his cell vibrating in his pocket, but neither of us stopped. His hands gripped tightly at the sides of my waist, while I dug my fingers into his shoulders—rising and falling. I pinned his bottom lip between my teeth, staring into his wild eyes, then kissed him hard, the taste of him driving me higher.

Cars passed, horns honked, the muffled sounds of passion lost in our kisses. We weren't quiet, and maybe we found our peak quickly because it was so daring. His head fell back, his neck strained, and muscles bulged while he fought the urge to bellow. I buried my face in his neck and, with some restraint, only bruised his shoulder a little with my teeth.

We slumped into each other's arms for a few moments before the limo made a sharp turn, rolling us to the side.

"It won't be long until we're in town," he said, kissing me one more time before I reluctantly dropped to his side and straightened my clothes. His gaze slid sideways at me, then he shook his head. "Sofia, you never cease to surprise me."

I grinned and clutched his hand in mine. "Good. I'm making that my new mission in life." After my heart settled into a normal rhythm again, I said, "By the way, when are we going back to Barcelona?"

"Remember, I've been off the grid for two weeks, so I'm not sure what's come up in my absence. I don't think I'll have to be in the London office for more than a week, but if you want, you can go ahead without me and I'll catch up."

It hadn't occurred to me we'd be separated. But then, I was officially a tourist, and while his job afforded him a lot of freedom, he couldn't live perpetually on vacation. For the first time in several weeks, my future came into focus, and I still didn't have a plan. Running off with Ryan had been an impulse, and while it was all part of our grand plan, I didn't want to lose sight of the fact that my life shouldn't be completely wrapped up in him.

Ryan pulled his cell from his pocket, and as he looked at the screen, the expression on his face shifted in an instant. "They couldn't wait until I got back into the office? I'm going to miss being off the grid." He planted a kiss on my cheek and said, "Sorry, I've got to take this call."

I leaned my head back on the leather seat, watching the now familiar cityscape coming into view, and thought about how I would miss our own bubble of island happiness, where time almost stood still.

"Yeah, James, what's up?"

I watched as he raised his hand, gripping his temples between his thumb and index finger.

"I'm the one who makes those decisions, not you. No. Don't forward that offer. I'm on my way in."

When he ended the call, he turned to me, his head shaking. "Vacation is officially over. Charlie will drop you off at the hotel. I might need to work late tonight."

"Bet you're glad we took advantage of the backseat now." I might have been radiating a triumphant grin.

With time on my hands and the luck of a sunny day in London, I planned a visit to Green's in search of another book. If I were going back to Barcelona, it wouldn't hurt to work on my language skills. Victoria must have books that taught basic Spanish. Besides, I did promise Josie that I would check in after my trip.

The mood in London somehow seemed lighter with the sun gleaming overhead—the tree-lined streets a sharper shade of emerald green, and smiles replacing grim lines once coats were shrugged off. My steps were lighter too in my Mary Janes, my skirt billowing in the breeze as I weaved through shoppers on the bustling streets of Notting Hill until I reached the lane and found the green door propped open wide. I paused for a moment, noticing a different display in the window and Oliver, who was placing a new release on a stand at the top of a pile. I waved to him through the glass, and he responded with a smile that lit up his features.

"Good day, Sofia. You're back! How was your vacation?"

"I highly recommend the Maldives if you enjoy sun, sand, and warm blue waters."

His eyes swept over me. "It definitely looks like you've had a bit of sun. You look quite lovely with some color in your cheeks."

Was I blushing? His gaze followed me when I reached for a book on the table marked New Releases. The cover attracted me at once. Against a background of a star-filled night sky was a silhouette of a woman, her face tipped upward and her arms held above her head as if she were dancing. I flicked through, catching snippets of a woman's voice, the intensity of her emotion radiating off the pages. It made me want to know more. I wondered, *how does love ever survive? Romance novels make it appear so easy, like happy-ever-after is a foregone conclusion.*

Oliver appeared at my side. "Ah, that's a good one you've got there, if you like romance novels. It's written by one of our own British authors."

I ran my hand over the smooth cover as if it were instantly transmitting the tone, one which resonated in my reconstructed heart. A few months ago, I couldn't have imagined even noticing it. "Honestly, I can't say that I've been a voracious reader throughout my life, but some novels seem to find me." I looked up at Oliver, whose expression told me he knew exactly what I meant. "I think this one has found me."

"That's how it goes. The reader knows when the voice of a writer is speaking to them."

"Have you ever tried your hand at writing?" I asked.

He shook his head. "Not yet, but I will someday. This shop has always kept me too busy. What about you?"

"Me? A writer?"

"You know," Oliver began, "they say everyone has one good story just waiting to be put to paper."

For a few brief seconds, I let myself imagine, and my thoughts drifted to pieces of a story not yet formulated. One that had floated through my mind in those moments when life was still. Then I thought of all the reasons I couldn't possibly write and changed the subject.

"Is Josie here? I'd like to say hello to her and the fellas."

Oliver stood aside and motioned to the corner. "Josie and John are here today, but Arthur has been taking some time off. Apparently, he met a lady and drives all the way to Surrey to see her several times a week."

"Good for him. It's never too late to find love."

"I suppose so, or at least a bit of companionship. I'm not sure we get second chances at love."

"A few months ago, I would have said the same thing, though I hated thinking that way. But life without love isn't really living; it's just existing. You never know what or who the universe will throw in your path."

Sadness colored Oliver's eyes as they bored into mine with such intensity I could feel the weight of his unspoken words. "You may be right about that."

Josie looked up from her book. Seeing me, she began waving a hand in the air, motioning me over. I excused myself to Oliver, relieved to end that conversation.What was he implying?I didn't know what had just happened, but my instincts told me to let it go.

"Will ya look at her, John, doesn't she look grand now?" Josie thrust an elbow, poking John in the arm. He nodded graciously.

"Thanks, Josie, but it's not hard to look grand when you've been in paradise for a few weeks." I thought about how sunshine could work miracles. Josie was wearing a pink flowered sundress, her pale cheeks now a rose-kissed blush.

"The islands are well and good, but I suspect your fella has more to do with the way you're glowing."

I rocked back in my chair and couldn't stop the grin curving my lips, then added, "Let's just say, as experiments go, this proved to be an extremely effective way to bond."

"I barely remember how to *bond*," John commented, ending with a well-placed harrumph.

"With Arthur taking off to meet his lady, you're sort of the last man standing here. Or sitting, rather," I said. "When are you going to date, John?"

He shrank in his seat, looking as if he wanted to disappear. "I'm not sure how Tillie would feel about that." A faint smile crept across his face. "Her spirit might be hanging 'round the house. Tillie could pop up and give a lady quite a fright."

"Don't be daft, John," Josie scolded. "Do you think Tillie would want you moping 'round that big old house all alone till you're buried six feet under?"

"But—"

"But nothing. I'd lay a wager that when Tillie knew it was time to leave this earthly world, she made you promise to go on with your life. She probably chewed your ear off about it."

He was quiet for a moment, then he shrugged. "She did say something like that a time or two."

Josie bounced in her chair, startling both of us when she let out a squeal. "I've got it! Widow Taylor lives just down the road a ways. She'd be a right good woman for you."

"Now, Josie," John protested, "don't be playing match-maker."

"You'd be a ruddy git not to give it a go." Josie's voice was stern, but there was warmth in her eyes when she gazed at John. "You're a good man, John, but your cooking is shite. A lady could teach you a thing or two."

John finally relented with a shrug of his shoulders.

"Now that it's all settled, I've got to run," I announced.

"Will you be back, love?" Josie asked.

"Of course. I'll need to find out how John gets on with Mrs. Taylor." I shot him a wink. "My schedule isn't set yet, so I'm not sure when I'm heading to Barcelona and then back to the States, but I'll pop in before I leave."

When I stepped out the door and headed toward Hyde Park on foot, I was suddenly struck by how much I missed Ryan. We'd been literally glued together for two weeks in vacation bliss. Now, I had nothing to do but wait for him to get off work. Hoping he had a break in his schedule, I pulled out my phone and sent him a text.

> **Lovely day for a late afternoon pint, don't ya think?**

Then I sat on a park bench watching two five-year-old children squealing with delight as they circled on one of those vomit-go-round amusement rides. As a child, I remembered the nausea every time I rode anything that went endlessly in circles. To my relief, they seemed unfazed when they got off, though they did stagger until they fell on the ground in a heap of laughter. A few minutes passed before Ryan responded.

> **I would love to, but I have a meeting in 30. Not sure if I'll be able to spend time with you.**

There were moments in life when a brilliant idea formed into a plan. This was one of them. I popped into the first cheese shop I spotted, picking out a sharp, aged white cheddar and a fresh baguette, as well as a wicker basket they had in a window display. Two doors down, the sommelier introduced me to a bottle of cabernet I hoped Ryan would love. The smell of freshly baked pies drew me into a store further down the block. I chose one meat and the other chicken with mushrooms. Still steaming hot, the clerk wrapped them tightly in paper boxes.

By the time I'd assembled my picnic basket, Charlie had responded to my text and was waiting at the curb.

"Where to, ma'am?"

"Ryan's office, please. He's working late, so I thought I'd surprise him with dinner. I suspect he hasn't had time to eat today."

He nodded, tugged at the brim of his hat, then pulled the car into the traffic, winding through the streets of London. Passing familiar sights—statues, storefronts, and corner pubs—I marveled at how quickly I had become comfortable in this foreign city. Comfortable with Ryan, too. Those two weeks together in the Maldives had opened my heart more than I thought possible. It was as if we'd climbed a mountain together, now relishing the wide-open view of possibilities. Now, it felt like part of me was missing when he wasn't by my side.

"The office is just up ahead, ma'am, but there's no parking here," he said, pointing to a glossy, modern high-rise. "Can I drop you at the corner?"

Scooping the basket onto my arm, I reached for the door handle. "Of course, Charlie. I recognize the building. Fifth floor, right?"

My feet hit the pavement, and I ducked my head to see him shoot me a thumbs up. The business district was such a contrast to the older parts of the city—modern, sleek, and seemingly out of place, according to my image of London. A conglomerate of high-rise buildings juxtaposed against London Bridge and the castle on the other side. *Progress,* I thought, *isn't always a good thing.*

I searched for my cell at the bottom of my purse, then stopped before arriving at his building to check the time. Six o'clock. He might still be in a meeting, so if he was still busy, I'd chat with Cara, then wait in the lobby. I had it all planned out.

Checking my makeup in the phone's mirror, I applied a fresh coat of lipstick. My pulse quickened at the thought of him finding me here; the look of surprise on his face. I could imagine his disarming smile, the sparkle in his eyes. I loved the way they softened when he looked at me. His eyes told me everything I needed to know.

The wine bottle rolled and clinked against the glasses as I started up the block, weaving through a tangle of people fleeing their offices for the day. They sprinted toward the metro, arms raised to hail taxis, their urgency creating a human river I had to navigate. Men in dark suits and women teetering on high-heeled pumps obscured my view ahead, but still my lips curved into a giddy smile. How could I be this excited to see him after only eight hours apart?

The straw basket bashed into my ribs, knocking the breath from me. "So sorry," came a voice from beside me. I barely registered the man—only caught a glimpse of his bald head—as my eyes remained fixed straight ahead, locked on Ryan.

Ryan.

I stopped dead. My feet transformed into lead blocks, anchoring me to the cement as if the sidewalk had gripped me in quicksand. People pushed past me, their shoulders bumping mine as I became a human traffic obstacle in their path. But I couldn't move—not an inch. I was transfixed.

My heart pounded, and the world began to spin as my gaze darted between his face—serious and drawn—and *her* face, etched with sadness. Or was it desperation? From a distance, it was hard to tell, but she seemed to be on the verge of tears.

Who? I mouthed the word, an unfinished question hanging in the air. I watched the two of them locked in intense conversation, face-to-face in front of his office door, their bodies angled toward each other with an intimacy that made my stomach clench.

Everything in me tightened. My instincts screamed *danger*; every nerve ending was on high alert. Maybe they were colleagues, I told myself. Maybe this was nothing but a business discussion gone emotional. But the way she looked at him—the raw emotion saturating her expression—confirmed my worst fears. I desperately wished for an invisibility cloak so I could inch closer, or some superpower to hear from a distance of a hundred feet.

Instead, I remained frozen, watching as the scene unfolded in agonizing slow motion. His hand moved to stroke her arm—a gesture so tender, so familiar, it sent ice through my veins. Ryan was comforting her, his expression soft—a look I thought was reserved for me alone. Intuitively, with every fiber of my being, I knew. She wasn't just someone. She was someone *important* in his life.

His fingers moved to her face, brushing away, what? Tears? Her face was pretty—with that sharp-edged jawline

I'd always envied, her sculpted nose punctuating wide-set eyes. Young, maybe thirty-five, with long dark hair that hung like a silk curtain down her back.

He reached for her then, his arms bringing her into an embrace. A sharp, knife-like pain penetrated my chest. Bodies weaved in front of me, and I stretched my neck desperately, cursing at the obstruction, my heart hammering against my ribs. It was impossible to tear my eyes away—as if witnessing a horrific car crash, I didn't want to see the carnage, but my gaze was drawn to the sight of them with magnetic force. There was nothing I could do but watch helplessly as the scene unfolded.

The crowd thinned, giving me an unobstructed view.

And then I saw it.

An involuntary gasp tore from my chest, raw and painful. No, no, no! The protest exploded in my mind like fireworks, bright and violent and deafening. My heart didn't just break—it shattered, my dreams splintering like glass hitting concrete.

Her body rested against his, and bulging between them, unmistakable and devastating, was her very pregnant belly. The baby bump rested against his body. The body I had rested against this morning.

A baby. A baby? The word swirled in my brain as I tried to conjure a reasonable explanation, but watching them—putting all the puzzle pieces together—I couldn't dismiss the answer right in front of me.

A deafening roar filled my ears, drowning out the city's symphony of car horns and footsteps and distant sirens.

Time became elastic—I wasn't sure if they held each other for seconds or hours because the world had become a watercolor painting left in the rain: time blurring, bodies passing like ghosts, traffic noise fading to white static. Any strength I'd possessed liquefied, my muscles quivering traitorously under my own weight. The picnic basket—my romantic surprise—dangled uselessly from my bent arm like a mocking reminder that, despite my big plans, the surprise was on me.

Then, they broke apart.

She—the nameless, glowing, pregnant woman who had just obliterated my world into a million pieces—walked out of sight as she turned the corner, taking my future with her. Ryan pressed his hands against the wide glass door but paused as it opened, as if some invisible force had whispered my name.

His head swiveled sideways, and his eyes found me hiding in plain sight among the crowd.

His eyes. Oh, his eyes. They told me everything.

Chapter Fifteen

Ryan

Rebecca? My ex-girlfriend's name flashed on my phone screen, and for a moment, I considered not opening the text message. James was in the middle of updating me on one of our clients, but my eyes kept drifting back to my desk, where my screen flashed with reminders. Reaching with one finger, I clicked and viewed the one-liner.

> *Ryan, I need to talk with you. Are you in London?*

What the-? Why is she contacting me now? It had been roughly eight months since she'd cut off all contact with me—since I broke up with her and she got pissed. I glanced at James. "What were you saying?"

"I said, Global Tech is interested in expanding, and they have their sights set on a Silicon Valley company. It's a start-up, but its stock just went public after introducing a new mobile app."

My phone pinged again, and my eyes reflexively darted to the flash. Rebecca, again. This was ridiculous, but proving I wasn't any better than a teenager with zero impulse control, I tapped to view the message.

Please, it's important. There's something I need to tell you and it can't wait.

"Hey!" James snapped his fingers in my face. "What's up with you today? I know you just got back from holiday, but could you please get your head back in the game here?"

I slapped his hand away, then straightened myself in the chair. "Sorry. Rebecca keeps texting me."

"Rebecca? That bird you were dating last year?"

"Yeah. I have no idea what she wants, but she says it's important. I haven't heard a word from her since we split up, and she pops up now? Really bad timing. But knowing her, she's not going to stop until I answer."

"Well then, you best get on with it, mate. She was an odd bird, if you ask me, but from my experience, women can be persistent if there's something on their minds."

"I'm not sure Sofia would be too happy about me having contact with an old girlfriend, and we had such a great time in the Maldives. Things are so good—the best, you know?"

"Simple answer, man. Don't tell her."

I shook my head. "That's not how we do things. I'm not going to lie to her."

"You don't even know what Rebecca wants, so it's not really an issue."

My phone pinged again, and I let out a growl when I read the message.

One way or the other, you are going to want to hear what I have to say. And there's not much time left.

That was it. *Not much time left?* Was she dying? James watched as I typed a response—short, to the point.

> **What's up?**

I waited, dots percolating on the screen, until her response appeared.

> *I can't do this by text. Meet me at that cafe where we used to go to lunch near your office. Can you make it in an hour?*

My finger hovered over the keys, and another text appeared, but this time from Sofia.

"Shit." I stared at James. "Sofia wants to meet me for a drink, but Rebecca is asking me to meet her in an hour. First day back and this happens?"

"Tell Sofia you're working and get this thing over and done with. You don't want her texts popping up when you're with Sofia."

"Fair point." I sucked in an anxious breath through my teeth and reluctantly confirmed with Rebecca, then sent Sofia a text. I hated lying to her, but I rationalized it by telling myself it wouldn't do her any good to upset her over nothing. Maybe Rebecca just needed closure. If I met up with her, I could put an end to everything once and for all. But despite my efforts to remain optimistic, my stomach clenched.

Rebecca's texts struck me as odd; she wasn't prone to hysterics, just the opposite. She'd always kept a tight rein on her emotions, making it impossible to feel a real connection with her. When we were dating, she had said she was falling in love with me, but her words had never reached beyond my ears. When our eyes met, when she touched me, I wasn't feeling it. But then, maybe it was because I hadn't been in the same headspace. One lone violin was cool and all, but when you were playing a duet, there was a synergy that magnified the piece—heightened the richness and intensity. With Sofia, I'd finally learned what love could be like when two people were equally invested.

The end had been inevitable, but Rebecca hadn't seen it that way. Nobody liked being dumped, but I supposed she felt blindsided. It hadn't gone down well when I'd abruptly left town after dropping the bombshell. I still blamed myself for being an insensitive jerk. I should have been more honest with her, realizing early on that I wasn't in it for the long haul. Avoidance had always been easier for me than confrontation, but now it didn't seem I had much choice—I had to meet with her.

When I stood and lifted my jacket from the chair, James said, "Good luck, mate."

I sucked in a heavy breath through clenched teeth. "Thanks, I have a feeling I'm going to need it."

The sidewalks were teeming with people dashing home in the after-work rush hour. What was normally a five-minute walk to the cafe took ten long minutes, battling to make my way through the people meandering past the shops like they had all day, and lost tourists holding maps, creating a logjam in the middle of the sidewalk. By the time I arrived, my irritation had doubled. I had to take a deep breath, steeling myself before I pushed open the door, then scanned the half-empty bar. Luckily, it wasn't packed and noisy, except for the sound of pots clanging in the kitchen and the sports announcer on the television over the bar. The smell of fried fish wafted from an open door, and my stomach growled in response. Then I remembered I'd been too busy to grab lunch.

Striding past a few men staring into their beers at the bar, I spotted Rebecca sitting at a corner booth in the back, twisting a napkin between her fingers. When her gaze lifted and she saw me, her lips pressed into a thin line. I forced a smile, but it wasn't reciprocated. *Shit.*

There was no turning back now, so I strode past the servers, then settled into the booth across from her. While my armpits were sweating, she sat bundled in a coat, even though the heat in the place was turned up so high the windows were steaming. I noticed immediately that there was something different about her appearance; her normally angular face was round like a cherub, and I couldn't help wondering how much weight she'd gained.

"Hello, Ryan, I'm glad you came. You're looking well," she said with more than a little formality in her tone.

I couldn't return the compliment and sound authentic, so I replied, "Thank you," then added the usual icebreaker, "How've you been?"

"Actually…" She hesitated for a moment, then slowly unbuttoned her coat, allowing the thick wool to fall at her sides. At first, I waited for her to finish her sentence, but my eyes darted over the edge of the table to her stomach, where the fabric of her gingham dress stretched taut over a large bulge.

My jaw dropped open. She hadn't just gained weight. She was pregnant. A slow trickle of realization descended to my gut, and nausea roiled in my stomach.

"Now then, lad, what can I get for you?" The gray-haired server's eyes were fixed on me, having glanced briefly at Rebecca, his cheeks rosy and pinched with a smile. Rebecca glanced down at the table and gripped a glass of juice. As she brought it to her lips, her hand trembled.

"Um, I..."

The man cocked his head and studied me while I sat there like an idiot, staring at her enormous belly. It could have been seconds or minutes later when he finally said, "Will you have a pint, mate?"

I nodded mutely, then ran a hand down my face. He must have thought I was completely daft, but his smile didn't falter as he turned and ambled to the bar. I swung my eyes toward Rebecca again; my tongue apparently paralyzed, unable to form words—to ask the question.

"It's yours," she said matter-of-factly. "I can assure you, and I'll take a DNA test if you don't believe me."

My head was swimming, caught in a swirl of questions and emotions and panic, as though I was trapped under a wave, struggling to determine which way to paddle toward the surface for air. I cleared my throat; my voice strained when I could finally talk. "How? We were careful."

Hurt flashed across her face, and the way she winced told me it wasn't the response she wanted but instantly readjusted her expression into a half smile. "I suppose one of your little fellas slipped past the condom."

"How far along are you?"

"Almost eight months."

My brain kicked into gear, calculating the math. The timing matched, but that didn't mean it was mine.

As if registering my doubt, she added, "I wasn't with anyone else, in case you're wondering. I learned I was pregnant a couple of months after we'd separated. I'd missed a period, but that wasn't unusual for me, so I didn't think anything of it, until I started throwing up. By then, it didn't seem right to... you know." Averting her gaze, she picked up her glass and swigged down several gulps of the juice, her eyes glistening now.

When the server placed the beer on the table, I didn't look up, just heard his footsteps trailing away, shuffling against the tiled floor. The buzzing in my ears muffled the conversations scattered through the cafe; the announcer's voice as he called the final score of a soccer game from the television's tinny speakers. Questions popped into my mind like bubbles. "Why did you wait until now to tell me?" I asked, not disguising the disbelief in my voice. "This just doesn't make sense."

Her chest rose as she filled her lungs before speaking, and her eyes fixated on the table between us, the tip of her finger tracing circles in the puddle of moisture left by her glass. "I wasn't sure if I was ever going to tell you. You made it clear you didn't want to be with me, so I didn't want you to think I was trying to trap you. This was my decision. I wanted to keep the baby, with or without you."

My heart sank. What if this child were mine, and she never told me? While I was still reeling with shock, an unexpected pain gripped my heart at the idea of my child existing in this world without my knowledge—a child growing up never knowing its father.

"But circumstances have changed," she blurted.

I shook my head, forcing my attention back to her. "How so?"

I thought I could do this alone, but I haven't been well. The stress of the job was affecting my health, so I had to quit. The doctor said I could lose the baby if I continued to work.

When she finished, the pretense of strength was gone from her expression. In her eyes, I saw fear and vulnerability emerging through her reserve, and something inside me loosened. Of course I'd take care of her and the baby—ignoring this development wasn't an option. Haunting memories of my sister surfaced—my failure to protect her; to keep her alive.

I didn't hesitate. "How can I help?"

When her gaze met mine, I saw her slump in relief, then her words poured out like they had been locked up for eight months, waiting to be released. "I don't expect a relationship, if that's what you think, but I'd like to count on you for financial support. The disability pay is helping me get by, to pay the rent and buy food, but I won't have money to buy things the baby will need. I don't have a crib or changing table or even diapers." A tear erupted from one eye while she blinked furiously against the flow, and I couldn't remember ever seeing her cry. Watching her hands wringing—fingers twisting together—I realized that reaching out to me for help must have been an agonizing decision. As a peace offering, she added, "You can be there for the birth, if you like, and... um, a baby needs its father, I suppose. It wouldn't be right to deprive it of knowing you."

Curious now, I asked, "You don't know the sex of the baby?"

"I'm choosing to do this the old-fashioned way. I'd like to be surprised."

I finally noticed the pint in front of me, the glass sweating onto the paper napkin, and grabbed it, downing half the glass. It was going to take a few more beers with a whiskey chaser to get through the rest of this day.

My mind was reeling again as reality gained a foothold. *I'm going to be a dad? Oh, God, Sofia. How the hell am I going to break this news to her?*

She had gone quiet, waiting for my response. Nothing about this situation was simple, and I chose my words carefully when I spoke. "Rebecca, it's going to take a little time for me to sort this out in my mind, but you can count on me for support. However, there's something you need to know." There was no easy way to tell her, so I just ripped off the band-aid, aware she'd feel the sting. "I'm in a relationship now—a committed relationship. My life and work are primarily based in San Francisco, so I'll have to consider these factors going forward." Her face crumpled, and despite her effort to regain a neutral mask, her bottom lip quivered. I pressed on before I lost my nerve, my tone softer now. "I'd like to be present for the birth and, of course, I want this child to know I'm its father. As you can imagine, this news has come as a shock, and I'm not prepared to give you more answers right now."

"I understand," she muttered.

"Don't hesitate to contact me, and I'll be in touch. I'll make arrangements to get whatever you need." With my mind spinning in a million directions, I had an urgent need to leave, to be alone so I could think straight. There were so many things to figure out—at the top of the list was how to tell Sofia. Oh, God. Sofia. My head was throbbing like I'd been on a two-day binge.

I downed the rest of my beer as she slipped on her coat. "Would you like me to walk you out?"

"I have to use the loo first, but yes. It seems like I spend most of my time in the loo these days," she said, attempting a half-hearted laugh.

It wasn't until she carefully lifted herself from the seat, her hands pressing against the back for support, that I saw the full girth of her belly. If it were any other woman, I wouldn't have even noticed. But knowing my baby was in there caused a wave of nausea to churn in my gut again. I *am not ready for this.* The words reverberated in my head, a pointless scream of protest. I spun on my heels and almost sprinted toward the bar to settle the bill.

I kept the conversation light as we walked down the street to my office where her car was parked, asking her about her sister and if she still lived in the same apartment. Her pace was painfully slow, and her breaths came in fast puffs, as though she were sprinting rather than strolling.

When we reached the front of my building, my steps halted, and I pivoted to face her.

"Thank you for telling me." I gently touched her arm because I noticed a few tears sliding down her cheeks. At least she wasn't sobbing in the middle of the sidewalk. She was probably keeping it together as best she could, despite the pregnancy hormones coursing through her body and brain. I was barely reining in my emotions, because as I said those words, there was a tug-of-war pulling me apart. Was I glad she told me? An hour ago, my life made sense. I was happy—Sofia was happy. Now, I was about to tear our world apart with this news. Yes, I wanted a family, but not this way.

She smiled, and I swiped my thumbs across her cheeks. "Everything will be alright, don't worry." On impulse, I pulled her into a chaste hug, careful not to press against her belly, but it was impossible to avoid contact with this beach ball protruding between us. It was the kind of hug I would give a friend, but still, the unwelcome weight of guilt settled over me as I thought of Sofia.

After I released her and watched her waddle away toward the corner, I pivoted and made to go back to my office, but for reasons I couldn't explain, my gaze was pulled in the other direction.

Sofia. The horrified look on her face meant only one thing. She'd seen everything, and she knew.

Chapter Sixteen

Sofia

"Is she...? Was she?" I asked, my voice barely a whisper. We'd sat in excruciating silence during the twenty-minute taxi ride home, and now, facing each other across the table, I braced myself for the truth.

"Was." Ryan rose from the dining chair and poured a glass of water from the bar, then handed it to me. My hand trembled as I tipped it to my mouth, unsure whether to wait or fire the questions circling like rabbits in my mind. The silence in the room was deafening. A police siren shrieked from the streets below, the sound a welcome distraction.

I watched him pace the length of the living room, loosen his tie, and drape his suit jacket carefully over the back of the chair. Then he let out a long, heavy sigh, thrusting his hands in the front pockets of his neatly pressed slacks. "We met here about a year ago. She worked at a bank, and we had a mutual client. It seemed like a good fit at first, both of us in the same field. Both of us wanted a family."

My hands tightened on the arms of the chair, gripping hard, as if I was steeling myself for a descent down a horrific roller coaster ride. The word "family" sliced me like a knife, piercing through familiar wounds. Ron's voice rang in

my ears, dumping me on his forty-fifth birthday. "If I'm going to have a family, I can't waste any more time." Then,
Ryan telling me he wanted kids of his own, the news coming
too late—after I'd already fallen for him. I forced myself to
keep listening, to stay rooted in my chair instead of bolting
out the door when my instincts were screaming, *run!*

"We dated for a few months, but I could tell something
was missing. I didn't feel the same way she did, and so
it didn't end well." He sank into the chair, and though he
avoided my gaze, I saw weariness, maybe fear, in his eyes.
"After we split up, she was angry with me, blocked me on
social media, and wouldn't have any further contact." His
shoulders slumped, and he looked at me as if pleading with
me to believe him. "We always took precautions, you know?
I never meant for it to happen like this."

Something in me shifted with the realization that Ryan
was in pain, too. I imagined his shock at the news—the
panic he must be feeling—and pushed my own fears aside.
Finally, I found my voice. Sounding stronger this time, I said,
"Intentionally or not, you are going to be a dad. There is
no disputing that fact unless you think there's a reason to
doubt her."

He shook his head. "The timing works out exactly, and
I believe she's being honest. She wasn't dating anyone else.
But I still might want a paternity test at some point."

"But why did she wait so long to tell you?"

"She thought she could handle it all on her own. I think
she was still hurting because I had walked away. The woman
let her pride stop her from informing me. Anyway, she texted

me today and asked me to meet her. She said it was important. I had no idea why until I saw her in the cafe."

I swallowed hard before asking the question that had been begging to be unleashed since the moment I'd seen them together. "What does she want now?" As soon as the words were out of my mouth, I realized it was the second most important question.

"She wanted me to know because she needs help. She's come to terms with me being a part of the baby's life—feels the baby is entitled to a father." As though saying those words caused him physical pain, he squeezed his eyes shut. "Of course, I want to provide for them financially, and soon, she'll need all those baby things, or whatever." He shook his head, his expression so unfamiliar. He looked completely lost. "Beyond that, I don't know yet how I can help her."

I hoped he hadn't seen me flinch. A carpenter was already going full speed ahead inside every inch of me, boarding up windows and erecting walls. Somehow, I held back the tears. Not only were my fingers numb from the death grip on the chair, but the numbness seeped to every part of me, defying me to feel anything.

My voice sounding surprisingly calm, I asked the most important question. "What do *you* want?"

"Honestly, I don't know how to answer that." He blew out a long breath and bolted out of the chair. "I can't—I need to think." Already moving toward the door, his steps quick and desperate, he yanked it open without even a backward glance.

The door clicked shut behind him, leaving me alone in the wreckage of everything we'd built together.

My chest constricted; unable to breathe, I sat frozen in that chair, too confused—too hurt even to move. The sun's light no longer illuminated the room. I allowed the darkness to consume me as the realization dawned—he doesn't know what he wants. Just this morning he knew, but now?

Fear seeped through my paralyzed state first.

What would I do? Where would I go? Will he come back, or has he gone to see her? I didn't even know her name, but anger spilled on top of fear. Why did she wait so long to tell him? If she'd only told him sooner, I never would have been in this position. He wouldn't be in this position. What if she wasn't being honest about the father?

So many what-ifs swirled inside my head, I feared vertigo would take me down if I tried to stand. Then, like ice melting after a freeze, the feeling returned to my heart. *Dammit, I swore I wouldn't let myself be hurt again.* This pain, this heartache, was far worse than anything I'd felt before.

I was suddenly homesick, wishing I was back in my own bed, retreating into the familiarity of my old life. That life may not have been exciting, but at least I was safe.

My laptop sat on the table in front of me. I opened the lid and typed, *flights from London to San Francisco.* But the thought of leaving started the avalanche. My eyes clouded, the words on the screen now only a blur.

And then it hit me—a flash of memories. Running away from Ryan the night we met, and again when I learned he wanted a family. I slammed the laptop closed. *Not this time*, I told myself. I'd promised Ryan long ago that I wouldn't run.

But I couldn't just sit here waiting for him, wondering if this was the end—it would drive me insane. I swiped the back of my hand across my cheeks, brushing away the unstoppable flow of tears while I dragged my carry-on bag from the closet, then randomly grabbed a spare set of clothes. This was the right decision. I'd give Ryan his space, and when he was ready, we'd sort it out. Still, my body shuddered with sobs. What if he decided to be with her and the baby? Why would he choose me when there was a ready-made family just waiting for him? Oh, God.

I sent Charlie a text asking him to pick me up, hoping he hadn't gone to bed early. Then, I scribbled a note to Ryan on the hotel's stationery, telling him not to worry about me—that I wasn't running. *Well*, I thought, *at least I'm not running back to the States.* Charlie arrived thirty minutes later, minus his usual black jacket and cap, wearing jeans and a T-shirt. I imagined him comfortably resting in his favorite chair in front of the television and instantly felt guilty. When his eyes fell on my suitcase, his jaw dropped, and his usual composure fell away.

"Bloody hell." He ran a hand through his thinning grey hair, then straightened his spine. "Right, where to, ma'am?"

My eyes brimmed, but I blinked back the tears. I couldn't trust that my voice wouldn't crack, so I passed him the suitcase in silence and climbed in the backseat. Once he was in the driver's seat, I said, "Please take me to another hotel. It doesn't have to be fancy. I just need a room in a safe neighborhood."

"My sister has a little bed-and-breakfast over near Earls Court. I expect she'll have a room available, but I'll ring her to be certain."

I stiffened in my seat, holding tight to my resolve while I barely listened to the one-sided conversation. Charlie set his phone down, and we rolled through the curve of the hotel driveway. "She said she'd be right pleased to have you."

"Thank you, Charlie. There's just one more thing." He tilted his eyes to the rearview mirror. "If Ryan asks..."

He shook his head. "Ma'am, if he asks me—"

"Just let him know I'm still in town and I'm not leaving." It didn't seem right to say more—to put Charlie in the middle of this more than I already had. He blew out a long breath. Neither of us spoke until we pulled into a driveway.

"Yes, well, here we are, love. It's not the Waldorf, but I think you'll find the bed quite comfy."

Mrs. Brown—Agnes, as she'd corrected me—closed the lace curtains, then patted the flowered bedspread. "Breakfast is served in the dining room downstairs at eight o'clock. If you need anything at all, just give us a shout." My makeup must have been streaked with tears, and I could barely lift my cheeks to meet her smile. She looked at me with sympathetic eyes, her hands nervously brushing against her housecoat like she didn't know what to do with this wreck of a woman who'd been dropped off on her doorstep. "Well then, I'll leave you to it."

As she turned the brass handle on the door, I muttered, "Thank you, Agnes. I hope it wasn't any trouble taking me in this late."

"Don't you worry yourself. Wasn't any trouble at all. Have a good sleep, love. Things always look brighter in the mornin'," she said, her voice artificially cheerful. The door creaked when she closed it behind her, and then I was finally alone. Even though it was tiny compared to the hotel suite, the antique furniture and soft, pastel colors made the room feel cozy.

I didn't bother to unpack. Bone-weary, my feet dragged across the floor to the bathroom, and once I'd brushed my teeth, I dove under the covers. I had no idea what I'd do next; a vast wasteland of the unknown lay before me, and I couldn't help but sink into despair. It wasn't likely that the morning would be any brighter.

Even as the sun streamed through the curtains, I knew there was no escaping the heaviness that had settled over me like a dark cloud, doubts raining down in buckets. Every time I tried to move from the bed, I fell back onto the pillows. Apart from putting on the complimentary robe I'd brought with me from the hotel, I didn't bother to get dressed. Apparently, pulling yourself up by the bootstraps was next to impossible when you were wearing flimsy hotel slippers.

The voice of reason attempted to console me. It wasn't like I expected happily ever after. Did I? It was sixty days, that was all. If it were a little less, no harm done. I fell back on the pillows and pressed one arm over my face. *Oh God, I did expect more. I want more. How did this happen?* I couldn't decide which was worse, wondering what Ryan was thinking or actually finding out for certain.

The day dragged as days do when one's thoughts are spiraling out of control. The only company I had was a brief visit from Agnes when she tapped on the door at nine-thirty, carrying a tray full of assorted muffins, some fruit, and a pot of tea. "You have to eat, love. If you'd fancy some roast and potatoes later, I'll bring it round at suppertime." I thought of telling her I wasn't hungry, that my stomach was sick with grief, but seeing the concerned look in her eyes, I just thanked her for her kindness. After she closed the door, I climbed back into my solitude and lost myself in the new book I'd purchased at the bookstore, listening to the drone of the vacuum cleaner in the next room and the constant rumbling of traffic outside my second-story window. Unfortunately, romance novels didn't serve as a distraction when it was the very thing you were trying not to think about.

When I finally summoned the courage to take the phone out of my purse, I saw twenty-two text messages from Ryan and three missed calls. **Where are you??** These texts of concern turned into anger. **Dammit, Sofia. Answer me!** And then to panic. **Please call me. I'm freaking out.**

We promised no ghosting, right? He was right. I owed him an answer, so I typed out a text letting him know I was fine but that I needed time to think. I was giving him the space he needed to process the... situation. Before he could answer, I tossed the phone into my purse and settled back under the covers. I didn't know when I'd be ready to face him, to hear what he wanted. When would I ever be ready to hear the sound of my life shattering?

Chapter Seventeen

Sofia

As it turned out, Agnes could make a mean roast dinner, though I only took a few bites and profusely apologized for my lack of appetite when she came to pick up the tray. I had ducked into the bathroom to brush my teeth when I heard a knock on the door.

"Coming," I mumbled with a mouth full of toothpaste and padded to the door in my bare feet. I hoped Agnes had read my mind and was waiting with a bottle of brandy. God, I needed a drink. But when I opened the door, Charlie was standing there, gripping his hat in one hand and rubbing the brim between his fingers. I pulled the toothbrush out of my mouth.

"I'm sorry to bother you, ma'am, but Mr. Hunter is quite worried about you." I glanced behind him, half expecting Ryan to be in the hallway. "He asked me to tell you he just wants to have a chat. He's waiting for you at my mate's pub."

I felt guilty that we'd put poor Charlie in the middle of this mess. His cap was spinning slowly between his fingers, and a fine sheen of sweat broke out on his forehead. I raised a finger to signal him to wait, then sprinted to the bathroom to lose the toothbrush. "Give me thirty minutes to shower and get dressed," I told him when I returned to the door. "I'll meet you downstairs."

Relief spread across his features, and if I didn't know better, I'd think he wanted to hug me. He placed the cap back on his head, nodded, then turned to leave, his footsteps thudding down the wooden stairs.

Despite my heart banging against my ribcage, I felt a strange sense of resignation when I stepped out of the car and saw the unassuming corner pub. I hadn't dressed to impress, having only slipped on a pair of jeans and a sweater. It seemed fitting that the sodium lamps were shrouded in a layer of fog, casting an eerie glow on the streets below to match my mood.

I thought I had my emotions under control, until I pulled open the heavy door and spotted him. My heart stuttered at the worried look on his face, his eyes weary and sad. I fought the urge to run and fall into his arms. Instead, my feet methodically stepped toward the table while I avoided his gaze. More than anything, I wanted to erase the sadness lying like heavy, damp air circling around us. To turn back the clock just twenty-four hours and climb back into our bubble where it was just Ryan and me. No ex-girlfriend—no baby.

"Hi," I said, my bottom landing on the hard wooden bench across the table from him. It sounded so ridiculously casual.

I hadn't known what to expect next, but it wasn't the words that rushed from him in an urgent stream. "Sofia, I'm sorry for leaving you alone. I'm sorry I didn't stop to think about how you were feeling. Of course, you would fear the worst. But I can't tell you what a relief it is that you're here with me now."

The muscles in my shoulders loosened as I allowed myself to relax just a fraction. A sliver of hope burrowed its way past my shield, but I held it at bay. "Ryan, I'm relieved to see you too, but you terrified me."

"You think I'm not scared?"

Our eyes met in the silence while I tried to put myself in his shoes. The pub was nearly empty except for a man throwing back a beer at the bar and a young couple holding hands across a table in the back corner. Ryan's fingers drummed nervously on the heavy wood tabletop. I scanned the dimly lit pub, searching for the server. It was definitely time for a drink. I finally spotted him slowly making his way to our booth, his body listing from side to side as he carefully favored one knee.

"Evening, what can I get you?" He brought with him a waft of beer-soaked air.

"Gin and tonic," I answered.

"I'll have a pint," Ryan added. "You're not really a beer drinker, are you?"

"Not generally. I prefer wine or a cocktail. I also prefer dogs over cats and always dark-haired men over blondes. Beach over mountains. My favorite color is blue. I had my first crush on a boy in kindergarten." I rambled like a lunatic—a lunatic desperate to bring us back to some semblance of normalcy—to who we were before yesterday.

He looked at me as if he thought I'd lost it. I wasn't entirely sure that he was wrong. But at least his fingers had stopped drumming on the table.

"Your turn," I said. "Tell me something I don't know about you."

"Okay," he said, shaking his head, his brows lifting with an unspoken question. "I already mentioned I had dogs when I was young, so I'm with you on that. Strangely, my favorite color is also blue. I harbor a deep dislike for lima beans, and I secretly wished I could be an artist when I was young. Of course, that was out of the question in my family."

"What do you want, Ryan?" I blurted. The question hung in the air between us once again. This time, he didn't run.

The server tottered over, carefully placing our drinks on the table. My eyes returned to Ryan's, waiting. The couple's laughter drifted through the bar, and it made me think about all the times we had talked and laughed—how normal things had been just a few days ago. Anxiety bubbled to the surface, my back stiffening against the wooden bench, but I was determined to hear him out. I had to know.

Ryan's gaze drifted to the corner where a fireplace glowed with burning embers. "Her name is Rebecca, by the way. I don't want to keep anything from you."

"When is she due?"

"She's almost eight months pregnant, so it could be anytime in the next six weeks. I guess you never know the exact timing." He paused before admitting, "I told her about you."

"Oh," I said calmly, like the thought had never crossed my mind. Like it wasn't the next question on my list. "And what was her response?"

"She tried not to let it show, but I could tell it wasn't the news she'd hoped for."

I gazed down at my lap. "You haven't answered my question."

His brows drew together. "I just did."

"No, the one just before the drinks came. What do you want?" Before he could answer, anxiety made me rush to fill in the blank. "Do you want to go to her? Take care of her?"

He reeled back. "No! After everything..." He shot me an incredulous look. "I don't get how you could think that."

Tears stung the back of my eyes. I cleared my throat, but it did little to stop my voice from wavering. "I left you once when you said you wanted a family. You convinced me that you'd give that up to be together. But now, it's not theoretical. It's real. Now, you have the chance." My voice broke—my greatest fear spoken out loud—and I crumbled.

His hand shot across the table and locked onto mine, tethering me to him as I was slipping away. Panic flashed in his eyes. "Sofia, nothing has changed." Tears spilled down my cheeks but I rolled my eyes. "Look, I'm so sorry. If I had known..." His fingers raked through his hair, as always, his tell when he was frustrated.

"I'm not blaming you."

He shook his head. "Let me finish." I stilled at his serious, intractable gaze. "If I had known, I would have told you upfront, but it wouldn't have changed anything. It wouldn't have changed how I fell in love with you. You asked me what I wanted. Well, here it is. I want you. Despite this... situation, I'm not willing to give you up. I'm not willing to sacrifice my life to be with Rebecca. You can't seriously believe I'd do that, right?"

"Stop," I insisted. "You don't know how you'll feel after the baby is born. You're about to experience something that will fundamentally rearrange your life." My voice wavered, and I released a shaky breath, trying to force back the emotions swelling in my throat. "Ryan, I can't just wait to see what happens and find myself blindsided if you change your mind. I know your priorities will shift once you meet your child, and I just can't..."

He let go of my hand; the absence of that small connection sent a chill across my skin, but it was the way the window in his eyes closed that scared me.

"So, you're just going to run?" He crossed his arms over his chest, his jaw clenched tight.

"I..." His steeled expression stopped me. In that moment, I realized we were both playing out our worst fears—anticipating abandonment. If I left him now, it would devastate both of us. I had to give us time to figure this out, even if it meant defying the urge to flee to safety. The idea seemed absurd, because Ryan had become my safe place. My voice softened. "I won't run, but I'm trying to understand where this is going. What do we do now?"

Silence filled the space between us. With each second passing, ice crept further through my veins. Were we both lost?

Ryan finally blurted, "We go on as planned."

"Just hang on for another three weeks until our contract ends? Pretend nothing has happened?"

In an instant, I saw the shift—the moment a lightbulb switched on in his brain, his eyes flashing the way they did when an idea was percolating.

"Look at it this way, if something unexpected happens that threatens to derail a business deal, you don't give up and walk away. You adjust course—find a way around the obstacle."

Resisting the urge to smirk, I said, "It's pretty hard to adjust course when a baby is on the way."

"But *we* can adjust course. Let's go back to Barcelona for the rest of... I mean, until the baby is born. I already told you, I'm not changing my mind after sixty days. We might just need to make some slight adjustments to our plans."

The words he'd used when he'd proposed the contract came back to me. "Reevaluate as things change. You did include that as a clause in the fine print. I just never expected a change like this." The absurdity of it all caused a smile to tug at the corners of my mouth.

Something released in him—maybe in both of us. He barked out a sardonic laugh, throwing his hands in the air as if gesturing to the universe, begging for an answer to this cosmic joke. "I never could have seen this coming," he quipped, draining the last of his drink.

Sadness and anger wound through me, tangling in knots like the roots of a tree. I wanted to pound my fist on the table—to protest the unfairness of it all. But what good would it do? If I'd learned anything in the past few months, it was that things could change in an instant—for better and worse. Instead, I sighed out a breath. "Life has a funny way of giving us what we need sometimes, not what we thought we wanted. The universe has its own timing."

He laced his fingers with mine, an intense yet calm look in his eyes that hadn't been there before this moment. "Screw the universe. Let's make a plan for at least the next several weeks before we figure out what follows. We'll decide our destiny. Where do you want to go?"

Letting his words sink in, I made the choice to trust him—to move forward instead of running or allowing myself to fall into a pit of despair. "I've been asking myself that question since last night. I'd like to go back to Barcelona for a couple of weeks before returning home." Instinctively, I knew Barcelona would ground us. It was where this had all started, and if we had to sort out our future, it had to be there.

"Let's do it. I can commute to London when I need to be in the office, and I can work remotely."

Out of the corner of my eye, I saw someone hovering, and turned to see the server timidly approaching as though torn between asking us if we needed anything and staying far away from this drama. Ryan caught his gaze, shaking his head. He ambled back to the bar, looking slightly relieved. "Can we get an apartment? I'd like it to feel like home, and a hotel would just feel like a vacation."

He smiled, and it was such a relief to see those dimples again. "I love you so much. You know that, right?"

"I do." I positioned a grin on my face, allowing the thought of us in Barcelona to block out the sadness threatening to derail our time together.

"Now, can we go back to the hotel?" he asked.

More than ever, I needed to feel his strong arms holding me, cocooning us from the rest of the world, convincing me it would all be okay.

Our clothes littered the floor, both of us peeling them off the minute we closed the door. His arm wrapped around my waist, pulling me next to his naked body under the sheet.

In the dim light of the moon cast through the sheer curtains, I found his lips with mine. As if careening through a wall of concrete barriers, I laced my fingers in his hair and kissed him hard—penetrating his mouth with my tongue, claiming him, devouring him with a fierce need. His response was instantaneous. Gripping my hips, he pressed himself against me, his tongue lashing wildly across mine. My skin blazed where he touched me, every inch of me feeling too raw, too sensitive, too vulnerable. I pulled my mouth from his and searched his eyes.

"I've got you, baby. I've got you." In his gaze, I saw unwavering love—clarity, as if there was nothing else in the world that mattered as much as our union. It was exactly what I needed to see.

The bed dipped, and I let out a whimper as I felt the weight of him shift on top of me, the words reverberating in my mind, freeing me. A few hours ago, I wanted to run far away from him, but at this moment, I could only think of doing the opposite. I wanted to fight for him, to hold on and never let go.

His lips trailed down my neck, kissing his way down to my breasts. Just as he raised himself, his knee prying open my thighs, my thumbs caught him at the front of his hips and I stopped him. He cocked an eyebrow.

"Turn over," I whispered.

"But I thought you liked me to..."

"Not right now." I nudged him and we rolled together, and then I was looking down at his impossibly beautiful face, half hidden in the shadows, my legs straddling him.

"Do you know how much I love looking at you? How much I love you?" My hands cupped his jaw, my lips claiming his before he could answer. His moan rumbled against my mouth when I lowered myself onto him, taking him inside slowly.

Maybe I wanted to convince him with undeniable certainty that what we had was better than anything he could imagine. Maybe I wanted to erase all the memories of anyone he'd been with before me. Or maybe I wanted to take control because I had no control over the forces dividing us. I was driven by an overpowering need to make him mine. To make us one again.

He shook his head, a wry smile curving his lips when I gripped his wrists and held them above his head.

"What?" I asked, dipping my head so I could feel his breath on my cheek. Drinking in the familiarity of his scent as I nuzzled his neck with the tip of my nose, moving my hips in long, languid strokes.

"You."

"Me?" He tipped his chin, and I kissed along the sculpted edge of his jawline until my lips rested a hair above his. My hips rocked, and satisfaction rippled through me at the sound he made—at the sensation of his response to me.

"Please don't ever leave me, Sofia," he whispered in my ear.

My heart tripped mid-beat. I released his hands and cradled the back of his head. "I won't. At least not for another few weeks." He pulled a face, and I curved my lips in a grin. "Don't even think about breaking our contract. That thing was ironclad. Unless you snuck something in the fine print about pregnant ex-girlfriends."

Thank God he laughed. I wasn't sure he would. A cloud lifted, and I saw relief sweep over his face, his furrowed brows relaxing. And just like that, we were tumbling, crashing—need spilling from our lips and bodies and souls. It was laughable to have thought we could control or stop the desire we had for each other, because something more powerful was controlling us both. Something we had uniquely created together, and I knew in my bones this love could never die. Just when I thought we'd hit our peak, another wave would come, and come again. Finally, when we'd banished all the fear—all the tension and sadness—we collapsed in a heap of tangled arms and legs. Our heaving chests slowed to shallow, even breaths, and my mind began to wander. He pulled me close to him, an arm wrapped around my back.

"It's going to be okay, you know. I promise."

My fingers traced the lines of his abdomen and slid against his chest, along his perfect skin and the cut of his muscles. I wondered how I could live without breathing in the scent of him every night. It was like being home. My new home. "We'll figure it out, together. Right?"

He kissed my forehead and wrapped me in a hold so tight, even as he drifted off to sleep, his arm refused to release me.

Chapter Eighteen

Ryan

"Ryan, I'm so sorry about the delay. I'm Dr. Webber, but you can call me Carrie." She extended her arm, silver bracelets clanging together on her wrist.

As I stood to meet her outstretched hand, my first thought was that her appearance didn't match the voice I'd heard during our phone consultation. She had a strong, commanding voice. The way she spoke reminded me of a pilot's reassuring authority crackling over the intercom. *Ladies and gentlemen, we're flying into some rough weather ahead, and the plane will experience turbulence. No need for alarm, but I'm switching on the seatbelt light. For the next fifty minutes, please remain seated with your belts fastened. I'll let you know when it's safe to move about the cabin.*

Her voice inspired confidence, like everything was under control. From experience, I knew that was exactly what I needed in a therapist. However, I'd imagined Dr. Webber to be younger, maybe taller. Instead, she appeared to be in her sixties, with a petite frame barely topping five feet. Her long skirt pooled around her ankles, and she wore a blouse that frilled at the neck. While her demeanor on the phone had convinced me she could help, now I wasn't so sure. Don't judge a book by its cover and all, I knew that. But in my mind, I equated strength and power with height, or at least a less... feminine outfit. I had to question whether that was a totally sexist assumption. I wasn't raised to think like that, so what the hell was going on in my head? Whatever it was, I couldn't just walk out now.

"You can come in now. I'm ready for you." I followed her along the tiled corridor and waited at her office door until she motioned me to a small couch, then positioned herself across from me in a leather chair.

Nothing ostentatious about her office—diffused sunlight poured through a large window draped with nearly sheer beige curtains, and a desk sat in the corner. A quick scan of the walls revealed only her license, a doctorate in psychology, and several framed photos of serene nature scenes.

Her gaze landed on my knee. Until then, I hadn't realized my leg was jiggling, heel bouncing against the wood floor. I froze. She continued without commenting.

"I'm glad we had the chance to speak on the phone and get the preliminaries out of the way so we can make the most of this session." She settled herself after retrieving a notebook from the table between us. "I understand you're only looking to come in once or twice, but let's see where this goes today, shall we?" This time I noticed the slight British accent threading through her words, but it wasn't too obvious. Maybe she'd lived outside of the U.K.?

I cleared my throat. "I really just need to clear my head. As I mentioned, therapy isn't new to me, so I'm sure I can accomplish what I need in one session."

Later, as Carrie's advice played on loop in my brain, I would cringe at the arrogance in that declaration.

"You were in therapy for quite some time as a teenager, right?"

I nodded. "Yes, on and off for a few years."

"Can you tell me about that experience?"

"Is that really necessary? It doesn't relate to why I'm here today." The annoyance leaked into my voice, but her expression remained neutral, a hint of a smile curving her lips. It reminded me of how I handled difficult clients. Damn.

I sighed, then rushed through the words to get this typical exercise over with, recounting the details without emotion. "I was in therapy after my sister died of a drug overdose and my family was falling apart. My father was defending himself in court on embezzlement charges, and my mother..." I ran a hand down my face, remembering how she'd lain in bed, unresponsive for weeks—maybe months. I'd tried to take care of her, but I was so fucking angry that I started getting into trouble. I finished simply, "My mother checked out."

"So, no one was taking care of you. How did you find yourself in therapy?"

The white noise machine whirred by the door, muffling footsteps in the hallway. The last thing I wanted to do was relive those years, but I had to give her something. "I got arrested for stealing cars. Actually, it was more of a business enterprise—breaking down cars and selling parts." Pride. I heard it in my voice. It shouldn't be there, but it was. "The judge ordered therapy. Either that or juvenile hall. I hated it at first. Wasn't until my third therapist that I finally understood what it was about. She's probably the reason I'm here today."

A pen rested between her fingers, and while I talked, she began writing in her notepad. It always irritated me when therapists did that—made me wonder what I'd said that was so important, so noteworthy. Seconds later, she stopped, placed her hands in her lap, and broke into a smile. I called it the *aha* smile—the expression therapists wore when they already had it figured out, just waiting for you to catch up. "What was it about that therapist that made it work?"

"Well, she didn't make me recount my entire history." I may have smirked. To my surprise, she laughed, and I decided to cut her a break. "She was direct instead of just nodding and saying 'hmm' and 'uh huh, how did that make you feel?' She confronted me with the choices I'd made and helped me climb out of the hole I'd dug myself into."

Carrie leaned back in her chair, her tongue pressing against the inside of her cheek. "Uh-huh. I see."

When I let out a laugh, she winked. She was good, I'd give her that.

"You've come a long way since then, and clearly you've made good decisions. So, let's get down to business. With your current situation, are you questioning your decisions now?"

"There's not a damn thing I can do about one of my decisions. Rebecca's pregnant, and I can't change that fact."

Her eyes shifted to the ceiling, deep in thought. "Tell me, Ryan, if you could go back in time and change anything about that situation with Rebecca, would you?"

My first instinct was to say *hell yes*, but I stopped myself. The clock on the wall ticked while silence filled the room, and I mentally ran through scenarios. If I'd stayed with Rebecca, we'd have a real family now, but I'd be miserable. If the condom hadn't failed or I'd never met Rebecca, I wouldn't be dealing with this crisis that threatened to destroy my relationship with Sofia. But then, I wouldn't have this chance to be a father.

Finally, I admitted, "I don't know. Being with Sofia makes it complicated. I try to sound positive for her sake, like everything will work out, but honestly, I'm drowning in all this and I can't let her see it."

She paged through her notes, nodding as if reminding herself of our phone conversation when I'd laid out this convoluted mess. Then she leaned forward, elbows on knees, and fixed me with her gaze—the intense eye contact making me shift in my seat. "Correct me if I'm wrong, but you're spending your time managing other people's feelings in this situation. Namely, Sofia's and Rebecca's. And possibly, it's not unlike when you tried to take care of your sister, then your mother."

Anger rolled up from my gut before I could push it back down. "Come on, the situation when I was a teenager was entirely different. Rebecca's pregnancy, the way Sofia found out... this whole thing was my fault and my responsibility to fix. Sofia doesn't even know I'm here."

The doctor's eyebrows drew together, her voice soft. "The situations are similar in that everything's out of your control, yet you're still trying to fix it. Your sister made her own decisions, and you couldn't change the devastating outcome. Your mother chose to stay in bed and abandon you rather than get help. Your father's bad choices created another crisis that affected the whole family, leaving you with a parent you could neither respect nor depend on." She reached for a pitcher on her desk, poised to pour water into a glass. "Would you like some water? I'm sorry I can't offer tea—my kettle isn't working, and I haven't had time to replace it."

When I shook my head, she took a few sips before continuing. I was still irritated, hearing my powerlessness laid out in such precise detail. "Now, where was I? Oh yes, the current circumstances. Rebecca has been entirely in control of the pregnancy—of when and how to inform you. She defines if and how you get to be involved as this baby's father. Sofia made the decision to leave you, and despite her coming back, you have no idea if she'll leave again. Your anger about your inability to control what everyone will do is emerging. But beneath that anger—and don't take this as weakness—is fear."

A protest bubbled in my throat, and I swallowed hard to keep it down. Everything she'd said was dead-on, but it was the word "fear" that triggered me. My damn knee started up again, jiggling in time with my racing heartbeat. "Alright, fine. But my fear is justified, right?"

"I never said it wasn't. In fact, I implied the opposite." Her face relaxed, eyes growing warmer. "Let's get specific. Name each fear so we can figure out how to tackle them."

My head began to throb, and I wanted to be anywhere but this office—even dental surgery would be less stressful. I blew out a long breath. "My biggest fear is that Sofia and I won't survive this together, that she won't be willing to deal with Rebecca and the baby in our lives."

Christ, it sounded even worse when I said it out loud.

Carrie nodded. "What's the next fear?"

The sun's rays had shifted, I noticed, my knees now illuminated in light. I casually slid my hands to the top of each knee to keep them still while I struggled to make sense of the thoughts and emotions tangling in my brain. "Rebecca worries me."

Carrie sat back and waited for me to elaborate, fingers intertwined across her stomach.

"If she were one of my clients, I'd describe her as a wild card—someone who could seem to agree to the deal but you suspect might back out at the last minute. More than that, someone who could potentially drop a bomb and blow everything up, causing damage to all parties involved."

Carrie's eyebrows shot up. "So, you see her as a threat to your security? And most likely Sofia's. What about the baby's?"

Anxiety seared through my chest, making it impossible to stay still. I struggled with an internal battle—the impulse to run and avoid this conversation nearly winning. Instead, I left my chair and stood staring out the window. Nothing much to see except a grove of trees swaying in the wind, their leaves falling like confetti, and a delivery guy attempting to park his oversized SUV in a tiny space. He was definitely going to sideswipe that Audi. Still watching the SUV backing up, then inching forward again, I said, "Honestly, I have no idea. I hope she's ready to be a good mother, but we won't know until she crosses that bridge. She's pretty emotional right now, but that's expected. I'm sure she's not happy with me, given that after I walked away from her, I ended up in a serious relationship with Sofia."

"That sounds concerning but not necessarily devastating. Do you think she'll change her mind about your involvement in the baby's life?"

"See, that's the other thing I've been trying to sort out." I was pacing now, her eyes following me as I moved from wall to wall.

"You told me you want children, and Sofia isn't a partner who can provide that in the usual way," she said.

"We discussed adoption, though I'm not sure Sofia would be happy starting over raising children. She'd be doing it for me. But now, problem solved, right?" As the words left my mouth, I knew she wouldn't let me get away with that.

She didn't hesitate. "Is it solved? Do you want to be a parent to this baby when you'd be forced to interact with Rebecca?"

I growled out the answer, clutching my head. "I don't know!"

"Ryan, just pause for a second. You're giving me whiplash." I turned to look at her, feeling more defeated than when I'd arrived. "Look, parents are often unsure of themselves and their commitment to a child until they actually feel the reality of his or her existence. That's especially true for men, because they aren't the ones growing the baby. Until you see the baby and hold it in your arms, this is just a concept. It's okay not to know what you want right now. She sprung this on you just days ago. Give yourself time to adjust."

Relief flooded through me as I sank back into the chair. Carrie nailed it, and I took some comfort in her giving me a break.

"Concerning the other variable—Rebecca's control over whether you're involved in this baby's life?"

"Oh, right." My life was like a game of whack-a-mole. I'd tackle one problem, and more would pop up from every direction.

"You do have rights as the father. You also have financial responsibilities. If you and Rebecca can't work this out, there are mediators and judges who can get involved."

"I've already assured her of my financial support, and right now she's asking for all the help she can get. She's amenable to my participation in parenting, but there's no telling how she'll react after the baby's born."

"Just to prepare you, she'll experience a surge of hormonal changes, coupled with sleep deprivation and new responsibilities. This could lead to behavioral changes. Expect her to be emotional; however, there are resources to help both of you adapt. You may need a therapist or home health aide to ensure her needs are met, which will help your communication go more smoothly."

"Great." I threw my arms in the air, then slapped the couch as they landed. "Now there's something else to worry about that I hadn't even considered." I was unraveling, but she continued, using a tone probably reserved for talking people off a metaphorical ledge.

"Things may go perfectly after the birth, but I think it's important to prepare you. Becoming a mother is no small task."

"No, you're right. I need to be prepared for all the variables. That's what I came here to sort out, so don't hold back."

"I'm glad to hear that because I have a feeling there's another fear lurking. Can you name it?"

Christ, does she have to be right all the time? There was something else, and I'd barely admitted it to myself. It had sifted to the bottom of the layers, since everything else involved people and outcomes I couldn't control. This one was squarely on me. I drew in a breath, but the words came out softly at first, though I could hear the desperation leaking out. "I'm afraid I won't be a good father. How could I be? I didn't exactly have a good role model. Committing to a 'concept' is one thing, and I told Sofia I wanted to create a family—to give a child a family better than the one I grew up in." When I paused and finally looked at Carrie, her face had softened, a knowing smile spreading across her face. "What if I wind up no better than him?"

"Oh, Ryan, if I had a pence for every time an expectant parent confessed that fear to me, I'd be... well, not rich but a lot more stable in my senior years." Her voice was so gentle yet confident. My fears immediately shrank by half. I flashed on that airplane pilot and wished I had that skill. On second thought, sometimes I did. In professional mode, I handled countless situations where it was necessary to calm nervous clients because whether it was a buyout or merger, the process was never straightforward. It was kind of my thing. I inspired confidence in clients, but I couldn't do this for myself.

Carrie broke into my thoughts. "No parent is perfect, but your willingness to learn from your past is a huge step toward growth. If we're lucky, each generation benefits from the knowledge gained by the previous one. Most of all, I see a man who not only wants to be a parent but will strive to be the best father he can be—not despite his past but because of his experiences."

I straightened in my chair, feeling emboldened, wishing my parents had given me the validation I needed. Carrie's gaze drifted to the clock, and I got the hint that our time was almost up.

"Look, Ryan, you don't need everything sorted before the baby's born. You only have to be prepared to roll with the changes as they unfold and accept that you don't control what other people do."

I snorted a sharp laugh. "Yeah... that's what I'm concerned about."

Her comeback was quick. "Do you always have control over whether a client accepts the terms and whether the deal goes through? You can set things up to the best of your ability, but in the end, it's their decision. This is no different."

"It isn't, yet it is. The stakes are high because it's my life we're talking about. If Sofia leaves me..." I shook my head, then locked eyes with hers. "I will be devastated—ruined. That, I can guarantee."

"Does she love you? Want to be with you?"

"I can say with confidence that she does. But—"

"Then it would be as devastating to her as it is to you if the relationship is lost. The stakes are just as high for her. When two people are equally invested, they tend to find a way to make it work."

"A pregnant ex-girlfriend showing up might just challenge that investment. Sofia usually runs, and I can't blame her this time."

"She ran because Rebecca's news was a shock, and she was afraid she'd lost you. But she came back, right?" I nodded. "Because you reassured her of your love and dedication. Believe me, that's worth gold to her. What the two of you have is rare, and you've both proven you'll fight like hell for it. Trust in your relationship. Trust in her."

Carrie's words and advice reverberated in my head during the taxi ride back, but I needed more time with my thoughts before returning to the hotel. Wandering London's streets, I barely heard the din of horns and traffic, the conversations as people passed. Before leaving her office, Carrie had asked if I was going to share my fears with Sofia. Even now, I was still weighing the pros and cons. Of course, she already knew I was afraid to lose her, but did I want to burden her with all the rest? I decided to let the dust settle first. Something was happening inside my brain—maybe recalibrating after hearing the doctor's assessments. This was my shit to sort out, and there was no reason to pile more worries on her.

So, I stopped mid-stride, turned around, and headed home—headed toward Sofia. Whatever else happened, we would weather the storm. Returning to Barcelona would be good for us. It was where we began, and our bond would grow stronger there, away from Rebecca and the firestorm she'd brought into our lives.

Chapter Nineteen

Sofia

T he last few days in London had been a whirlwind of travel preparations, apartment hunting, and last-minute sightseeing. I'd thrown myself into anything that might distract me from what was coming—the birth that would change everything between Ryan and me. I'd reduced the inevitable to a single letter—B—because apparently, my coping mechanism involved turning life-altering events into some kind of emotional shorthand. It wasn't as if I'd magically forgotten what was facing us, but I was choosing to kick it backstage, out of the spotlight, instead of letting the uncertainty eat away at the good moments.

The day before our flight, I visited the bookstore one last time. Oliver's face fell when I told him I was leaving London; a look of disappointment I hadn't expected.

"But... you'll come back to London again, won't you?" he asked, pausing mid-unboxing of what looked like a literary treasure trove. "I mean, you're always welcome here."

The bookstore had become my anchor in this sprawling city, the one place where I didn't feel like a tourist wearing an invisible sign that screamed 'lost American.' Maybe that's what prompted me to scribble my email address on a napkin and slide it across the counter.

"In case I don't make it back for a while, I'd love your book recommendations."

Oliver's face beamed with a smile. "I'd be delighted to keep in touch."

"Thank you, Oliver. That means more than you know." The words stuck in my throat because, honestly, my future was about as clear as London fog.

When I checked in with the lonely hearts club—though I'd have to rename them the "second chancers" at this rate—Josie straightened herself in the chair, shoulders back, a full-wattage smile on her face.

"Got myself a new fella," she announced, practically glowing. "Too early to tell, but he's got all his teeth, a full head of hair, a steady job, and a pension that'll set him right in his old age. Plus—and this is the real miracle—he's actually single and doesn't live with his mum."

Arthur was still making his pilgrimages to Surrey, but now he was practically moved in. "I still don't know what a pretty bird like her sees in that old bugger," Josie couldn't help adding, "but the shagging has surely lifted his spirits."

Even John looked more animated than I'd seen him. Apparently, Widow Taylor had hung a "permanently closed" sign on her dating life, but he'd taken Arthur's advice and joined an over-fifty dating site. "Mind you, most of the women are older than my Tillie, and they leave their walkers out of their profile pictures on purpose. But I have a little company every fortnight or so."

When they asked about my "fella," I forced a smile and delivered the highlight reel—all sunshine and romance, conveniently editing out the pregnant ex-girlfriend plot twist. Some stories were too exhausting to relive in the telling.

But Madison got the full, unvarnished truth via email. Her response arrived just as we were heading to Gatwick:

To: SofiaDrake01@gmail.com
From: Madison555@gmail.com
Sofia, tell me this is some kind of crazy misunderstanding! Or maybe a love-crazed ex-girlfriend's plot to get him back? I'm going to check your astrological chart because something is seriously off here. Don't roll your eyes at me. I'm just trying to understand why this is happening to you. There must be a reason, we just don't understand the grand plan yet. Call me later, okay? Sending you a big hug. Enjoy Barcelona and don't worry about your house. All is well here. And yes, Roger and I are doing fine. Kevin hasn't dared to contact me. XO, Madison.

I typed back quickly as the plane's engines began their pre-flight symphony, simply saying, **Can't wait to talk! Barcelona, here I come.**

After switching to airplane mode, I turned to Ryan. "I think I'm going to miss Charlie."

The corner of his mouth twitched with barely contained amusement. "You'll have to stop hugging him at every opportunity, though. The poor man breaks into a sweat every time you get near him."

"You can take the girl out of California," I shrugged, "but apparently, you can't take the California out of the girl."

He leaned over and kissed my forehead tenderly. "Don't ever change who you are."

"I'm still me—just Sofia 2.0. All the original features, plus some significant updates that hopefully make me less likely to flee when things become complicated."

"Sofia 2.0," he murmured against my hair. "I can't wait to discover what comes next."

"And I will enjoy surprising you," I said, my mind already wandering to decidedly R-rated possibilities involving airplane blankets and zero shame.

Apparently, I was full of surprises these days—for him and myself.

Summer was officially ending, but Barcelona hadn't gotten the memo. The air hung thick and warm, buzzing with a tourist energy that felt electric against my skin. Our taxi driver navigated the maze of lost tourists in rental cars like a Formula One champion, weaving down Via Laietana toward El Born.

Ryan would've preferred staying uptown where the streets were wider and the tourists fewer, but in the end, he deferred to me. Possibly it was his penance for bringing a pregnant ex-girlfriend into our lives, but to his credit, he gave me carte blanche to find an apartment for us. I wanted to be right in the heart of it all—the noise, the chaos, the ancient alleyways that sometimes smelled like they hadn't been cleaned since the medieval period. Though the streets received a nightly hosing down, some odors born over time were impossible to eliminate. It was Gothic Barcelona in all its grimy, gorgeous glory.

A gust of nostalgia swept over me as we pulled to the curb opposite the cathedral and heard the musicians playing for the crowd. The music had seeped in through my pores, and though I hadn't realized it at the time, the sights and sounds of the city had planted the seeds of a dream.

Our apartment was a far cry from my previous budget accommodation, which had come with its own cockroach colony. With Ryan's resources, I'd found us a penthouse with a terrace that came with a breathtaking view across gothic spires and terracotta rooftops all the way to the shimmering Mediterranean. The space felt light and airy, with sea breezes circulating through the large balcony doors.

"Do you like it?" I asked as he wheeled my suitcase into the bedroom, his eyes already cataloguing the king-size bed like a man with very specific plans.

"I think this will do just fine." Before I could blink, he'd lifted me as if I weighed nothing and deposited me on the crisp white linens. "I think we need to finish what you started on the plane. That was cruel and unusual punishment, don't you think?"

His fingers found the buttons of my blouse just as his phone erupted like an angry electronic bird.

The spell shattered. "Do you need to get that?" The question came out more loaded than I'd intended, because I had to face it—I would always wonder if it was her calling, needing him, pulling him away from me.

He slipped the phone out of his back pocket. "It's Steve from the office. I'd better take this."

Of course you do, I thought, hanging clothes in the closet while his voice grew increasingly tense behind me. Welcome to the new normal—competing with conference calls and quarterly reports for attention.

"I'll need to work for a while. Sorry," he said, phone pressed to his ear, his mood already shifted into serious financier mode.

"No problem. I'll go get some groceries." I grabbed the granny cart from the entryway. I never understood why it had earned that name, because everyone in Barcelona had one, regardless of age or actual grandmother status. After all, it wasn't like you could pull your SUV into a parking lot and load up the trunk.

My feet remembered the route to the market, which surprised me, but I was still dubious about finding my way back to the apartment without the aid of GPS. I managed to buy bread, pointing mutely at a round loaf while the cashier rattled off something about "cortado."

"Oh, sí, cortado, por favor," I responded, feeling like an absolute genius when she actually sliced it.

At the fruit stand, I played grocery store charades, pointing and smiling while fruit flies conducted aerial maneuvers around the ripe fruit. A fan circulated the sweet smell of berries and melons and peaches; the heady combination wafting through my nostrils. The vendor and I communicated in a combination of Spanish and hand signals; me pointing and saying *"vale"* because I'd heard the locals repeating this word everywhere I went. The pronunciation actually sounded like, *"baalay,"* The tone undulated like a song, bouncing from one octave to another, then syllables slammed into each other in a rush at the end. "Vale... vale... sí... *vale, vale, vale."* For all I knew, I'd agreed to buy several kilograms of kale. Fake it till you make it, right? At least I sounded like a local.

By the time I reached the apartment, I had decided on a plan, because having a plan meant I could avoid spiraling out of control. "I'm going to enroll in language school," I announced to Ryan's back.

"What? Oh, that's a good idea," he responded without looking up, absorbed in the digital wonderland of mergers and acquisitions.

I wheeled the groceries into the kitchen, a little annoyed, but could I be? I reminded myself that his job involved juggling several potential deals at the same time and that I would always have to compete for his time.

While I prepared pan con tomate—rubbing garlic and fresh tomato over toasted bread, then drizzling it with olive oil—the pieces finally clicked into place. Since my arrival in London, I'd been drifting like a tourist in my own life.

Ryan had his purpose, his trajectory, and now his pregnant ex-girlfriend to factor into every decision. But what did I have?

The aroma of garlic and fresh bread filled the kitchen, and just as I bit into the toast, the flavors exploding on my taste buds, Ryan called out, "What are you making in there? Smells good."

I laughed—well, actually honked. "Hah! So, now you're paying attention. Typical."

He appeared in the doorway, barefoot and confused. "What?"

"Nothing," I said, offering him the plate. "You barely acknowledged me when I came in, but the smell of food sure got your attention. I see where I rank."

He demolished half a slice in one bite, eyes rolling back as he savored it. "Damn, that's good. And I'm sorry, Sofia. Working from home is going to be an adjustment for both of us." Then he planted a garlic-tomato-flavored kiss on my lips.

"I know," I said between kisses. "We'll get the hang of the routine. As I mentioned, ahem... I'm going to start studying Spanish, so I'll be busy too."

"Right, I did hear you." His phone chirped from the living room, and he had the grace to look apologetic. "Great idea. We can practice together."

"Go," I said, practically pushing the plate into his hands. "Take your carbs and conquer the business world."

After he dashed from the kitchen, I padded to the bedroom. Propped up on pillows, I opened my laptop and found myself drowning in language school options. Most started at nine a.m.—which was basically the middle of the night for a recovering night owl like me—but ran only four to five hours. That would leave my afternoons free to enjoy the rest of my time in Barcelona.

I enrolled in a week of classes near El Born, starting Monday, with a sense of accomplishment that there was at least one thing I could control. If nothing else, it would distract me from counting down the minutes until our contract was due for renegotiation. My gaze broke from the laptop screen, shifting to the sound of his voice in the next room, the speaker magnifying the conversation—a battle to claim a prospective client.

That damn spotlight moved back to center stage, and I had a sudden urge to march in there and say... what? What could I possibly say that would bring me the certainty I craved?

Even from the start of this crazy idea, neither of us had discussed what would happen next. Until Rebecca came along with her plot twist, there hadn't been any reason to question what came after the sixty days.

I lay back on the pile of pillows, staring up at the curved, wood-beamed ceiling and focused on his voice—the comfort of his presence. Yet the foreboding feeling in my gut wouldn't subside. As much as I needed resolution—to get out the poster paper and plot the course—the future was impossible to predict. There would come a time when we'd have that discussion. The only question was when.

"It's so good to hear your voice! It feels like forever," I whispered into my phone. I'd left Ryan snoring in bed, quietly shutting the door and curling up on the living room sofa in the dark. A cool breeze drifted through the open balcony doors, and I heard the church bells chime with twelve loud gongs. It would be three o'clock in California, just about time for Madison's break. Ryan and I had gone out for a late dinner and then collapsed on the bed to watch a movie. He'd drifted off sometime before the final credits rolled on the screen, his head resting on my shoulder.

"Oh my God, you even sound different," Madison's voice practically bounced through the speaker. "I bet I won't recognize you."

"Well, what do you expect? World travel and great sex will do that to a woman."

Madison let out a whooping sound, then added, "You go, girl."

"Speaking of great sex, how's Roger?"

"He's fantastic—*we're* fantastic. It's the real thing, Sofia. I didn't know it was possible to feel this way again at our age, but here I am, acting like a lovesick teenager."

A pang of envy bubbled to the surface. Her relationship had a fighting chance, while mine was teetering on a cliff edge.

"I'm at work, so I don't have much time," Madison contin-ued, her voice nearly a whisper. "Listen, I know you're going through a crisis, so I'm not sure this would be a good time, but Roger suggested a trip to Barcelona while you guys are there. You know, to show us around. What do you think?"

Until that moment, I didn't realize how much I missed my best friend—the familiarity and comfort of someone who knew exactly what I needed without me having to ask. Roger might have thought this was his idea (she was that good), but I didn't have a doubt this spontaneous trip was her doing. "Oh, Madison, it's a brilliant idea! When can you come?"

"Do you realize you've developed a British accent?"

I laughed. "Well, you should hear me in England. I sound like bloody Mary Poppins again. I did the same thing in my twenties."

"Ryan probably wouldn't know who that was, would he?"

"Definitely before his time."

"We could fly out next Friday, stay a week. Given your timeframe, maybe we could fly back together—if you're still coming home. Oh, and send me some hotel suggestions?"

The question of going home stirred up emotions I wasn't ready to face. "Yes, I'm coming back, but I don't have a flight yet. I'll research hotels tomorrow. I can't wait to see you."

"Same here. And, Sofia? Try to stay calm. I really think everything will work out."

Her compassion undid me. My careful composure dis-solved like sugar in rain, and I found myself curled in a fetal position on the couch, crying for everything uncertain and beautiful and terrifying about my life.

After forty minutes staring out at the night sky, I heard the lone chime of the Gothic cathedral's bell marking the hour. I crept back to bed, pressed close to Ryan's warmth, and promised myself to stop borrowing trouble from tomorrow. Our moments together were too precious to waste.

Chapter Twenty

Ryan

Time had become my enemy. Some days, I could almost hear it ticking past—a persistent, obnoxious clock inside my head. I wanted to dropkick that clock into oblivion—to have more time with Sofia before everything changed in ways I couldn't yet imagine. She must be feeling it too, because there had been moments when her tension was palpable. It was like being next to a hot stove, anxiety radiating off her in waves of heat.

Twenty-four hours wasn't enough when every moment mattered this much, especially when most of my days were consumed by work, when I'd rather spend every minute with Sofia. But I was glad her time was filled with language classes, homework, and the afternoon excursions she took to explore on her own. It made her happy and eased my guilt about only being available in the evenings. She didn't complain—maybe she was hiding her anxiety—and her glow had returned since we'd been back in Barcelona.

Since I was working from home, except for occasional escapes to a café when I didn't have phone meetings scheduled, she made herself scarce during the day. I heard the solid *thunk* of the apartment door closing, then her feet tiptoeing to the closet in an attempt not to disturb me. Whenever she was near, I got distracted. Especially now, when she was changing out of her swimsuit. I closed my laptop, letting my gaze roam over her body. She caught me staring.

"What?" She said it so innocently, but I saw the playful glint in her eyes. She knew exactly what she was doing to me.

"I was just wondering how your classes were going."

"It's torture. I feel ancient. Most of my classmates could be my children, and even the teacher looks like she should be carded at bars." She caught my gaze, and her cheeks flushed pink. "What? Why are you looking at me like that?"

"From where I'm sitting, you don't look like anyone's mother. Not many women at any age can pull off a bikini like you do."

"Oh, stop." She pulled a white cotton dress over her head, then flopped into my lap, the fabric billowing at her ankles. "And did you know your brain can actually hurt from learning verb tenses? There are four different ways to describe the past. Four!"

"Yes. The preterit—"

"All right, show-off." She wrapped her arms around my neck and kissed me, effectively ending that conversation.

"Hello, gorgeous. I missed you today," I said. She looked fresh and adorable without makeup, wild brown curls framing her bronzed cheeks. "Sorry I couldn't make it to the beach. Work's been insane."

"That's okay. If you'd been there in those criminally tight swim trunks, I wouldn't have finished my homework. You're very distracting."

"Oh, really? Hm. Well, I have a plan to distract you later."

"You? With a plan? I thought I was the planner in this relationship."

"You deserve some special treatment." My lips skimmed her neck, and I felt her skin erupt in goosebumps. "I've been neglecting you."

"You'd better watch it, or I might ruin your plans for later." Her eyebrows bounced, her gaze turned sultry, and I almost took her up on it. "I'm going to take a shower and get dressed. It's Friday night, and apparently, you're taking me out."

"Wear something sexy," I called out as she walked away.

She spun around, hands on hips. "You're supposed to think I'd look sexy in a garbage bag."

I laughed, partly at myself for making that stupid comment. "Point well made."

An hour later, she emerged from the bedroom in a black silk dress that hugged every curve, slit up the thigh, with a neckline that showcased her breasts like fine art. Her heels clicked against the wood floor as she cat-walked to the couch where I was waiting, scrolling through emails.

"Sexy enough?"

"Holy shit." My mouth fell open. "Where did you get that dress?"

"Harrods sale," she said casually, as if it was no big deal—as if she didn't know what effect it would have on me.

"That dress couldn't be more perfect if it had been made for you." I rose and held her by the shoulders while I studied her at close range. "You should wear that to class. Nobody's mother looks like that." Then I realized what I'd just said. "Scratch that. I just got an image of those young boys drooling over you."

"You're picturing yourself at that age, aren't you?"

"I don't even want to go there."

"Mrs. Robinson?"

I shook my head and ushered her out the door. "Let's go before I change my mind about leaving this apartment."

"Reservation for two, Ryan Hunter."

The hostess let her gaze linger on my face for too long. *Really, lady?*

As she showed us to our table, I watched Sofia's face for her reaction, and it was exactly as I'd hoped. Her lips parted, and her eyes went wide as she took it all in. Everything about Mirabé screamed elegance—white linens, fabric-draped chairs, and floor-to-ceiling windows that displayed Barcelona like a living postcard. From our perch atop Mount Tibidabo, the city spread out below us in a golden tapestry that still took my breath away. It was one thing to observe the shifting architecture while exploring on foot, but from this elevation, we could clearly see the modern Eixample district's grid design—laid out in straight lines, appearing like squares on a chessboard—then the abrupt transition into medieval Gothic, with its chaotic, winding alleyways snaking all the way to the water's edge.

"I'm glad I dressed for the occasion." Her gaze traveled out the window, and she blew out a breath, aiming for a whistle, but it came out as a wisp of air mixed with saliva. The sunset blanketing the hillside reflected an amber hue on her skin, and my God, she looked breathtaking. "This view is insane."

"I thought you'd like it." Making her happy, seeing the look on her face when I surprised her with places I'd discovered—it motivated me to never stop giving her more.

When the server appeared, I ordered champagne. I'd been waiting for the right moment to share my big news, and tonight we were celebrating.

"Champagne instead of cava? You're going all out tonight."

I cleared my throat. "It's time to celebrate the good things coming our way, and I have a lot to be grateful for. You are at the top of my list, of course."

Her eyes went soft with the unmistakable look of love that always grabbed me right in the chest, and I couldn't help the smile breaking across my face. "Sofia, I've received some good news. I'm being promoted to head up the London office."

Her entire expression changed. I could see the wheels turning because her eyes were practically vibrating in their sockets. This wasn't the response I had been expecting, but her voice sounded cheerful when she spoke.

"Congratulations!" She raised her glass. "To wealth and early retirement. Nice work on the plan."

"Thanks. It'll take time to reach my goals, but this is a major step. The board is announcing it next week. I guess my work on the Dubai deal opened some serious doors."

She set her glass down on the table—hard. "That was a close call. I'm glad you did the right thing."

I cocked my head, trying to figure out what in the hell was going on. Didn't she understand what this recognition meant to me? I enunciated each word this time, with more volume than was necessary. "Turns out, Omar appreciated me for preventing a disaster. He must have put in a good word with management."

Sofia offered another toast, her voice competing with the couple at the next table chattering in Catalan, and then I launched into an explanation of my new responsibilities, hoping she'd get the significance of this promotion.

"So, you'll be based in London full-time?" she asked. While her voice was light, her jaw clenched so tight the muscles in her face twitched.

"Yes, less traveling," I said hesitantly. "Sam's covering for me in San Francisco—you remember Sam from game night at the bar?"

"Of course. How is he?" Her fork hit a croquette with a stab that nearly upended the plate.

"He's good." I let my cutlery drop onto the plate. Enough was enough. "Hey, is something wrong?"

"I was just thinking how convenient it is that you'll be in London. Closer to the baby. But not in the Bay Area."

"Oh," I said, releasing a long breath as realization crashed over me. "This doesn't have to affect us, Sofia. Everything's happening so fast, I haven't had time to process what comes next."

"You're right. We haven't made any plans past next week, let alone what will happen at the end of sixty days."

"Look, we'll go back home, take care of business, then you'll come with me to London." It was simple, wasn't it? I picked up my fork and speared a potato, then stopped midway to my mouth when I saw her gaping at me like I'd just said we were moving to Mars.

"Hold up. How do you see this new family scenario playing out? Shared custody on weekends? Am I changing diapers or waiting on the sidelines in London while you're with Rebecca and the baby—an extra in this play?" Her voice bordered on shrill, and I shot a glance at the tables nearby to see if anyone noticed.

"Whoa. Sofia, aren't you jumping the gun here?" I took a breath, searching for an answer that would satisfy her, but came up empty. "How am I supposed to know what the arrangement might look like? A lot will depend on what Rebecca wants, but I'm telling you everything is going to be fine. It will be you and me in London, then we'll figure out the details."

"Ryan, you're acting like our lives aren't about to change dramatically. Questions are circling us like rabbits, and you're pretending everything is resolved."

I opened my mouth to answer, but she cut me off.

"Even setting aside our contract renegotiation, I can't keep following you around the world. You have your job and a baby on the way. I'm unemployed and, well, drifting—just following you around, if I'm honest." She leaned across the table and held my hand in hers, her voice softer now. "You have your course set. If I'm going to be my own person—not just your shadow—I need to decide what I want out of life."

"Do you remember what you told me about your goals?" My mind drifted back to that day in Big Sur when we'd first shared our hopes and dreams—when I had stupidly told her I wanted a family. The day our wishes burst like a piñata, complications spilling out like sour candy.

"I think so."

"Babe, you're there. Think about it."

While the server presented a paella the size of a car tire, Sofia began recounting her list.

"I said I wanted love—check. Maybe it was too much to ask for uncomplicated love, but here we are."

I shrugged. "Yeah, well, you probably should have qualified that."

She smirked at me. "I wished for a partner to share adventures with—check." Now she counted them off on her fingers. "The freedom to explore new possibilities for my future—well, sort of. Yes, I have the freedom, but there hasn't been a sign, a revelation, or even a tap on the shoulder to point me in a direction. As for my goal to unearth my inner adventurer—take chances and carpe the hell out of diem—I'm just getting started."

In a way, she was on this marathon trek, and her face beamed as if she could see the finish line ahead. I took it all in, spooning rice and shellfish onto her plate, catching her wince at the sight of the giant prawns with their beady black eyes. She gazed out the window with a pensive expression. I sensed something was shifting in her. Below us, Barcelona transformed into a carpet of twinkling lights, and I watched as her lips curled into a smile.

"You're smiling but not eating. Want me to decapitate the shrimp?" I asked.

She took a sip of champagne. "No, I can handle it." She picked up her fork and finally began eating, then paused. "I'm just happy and grateful that we're together, because time with you is a precious gift. I don't have all the answers yet, but if I dwell on the what-ifs instead of making memories with you, that would be a total waste. After all, I've trusted you this far, and you haven't let me down. So, I'll live in the moment. Right here, right now, with you. I'll figure out the rest later."

Relief washed over me. We were going to be okay—we had to be, because I couldn't lose her. I'd hoped this evening would help us forget about the complications, even for a while. My plans for tonight were just beginning, and finally, things were looking up.

"I have no doubt you will. But do it tomorrow. The night is still young."

As we left the city lights behind, driving past deserted beaches that stretched like pale ribbons against the dark sea, our heads bobbed to the tunes on my playlist. All old-school music—classic rock and funk. My parents used to play this stuff when I was young. I remembered the songs because they reminded me of the times the music made my parents happy—times when we all got along.

When "Tower of Power" came through the speakers, Sofia began belting out lyrics like she was auditioning for a soul revival. I pulled into an empty parking lot at the edge of a beach while she was in the middle of singing, "You're still a young man, babe," when I reached to power off the car.

"Wait! Leave it on."

I obeyed, dimming the headlights as the engine fell silent, and blasted the volume to ten. Joining her in a duet, I pantomimed the song, hand over my heart and really selling it. This sent her into fits of laughter, but she managed to fill in the harmony with the backup singers in a soprano voice. "You're too young to love."

With the click of a button, my seat shot back so I could place one knee on the floor. My voice went deep as I hammed it up, palms pressed together. "Down on my knees... um huh... heart in my hand." I added hand gestures, forming my fingers into a heart shape. While I kept singing, mostly with a straight face, she was doubled over in laughter, squeezing her thighs together as if she had to pee. Yeah, it was totally corny, but I hadn't had this much fun letting loose in ages.

"I'm hearing this song in a whole new light," she said when I turned off the sound, still clutching her stomach.

"Never underestimate a young man in love." I brushed the stray wisps of hair off her forehead.

"Thank you," she said in a soft voice, her sweet face tipped up to mine.

Looking into her eyes, warmth swelled from somewhere deep and uncharted—as if she'd found an abandoned chamber inside me, dusted it off, and made it home. I should be thanking her. Instead, I asked, "For what?"

"For not giving up on me. You could have quit when I ran from you the first night we met, or when I broke it off after our Monterey trip."

"Or when you left me in London," I interjected.

She slid a hand down her face. "Yeah... that too. I'm surprised you didn't just walk away."

"Not a chance. I knew. Don't ask me how, but I knew you were the one from the moment we met."

Tears pooled in her eyes. "How do you have this effect on me?"

"Believe me, it's mutual. Now, let's go have some fun." As we stepped out into the salty air, I said, "Lose the heels. You don't want to ruin them."

She kicked them off, and I toed out of mine, then I grabbed a blanket from the trunk. We walked barefoot to the water's edge, the sand cool and damp between my toes. The deserted beach stretched endlessly in both directions, lit only by the moon and the stars dotting the sky with a million pinpricks of light.

"Looks like we have the whole place to ourselves," she said, watching waves erase our footprints.

"I was counting on it." My hand found the back of her neck, fingers threading through her hair as I pulled her close. I kissed her—tenderly at first. When her lips parted, all the pent-up desire I had for her poured out, and my body instantly responded.

With my pulse racing, I broke away. "Do you remember our first kiss on the beach?"

Her eyes caught the moonlight, gold flecks reflecting in the green of her irises. "How could I forget?"

"Did you know how much restraint it took not to do this?" My fingers gingerly lowered the straps of her dress, one shoulder, then the other. The silk pooled at her feet.

"Here? Really?" Her voice lilted, but the sexy tone and the way her eyes flashed told me it wasn't a question. It was a dare.

She watched as my fingers worked the buttons on my shirt. I shrugged it off while kissing my way down her neck, then the crest of her breasts. She arched against me, giggling as my tongue lashed her stomach, her muscles twitching.

"Oh, so you're ticklish right there?"

"No, no tickling," she begged, her laughter mingling with a gust of wind that smelled of the sea.

She backed into the gentle waves as I shed the rest of my clothes. Her gaze drifted upward, to where a shooting star carved its path across the inky sky, and she closed her eyes. I couldn't take my eyes off her face. A smile played at the corners of her mouth, and her skin glowed in the moon's reflection.

"What did you wish for?"

"It doesn't matter. It can't get any better than this."

With a giddy grin, she launched her body against mine, and I caught her, my hands supporting her ass while her legs wrapped around my waist. I spun her in circles, her head tilted to the starry sky. She giggled with pure abandon, and God, I loved the sound of her—happy. We were both dizzy by the time I lowered her to the blanket, the feel of her soft skin against mine driving me crazy. This wasn't the same person I'd met that night in San Francisco. This Sofia was bold, free, radiating a boundless hunger for life. Hell, she was free-falling off a cliff daily with me—the very thing she'd sworn she'd never do.

Tumbling onto her back, her eyes scanned the sky, tracking the gulls flying overhead, their caws drawing her attention. Her expression shifted, became pensive, and I asked, "Are you okay?"

"I'm memorizing everything about these moments and filing them under: Highlight reel with Ryan."

"Oh, you have a file on me?"

She propped up on one elbow. "A thorough and complete file, but I highlight the best stuff. We make memories every day, and I don't want to take them for granted or forget the details. Like tonight, how it feels to be naked with you, uninhibited, the scent of the sea in the air, and the mist on my skin." Her fingers stroked my cheek, and I stared at her in amazement.

For the millionth time, this woman blew me away. I couldn't imagine my life without her, and the thought made me pull her close, cementing these memories in my own vault. She didn't have to spell it out, because we'd both known loss and life didn't come with a happiness guarantee, but she was teaching me how to appreciate every moment together. Because in a world filled with uncertainties, that was all any of us really had.

Chapter Twenty-One
Sofia

Journal entry - day 41

I've decided not to share this entry with Ryan. Things are getting real now, and since I don't have poster paper to chart my options, this journal will have to do.

There's a question booming in my head—loud, insistent—and I can't ignore it any longer. Who am I now?

I've been a daughter, a mother, a wife, a divorcee, and now a girlfriend. I've been someone's therapist or boss. I'm too young to be considered a 'retiree.' I certainly haven't put away enough money to live comfortably for the rest of my life doing nothing—just drifting without a purpose or goal.

I got what I wanted: a wide-open path with infinite possibilities and the love I was craving. Now what? Ryan is heading down his own path. So, I have to ask myself now, at this juncture, what do I want out of life?

Breaking from the script has me filled with trepidation and confusion. The only thing I truly know is that I want more—more new experiences and places to discover. More fulfillment than my life held in the confines of the suburbs. I feel like a kid who's finally been given the keys to the candy store, and I'm staring at the chocolates and brightly colored wrappers, salivating at the possibilities.

If I'm to redefine myself, I can't go back to living in the same house, the same neighborhood where I felt suffocated, where my dreams were reduced to rubble, where I allowed my spirit to wither. I've come this far, I'm not turning back now.

So, what does a woman of forty-nine do when she finds herself falling out of love with her old life? Anything she damn well pleases. Hopefully, I'll excavate other parts of me that have been buried, and in the process, I just might learn what I'm supposed to do with the rest of my life—without the constraints of the labels that have defined me. But I realize now that it's up to me to find my way forward, instead of following someone else's lead.

To: SofiaB1@gmail.com
From: Oliver@greensbooks.co.uk
Dear Sofia,
I hope you don't mind my taking the liberty of writing to you. I trust all is well with you in Barcelona? You mentioned that you'd like to receive recommendations for new novels, and I wanted to let you know that the author of the last book you purchased has just released a sequel. Pity you won't be by the bookstore to see the display, but you may look for her series online.
Pursuant to our last conversation, I am also attaching a link to an online writing course. I hope you don't think me too bold, but do take a look and see if it holds any interest. One never knows what talents lie hidden, waiting to be discov-

ered.

With fond regards, Oliver

His words rang in my mind long after I shut my laptop, then hopped in a taxi near the cathedral, setting out for the airport.

"You're awfully quiet." When I didn't respond, Ryan leaned hard against my shoulder just as the taxi made a sharp left turn onto Gran Via. "Aren't you excited about seeing Madison?"

I shifted in my seat to face him. "Please don't laugh, but what do you think about my becoming a writer?"

"I didn't know you had ever considered it, but why not?"

"It's probably a silly idea, but the owner of the bookstore sent me information about a writing course. Oliver seems to think I should give it a try."

"Wait." He shook his head, then peered over at me. "This man is writing to you?"

I pulled a face. *Seriously? He's jealous?* "I gave him my email for book recommendations. Do you have a problem with that?"

The driver's eyes appeared in the rearview mirror, stealing a glance at us. I wondered if he spoke English or simply recognized the universal pitch that made men's eardrums bleed.

"I might, if the guy's interested in you. You spent almost as much time in that bookstore as you did with me."

"Do you really think I'd flirt with another guy when I came to London to be with you?" He opened his mouth, searching for some defense, but I cut him off. "You—with your arms around your pregnant ex-girlfriend—are worried about a guy emailing me book recommendations?" I let out an exasperated growl. The driver pulled up at the airport and stopped abruptly, jolting me forward against the seatbelt. A sudden burst of anger propelled me out of the car, my feet hitting the curb with purpose. I paced back and forth, fuming, narrowly missing a collision with a frantic traveler who bolted toward the departures door, his carry-on rolling over my toes.

My head felt like a pressure cooker ready to blow. Ryan was paying the driver, shooting worried glances in my direction. Maybe I was overreacting; nothing about my fury made sense.

And then it hit me like a slap. As much as I'd tried to be understanding for Ryan's sake, part of me was furious about this woman coming between us. Furious that I wasn't younger—that I was a decade past being able to give him what her body was preparing to deliver.

Ryan stepped out of the taxi and came around to face me, placing his hands on my shoulders. "Are we having our first fight?" The corners of his mouth twitched, but I kept my arms crossed and my lips pressed tight, stubbornly clinging to my righteous anger.

"I'm sorry," Ryan said, his voice annoyingly calm. "I guess I'm on edge and probably worried these days, though I didn't want to admit it. You're probably feeling the same."

People rushed past us, wheeling luggage through the revolving door. Out of the corner of my eye, I saw a couple embrace. The teary-eyed woman broke away and disappeared inside, leaving her lover staring after her like he'd lost his whole world. Would this be us soon? Saying our final goodbyes? My anger melted into sadness, tears stinging behind my eyes.

"I am more than a little worried," I admitted, my voice cracking. I bit my lip to stop it from trembling. As much as I didn't want him to see me like this, I couldn't hide my vulnerability anymore.

"Come here." He wrapped me in his arms, and I pressed my head against his chest, fighting against becoming another heartbroken woman losing it at the airport. "It's going to be okay. We've got this."

I mumbled into his soft linen shirt, gripping his broad back. "How?"

His chest rose and fell with a deep breath. "I'm not sure yet, but I know I love you and I don't want to let you go."

I sniffled and buried my nose in his shirt.

"Did you just wipe snot on my clean shirt? You did, didn't you?"

Admittedly, it was a minor but satisfying payback. I peered up at him and suppressed a smile. "Maybe."

Just like that, the tension lifted. I sagged with relief. "I guess we'd better go meet Madison and Roger."

"Wait, your mascara's smudged." He wet his thumb and wiped under my eyes. "There, perfect."

If this man was willing to deal with my meltdown and snot on his shirt, yet still fix my makeup, I had little doubt that somehow, he'd stick with me despite the obstacles that were about to multiply like rabbits on espresso.

It would have been impossible to miss Madison emerging through the sliding doors from baggage claim. Among the rush of locals with toddlers and college kids weighted down with backpacks, she stood out like a beacon. Skin-tight jeans hugged her curves, topped with her signature animal print blouse. Her black braids, trailing halfway down her back, were perfectly intact despite the transcontinental flight. I waved from behind the metal barrier. "Madison!" I squealed.

"Sofia!" Her hips swayed as she pranced toward me in high heels. We collided, holding each other like we'd been apart for years rather than months. Over her shoulder, I saw Roger approach, pushing a loaded luggage cart, his tall frame towering over the crowd.

"Roger, glad you made it. How was the flight?" Ryan extended his arm, gripping his in a firm handshake.

"Longer than I'd expected. I don't know how you travel to Europe so often. Still can't believe I'm halfway across the world, but I'm stoked to be here." He cocked his head, his bloodshot eyes brightening as he looked at Madison. "Looks like the girls are pretty happy too."

"You have no idea," Madison exclaimed. "Thanks, babe. I'm so glad you suggested this trip."

Roger shot Ryan a wink. "Was it my idea? As I recall, you planted it, but I'll take the credit."

Madison linked her arm through mine, and we followed the guys into the elevator, then waited in line for a taxi. While

Ryan helped Roger with the luggage, Madison whispered, "Are you okay? Your eyes are a little red."

"We had a tense moment, but considering everything, that's normal, right?"

"Honestly, I don't know how you're holding up so well. With a baby due and your contract ending, 'tense' is an understatement."

As we piled into the taxi—me sandwiched between Madison and Roger—I linked my arm through hers, her presence grounding me like an anchor.

I wasn't sure who looked more awestruck as the city's architecture flew by. The port came into view, sunlight dancing across inky blue water, the tarnished bronze statue of Christopher Columbus looming at the bottom of Las Ramblas. Not long ago, my eyes had drunk in every detail at first sight of this city. My head whipped between them like a bobblehead as I gave running commentary while they pointed at unfamiliar architecture, lacy iron balconies, and terrace restaurants stacked one after another, diners enjoying lunch alfresco with views of the sea.

"This is stunning! I had no idea," Madison exclaimed, while Roger appeared speechless. Madison elbowed him in the ribs.

"Man, you guys are lucky. I can see why you love it here."

Ryan rotated in his seat. "Roger, want to catch a Barca game this week?"

"Are they playing at Camp Nou?"

"You're in luck. There's a game tomorrow. I doubt the girls would mind having time for themselves."

Madison planted a kiss on Roger's cheek. "You guys go have fun," she said. "I'm sure we can find something to do."

Roger leaned forward, a hand on Ryan's shoulder. "You know they're dying to talk about us."

Ryan caught my eye. "Why do you think I suggested it?"

For the millionth time, I marveled at how quickly this man had learned to read me.

"Didn't I mention you should bring practical shoes?" I browsed the racks at a tiny shoe store tucked in an alley and handed Madison a pair of espadrilles. A shopping trip was necessary after watching Madison hobble over uneven stone pavement in heels. "Here, your first pair of Spanish-made shoes. I'm sure it won't be the last you tuck in your suitcase."

She slipped into the wedge sandals, parading in front of the mirror while the shop owner lavished her with compliments, spoken in Spanish. "*Son cómodos, sí? Guapísima!*"

"What did she say?" Madison looked at me blankly.

"She thinks you look beautiful in those shoes and asked if they're comfortable."

"Wow, you're really picking up the language. And yes, these are a relief. I'll take them."

After Madison dropped her heels into the shopping bag and we set out for a tour of El Born, she asked, "How are the language classes going?"

"*Poco a poco*, as they say. Little by little, I'm improving, but at my age, my brain isn't as quick as it used to be. Maybe the RAM is maxed out."

"I doubt that. Everything else seems to be working fine at your age."

"You're referring to sex?" An elderly woman shuffled past, her steps careful on the uneven ground. She shot me a disapproving glance, and I pretended to ignore her as we strolled in the opposite direction, waiting until she was out of earshot. "There's no problem there. With Ryan, I'm having the best sex of my life."

"Are you over your freak out about the age difference?"

Pausing in the alley, I let my gaze drift to the ancient stone walls flanking us, to balconies draped with linens and underwear hung out to dry. Ahead, the stained-glass windows of Santa Maria del Mar Cathedral gleamed, the sun illuminating figures of Mary and baby Jesus. On my first trip, I'd visited often, resting on wooden benches, examining religious scenes carved into alcoves. The benevolent guardian angel statues seemed comforting.

Though I'd never been particularly religious, this cathedral inspired spirituality. Maybe it was the intimate size, the dim lighting, or some quiet, invisible force within its angled walls, but during meditation, I'd sensed a power greater than myself. I'd silently prayed for acceptance, courage, and direction, sending requests into the universe. This was where I'd opened myself to love and battled doubts. While the battle sometimes raged on, the skirmishes were more manageable now. I'd learned not to let them force my heart back into a steel cage.

Finally, I faced Madison, answering with conviction I was only now grasping. "Right now, nothing matters except the love I feel for this man. Age doesn't feel like the elephant in the room anymore, but the baby is a painful reminder that we're at different life stages. Will I freak out tomorrow or next week? Probably. But whatever happens, I know he loves me."

"I'm so damn proud of you. And happy for you. Sad too, but I'm keeping positive thoughts that happiness wins." Her hands gripped my shoulders, looking me straight in the eye. "And if you freak out, I'm here. You know that, right?"

"I know. Your name is listed as my emergency contact. It's labeled: 'In case of freak-out emergency, call this numb er.'"

At that, she laughed, the sound bouncing off stone walls.

"Let's duck into the cathedral. The air is stifling in these tiny alleyways."

Her nose crinkled. "It smells like pee here. Is it from dogs? From what I've seen, dogs might outnumber people two to one here."

As if to demonstrate, a dog the size of a large rat lifted its leg while its owner waited patiently, the yellow stream pooling in the cracks of the stone walkway.

"Yes... presumably. But late-night partiers also relieve themselves on the walls."

"Eww."

Most of the time, I didn't mind the smells because they were offset by the scent of prawns sautéed in garlic wafting from restaurant kitchens or—my kryptonite—the fragrance of freshly baked bread from the three patisseries on each block. Like everything in life, there were trade-offs.

> **Hope you're enjoying time with Madison. Where are you now?**

Ryan's text sent warmth through me, lifting my cheeks in a smile. I couldn't help it. He always had that effect.

> **I really am! Thanks, hon. We're sitting on a rooftop terrace, having tapas and sangria.**

> **Sounds perfect. Roger and I have arrived at Camp Nou. Meet up later?**

> **Sure, but Madison and I will be well lubricated by then.**

> **Hah! Just the way I like you.**

> **Bad man, that's not what I meant. Xo**

Madison was tapping on her phone. I knew the answer but asked anyway. "Roger?"

She smiled. "Yes, he checked in too. Says he misses me."

"You guys are pretty cute together." I propped my feet on an empty chair, my sundress hiked around my thighs as I sunned my legs. "How's the sex? Come on, details please."

Her grin answered before she spoke. "I gotta say, dating a younger man is perfect. Though he's not as young as Ryan, he's got the stamina and drive to keep up with me. He's not lacking in skills and has this technique—"

"Can I get you anything else?" the young blonde server interrupted, bending over our table as she gathered empty plates, long hair tossing in the wind. Her timing was annoying. I wanted to hear Madison finish that sentence.

"We'll have another half liter of sangria, please." As she turned to leave, I couldn't resist my mischievous impulse—Madison's influence, probably. "Wait. If you don't mind, we're discussing men and sex. What would you say is your favorite quality in a man during sex?"

Her face flushed red, the tray tilting precariously with someone else's drink order. "I'm not sure," she stammered. "I've never thought about it like that." She studied the sky for a moment, then, as if the heavens delivered an answer, she giggled. "I guess it helps if he's hot."

I nodded and smiled. She pivoted and fled like I'd set her on fire. "And there you have it. Experience trumps youth. You'd easily answer that question, right?"

"Hell yes. My list—my long list—is stored on Google Drive."

"Really? I thought I was the only one. I could name the most important things I need in a man—both in the bedroom and as a partner. But in my twenties? I didn't have a clue."

"I still can't believe you asked that poor girl about her sex life." She cackled, a laugh that made the couple at the next table glance over at us. "At least there's some satisfaction in getting older."

"We have no choice but to find the bright side, because let's face it, hot flashes and sore joints are no joke."

"I'll drink to that," Madison said, tipping her glass until orange slices fell on her nose.

"I'm so glad you're here, Madison. I've really missed having my friend to confide in."

Her eyes filled with concern. "Have you considered what you'll do after the baby is born? What about the contract?"

I let the question settle, its weight dampening my mood. I peered over rooftops—the domes and spires punctuating a magnificent city view. "Ryan wants me to come to London, but I don't think it's wise. He'll need time to work out how to be a father, and I need time to figure out who I am now, apart from him—at least for a while. Then we'll see." Madison nodded in agreement. "But one thing's certain... I don't want to trade this view for a lonely suburban house. I've tasted the life I've dreamed of, and I'm not giving that up."

"Then don't. Stay here. I'm happy to visit." She shot me a wink. "This sangria is worth the trip."

I snorted. "Seriously, it can't be that easy to move to Spain long-term. I have no idea what's involved in becoming a resident. What about my house? And there's my family to consider." I shook my head, my voice rising as I protested. "How can I just up and move to Barcelona by myself when I don't know anyone in this city?"

Madison waited, arms crossed, while I finished my rant. Leaning in like a mother about to lecture her teenager, she gave me the same determined look that had convinced me to take this Barcelona trip. "You'll figure it out, so stop doubting yourself. You're a warrior princess! You can do whatever you set your mind to." Her words sounded like a mantra—one I'd probably need to repeat daily if I were to convince myself.

"Can I record you? My positive affirmation app isn't cutting it."

She leaned back, refusing to let me derail her confidence-building mission. "Sofia, you've climbed mountains before and always made it to the other side. If this is what you truly want, go for it."

My groan only spurred her on.

"Get on expat sites, do research. Lots of people retire in foreign countries. It can't be that hard."

I sighed. "Vale. Vale."

"What?"

"Never mind. I'll consider it."

"I think you scared off the server. She forgot our drinks." Madison looked longingly at her empty glass.

"Let's get out of here and take a walk. There's a little bar with a view of the Barcelona Cathedral."

Maybe it was Madison's faith in me, or maybe it was how this city had drawn me in from the first moment, but as we meandered through the streets of El Born, I gazed at apartment buildings with new interest, noticing Spanish signs: "*En Alquiler.*" I checked my phone's translator to confirm what I suspected—these apartments were for rent.

"Madison, look." I stopped in front of a gated entrance and pointed to a fourth-floor balcony. Her gaze followed my finger. "That one's for rent."

While the building across the street blocked the sun from reaching the lower floors, this balcony was flooded with light. Aged green shutters were open, revealing shiny, new, double-paned glass doors.

On the iron-railed balcony to the right, a white-haired woman stooped to water plants with a large pitcher, the tangle of vines and flowers so thick it looked like a Jumanji scene. I worried slightly about her safety.

I surveyed the narrow pedestrian street, checking left and right, noting countless shops and restaurants—several pharmacies, a mini-market, pizza takeout, a falafel place, even gelato. What more could anyone need?

The street hummed with activity. Tourists snaked through the alley's bends in an endless stream of curious faces. Skateboarders whizzed by at lightning speed, wheels clacking on stone pavement. Locals trudged home, lugging groceries in heavy carts. Young, old, and everyone in between, going about their everyday routine on this street.

I tried imagining life without a car: spending days hanging damp laundry on thin lines over the balcony, making three grocery stops instead of one supermarket run. What it would be like trading modern conveniences, a backyard, and my own house for a rented city center flat.

"What are you doing?" Madison asked.

I pressed my nose to the glass entrance door, shading my eyes to see inside. "Checking for an elevator. Ha! Yes, there it is."

Just then, a man in jeans and a sports jacket appeared on the other side. I reeled backward, feeling like a spy caught in the act.

Once outside, he spoke in Spanish. My guilty conscience interpreted his words to mean something like: "*What the hell are you doing here?*"

Utterly mortified, I held up my palms. "Sorry, I speak English."

His brows arched with surprise, as if he'd assumed I was Spanish. At least I looked the part, even if I couldn't manage the language.

After a moment, he spoke again. "Can I help you?"

"Oh, well, um..." I stumbled over words. What could I say? It seemed ludicrous, but I plowed ahead. "There's a sign in the window up there. An apartment for rent?" I pointed upward, an unnecessary gesture, I realized, then closed my hand. "I'm considering renting an apartment in Barcelona."

He shook his head. "This isn't a vacation rental; it's for long-term lease."

Before I could reconsider, I answered in a small voice, "Yes, that's what I'm looking for."

He smiled then, and I was relieved he didn't dismiss me with a wave, saying, "*silly woman, what could you be thinking?*" Because I was telling myself those words. Instead, he pulled out his phone. "I live in the flat above, on the fifth floor. I know the owner. If you give me your number or email, I'll pass it on and tell him you're interested."

I turned to Madison and gave her the look that said, "*What the hell do I do now?*" The I-told-you-so grin plastered on her face provided the answer. She held her palms upward, toward the sky. "The universe gives us what we need."

Her expression so knowing, so serene, I almost chanted *namaste*.

I didn't tell Ryan about the apartment that evening. We were having too much fun dancing at a bar in Paseo del Born, despite the cramped quarters. The entire bar had the square footage of Ryan's bathroom in San Francisco. Madison and I danced to salsa and Reggaeton music in the space between tables, people pressed so close you could smell beer on their breath. Ryan and Roger rocked in place—humoring us with two-step moves while we literally spun circles around them. Beer glasses hovered above gyrating bodies while "Despacito" blared on the speakers.

Nor did I mention it over the next few days as we toured Barcelona, stopping at Sagrada Familia and Parc Güell, two of Gaudí's famous masterpieces. We walked until my feet hurt, even in practical shoes, covering territory from Las Ramblas to Port Olímpic. Madison didn't complain once about her feet since she'd traded espadrilles for comfortable sneakers. Roger now towered over her in flats. He teased her once, calling her "shorty." The look she shot him served as a warning: *You're sleeping on the couch tonight, buddy.*

I loved how Madison appreciated everything about Barcelona, trying new and unusual foods. "Am I really eating octopus?" she asked, slicing another piece of the grilled delicacy. Mealtimes became the main event each day, paella and sangria quickly becoming her favorites. Roger was less adventurous, sticking to burgers and fries.

I checked my email daily—sometimes several times—anxiously waiting for news about the apartment. I didn't tell Ryan because it seemed so absurd to even consider a move to Barcelona alone. As long as it remained a fantasy, I could protect it and keep the dream alive. I nurtured the fantasy from a seed, and through the week, it grew into a full-grown tree. But by Thursday, when I saw the owner's email inviting me to visit the apartment, I knew it was time to tell Ryan.

However, I didn't anticipate he would be the one delivering a surprise.

Chapter Twenty-Two
Sofia

"**H**old on. What do you mean you're having contractions? Isn't it way too early for that?"

I'd just walked through the door of the apartment, having spent the afternoon shopping with Madison. My arms were loaded with bags of new outfits I probably didn't need, but with Madison, shopping was more like a fishing expedition. If you didn't come home bearing at least several trophies, she considered it a total waste of valuable time.

At the sound of Ryan's voice—tense, urgent—penetrating the wall of our bedroom, I stopped dead at the word "contractions." From the living room, I heard the conversation on the speaker as I stood rooted in place. My heart dropped as *her* voice rang out, matching Ryan's urgency.

"At first, the doctor thought they were a sort of false labor—Braxton Hicks, I think she called it. But then, after a physical exam, she said I'm at risk of going into labor. Oh God, it's too soon. Ryan, I'm scared." Her panic was palpable, the words spilling out too quickly, a muffled sob rising from her throat.

"It's going to be okay," he said calmly, forced reassurance threading through his voice. I pictured him raking his hands through his hair, his brows knitting together. "Tell me, what are they doing to slow it down?"

She sniffled, then cleared her throat. "They gave me some sort of medication and told me to stay in bed. I can't do anything but lie there, waiting to see if this medicine will make a difference."

For a few seconds, Ryan didn't respond. The only sound I heard was my pulse pumping in my ears, drowning out all the positive mantras, filling me with dread.

Rebecca broke the silence. "I just thought you should know." There was an expectant lilt in her tone, as if she was waiting for an answer to a thinly veiled plea.

"Of course. I'm glad you called." His voice sounded calm and reassuring, but I wasn't convinced he meant what he said. "When do they think it will be safe to deliver the baby?"

"The doctor says it would be better to wait another week, possibly two."

"Is your sister there with you?"

Even from a distance, I heard a heavy sigh. Her voice emerged weak, vulnerable. "No. She's been sent to New York on business—to the head office. There's some sort of marketing meeting. I called her, and she said she'll try to get back early next week."

It didn't take a rocket scientist to guess where this conversation was headed. She was playing the role of a helpless maiden, baiting Ryan to mount his horse and save her. Damn those fairy tales.

"Well then, I'd better get on a plane."

This time, I was sure I heard the pop of our bubble bursting. My arms went limp, shopping bags crashing to the floor. Everything in me sagged. I wrapped an arm around my waist, feeling as if I'd just been punched in the stomach. His words blurred, drowned out by the whooshing sound in my ears.

I barely made out Ryan saying, "I've got to go, but I'll call you later. Just rest."

Moments later, he appeared through the doorway, his gaze resting on my curled shoulders, my hand on my stomach—everywhere except my eyes.

"You heard?"

I nodded.

"I have to go. Rebecca needs my help." He paused, keeping his distance from across the room—the divide between us suddenly a chasm the size of the Grand Canyon. "I told her I'd be there for the birth, but it seems it might happen sooner rather than later."

I nodded again, unable to unscramble my thoughts, unsure of what to say. Rationally, I knew what a supportive girlfriend should say: I *totally understand, of course you should go to her. Best of luck, I hope everything goes well with the birth of your baby. You're going to be an amazing dad. Don't worry about me, I'll be fine.*

But I wasn't fine or rational. In fact, I wasn't sure if my lunch was about to become projectile vomit all over the sofa if I didn't make it to the bathroom. I ran for it and slammed the door behind me, sucking deep, calming breaths into my constricted chest. In for five, I counted. Out for five.

"Sofia, please." He knocked on the door. Relentlessly. "Let me in and we can talk." Silence. His voice penetrated through the door, sounding desperate now. "I don't know what to do. I don't know what we should do. This is an impossible situation. Whatever direction I take, someone is going to be hurt." And then he added in a voice much smaller than his large stature would suggest, "Including me."

The trembling in my limbs slowly subsided, and once I was certain my lunch wouldn't erupt from my stomach, I opened the door. His eyes met mine and my heart splintered at the weariness on his face, as if holding the weight of our sorrows and fears and hopes had beaten him down. I could read his thoughts—his fears about becoming a father, losing me, losing the baby if something went wrong.

A voice in my head screamed, *it isn't fair.* But then, who said life was fair? Shit happened, in my experience, but we had to choose how we dealt with the mess.

I swallowed hard. "The most important thing right now is the life of this baby. And you'd better get used to baby-comes-first, because that's the way it's going to be for the next eighteen years or so."

I dug deep, remembering what it was like to have a new, vulnerable baby. How my priorities rearranged on a molecular level with the force of a biological imperative. He didn't know it yet, but he would love this baby more than anything in the world—protect it at any cost.

He stared at me, wide-eyed, as if he expected me to bolt. I gave him the reassurance he needed, even if the words rang hollow in my ears. "Look, you've got this. And you've got me, whatever happens." I watched with satisfaction as his shoulders sagged with relief.

"I expected to have more time with you, before..." He reached out a hand and tucked a strand of hair behind my ear, the end of that thought dangling unfinished—a mirror of our relationship. "You go back with Madison, and I'll join you when I can. We'll figure things out then. You know, renegotiate the contract and all." The corners of his mouth quivered into a smile.

"Ah yes, the contract. I think you'll owe me a week or two for reneging." My voice rang out playfully, trying to ease his worries. But it was impossible to pretend I wasn't crushed. He always saw everything in my eyes.

He took me in his arms, our bodies pressed together, our chests rising and falling in simultaneous heavy breaths. The minutes ticked by as we stayed locked in a silent embrace; neither of us wanted to let go.

I didn't accompany him to the airport. The scene of lovers parting was too fresh in my mind, too painful to live out that prophecy I'd predicted. I preferred to watch him as he got dressed the next morning, soaking in the way his broad shoulders shrugged into a shirt, the cut of his waist as he pulled on a belt. Memorizing the scent in the air that was him—a mix of body wash and spice. It was easier to pretend he was going off on a business trip as he closed his suitcase. After all, we'd soon see each other again. Right?

I had to keep pretending as he kissed me goodbye, my mind blocking out thoughts of how his life would be inexorably changed. I didn't think about how I wanted to tear his clothes off and pull him back into bed—begging him to stay. I didn't cry until the door closed behind him.

"Hola, you must be Sofia. Come in." From the doorway of the apartment, he ushered us inside. Based on the emails we'd exchanged, I'd learned that the owner wasn't Spanish but German. He spent most of his time in Barcelona, managing the flats he owned.

I didn't know why I'd pictured Neil as an older man, so when he opened the door and I came face to face with a handsome man in his early forties, my eyes must have betrayed my surprise.

"Hi, I'm Madison, Sofia's friend," she announced, stepping inside.

"Ah, you're the support person she mentioned. Will you be living here too?" he asked.

"I wish, but no. My life is in San Francisco. This is all about Sofia."

"Feel free to look around. As you can see, this apartment has been recently renovated."

I nodded, already scanning the living room, my eyes drawn to the light flooding through the open balcony doors and a faint but delectable smell of freshly baked pizza wafting in on the breeze.

"So, you're from California? My last tenants were from New York. A lot of American expats have found their way to Barcelona. Will you be working here?"

I peered around him, inspecting every inch of the open floor plan—the living room on one side, the L-shaped kitchen on the other. The entire space was a quarter of the size of my living room, but this wasn't about comparison; it was about change. The building was probably constructed in the 1800s—the antiquity, the ambiance—that was the change I craved. Yet everything looked surprisingly new inside, apart from the original wood shutters that framed the balcony doors.

"No," I answered absently. "I'm considering working re-motely," I lied, still unsure of a plan or how I'd make this work, but I couldn't divulge that to Neil.

"Oh, that's perfect then. You shouldn't have any problem getting a visa to live here."

I pulled my attention back to the man blocking my view. "Mr. Meyer, is it? I haven't investigated the process. Is it lengthy?"

"It's Neil, please. I'm not certain about California, but my last tenants applied through the Spanish consulate in Manhattan. They had their visas within a month. You'll have to prove you have the income to live here and go through a background check, but the rest are minor details. Once you arrive, the Spanish government puts you through a few more steps to be granted official residency, but you can find help with the process if you don't speak the language."

Madison nudged me on the shoulder. "See, it's not that hard. Can't you just picture yourself here?" She walked ahead into the living room, her sneakers leaving dust prints on the gleaming hardwood floor. I really could see myself there. I imagined sitting out on the tiny balcony overlooking the street. There was just enough room for a small table and two chairs. I pictured Ryan and me sitting on the balcony together, making dinner as we jostled for space in the small kitchen. More than anything, I wanted to keep this vision of our future alive, but it couldn't come at the expense of sacrificing my own direction.

As I stood on the small slab of brick and leaned against the iron railing, I felt as if I'd stepped into my dream—the one Ryan had inspired—the one I wanted us to share together. Having looked at these balconies from below so many times while he'd shown me the city, now I had a view of bustling activity on the street beneath me. An old man sat at a table outside a small café, sipping coffee. Shop owners lingered outside their windows while puffing on cigarettes, chatting with each other as though in a tight-knit community. Customers perched on a bench with slices of sizzling pizza. The sound of life—voices in conversation, Latin music drifting through the air—lifted me into an alternate universe, far from my solitary existence back home.

"The apartment is furnished. Basic IKEA, but it's all new." Neil gestured to the IKEA couch (its label still attached) and the basic dining set. The refrigerator, apparently recently delivered, still had the energy label plastered on the front.

"Down the hall, you'll find the bathroom." I peeked in and saw beige-tiled walls, a large walk-in shower positioned at the back. We passed a small, windowless bedroom, which held a double bed, leaving room for little else, and entered the master bedroom. "As you can see, the beds are brand new." A foam mattress, still wrapped in plastic, rested in a white bed frame. Two small nightstands flanked the bed. It would take a lot of work to make this feel like a home. Home. It had become less about a place since Ryan. Being with him was my home—where I felt safe and warm and loved.

Almost absently, I followed Neil as he ushered us over to the glass door in the bedroom, presenting us with a utility balcony. "This is the only terrace in the building. You have your washer here." He gestured with his arm outstretched like a game show host unveiling the grand prize. It was nothing like the terrace where I was staying with Ryan. I stared at the brick slab, all four feet of it, and the view of weathered stone interior walls, barely a shaft of light tunneling through. But I could see its value—a small outdoor area that afforded some privacy and quiet, not to mention a place to hang laundry that wasn't strung on three tiny clotheslines directly over the street.

"Well, what do you think?" Neil asked when we returned to the front doorway, handing me a flyer with a picture and information written in Spanish. I almost laughed. I'd be trading my American-sized house with all its conveniences, all my things, to start over in a small apartment. But the thought of living here—in the heart of Barcelona—set fire to a dream.

When I took a quick glance at the paper and noticed the rental price, I realized it might be possible to pull this off. In San Francisco, you couldn't find a garage to rent for this amount. For twelve hundred euros, I could have a fully furnished, renovated apartment in the center of the coveted historic district.

"I love it. I'll be returning home this weekend and will check with the consulate first thing Monday. Can I get back to you then?"

"There are a few other showings scheduled, but to be honest, I'd rather rent to an American. In my experience, they take good care of the property." He shook my hand firmly and said, "I'll wait to hear from you."

When I looked over Neil's shoulder, I saw Madison flitting from room to room, clicking photos with her cell phone. She tucked the phone into her purse and joined me in the doorway. "I'll send these to you just in case you need a second look."

I thanked her, knowing all the while I'd already imprinted every image in my memory. We stood shoulder to shoulder in the shoebox-sized elevator, its gears grinding as we descended the four flights. I stared into the mirror the entire way, partly to combat my anxiety while I waited for the steel doors to open. Elevators always made me nervous, let alone one of questionable vintage.

Examining my reflection, I dressed differently now, having adopted the casual-chic style of Barcelona. My blue high-top sneakers matched the long, flowing skirt, complemented by a crop top. The ensemble was a far cry from the American jeans and loose T-shirt that had become my attire outside of work hours. I felt pretty in these clothes. Moreover, I felt like a different person—transformed like a shape-shifting toy.

Granted, the transformation had taken almost two months instead of seconds, but I didn't want to shift back to the way I was before. Nothing about my life was simple or predictable anymore. But seeing the way my eyes reflected a spark that wasn't there a few months ago, I decided that complicated, messy, and exhilarating suited me.

Madison's gaze slid toward me in the mirror. "Well? What did you think of the apartment?"

A slow smile swept across my face. "I think I've just met my new life."

"I support you one hundred percent, but are you hoping and planning that Ryan will join you here? Because given the situation..." She hesitated, but I knew the end of that sentence.

"I can only make plans for me, but I still hold on to hope that our plans will somehow sync. I don't know how, or what course his life will take, and I don't have control over those factors." Our eyes met, and knowing her so well, I predicted exactly what she'd say next.

"Damn, girl, you're relinquishing control? You've risen to a whole new level of carpe diem."

She linked her arm through mine almost possessively as we traveled down the cobblestone street. After all, I had to give her credit. If it hadn't been for her nagging me to take that trip to Barcelona in the first place, I'd never have realized the possibilities now materializing before my eyes.

Chapter Twenty-Three

Ryan

It was back to shepherd's pie—Wednesday's daily special. I stared at the white melamine plate where mushy peas sat in a fluorescent green mound, untouched and unappetizing. My fork hovered mid-air above the pastry crust, but I couldn't bring myself to take another bite. The clatter of dishes ricocheted off sterile walls, each sound like fingernails on a chalkboard against my frayed nerves. After seven days of hospital cafeteria food, I'd exhausted my options and was now on round two of the weekly rotation. The thought of enduring another week trapped in this antiseptic maze made my stomach turn.

But I reminded myself that the previous week—waiting on Rebecca hand and foot while she was confined to bed rest—hadn't exactly been a picnic either.

I couldn't deny feeling somewhat relieved when the doctor admitted her after the contractions started again. At least here, the professionals could monitor her properly. A massive weight had lifted from my shoulders, yet guilt gnawed at me for wanting to leave her in the care of doctors and get back to my life. But I couldn't abandon her to face this alone in a sterile hospital room. Leaning back against the unforgiving plastic chair, I battled another surge of resentment rising like bile in my throat. God, I really hated hospitals.

"*Rebecca needs you to stay strong, Ryan. We'll keep her in for observation, and hopefully the medication will postpone delivery for another week. At thirty-six weeks, the lungs should be fully developed.*" The doctor's words had initially sent me spiraling into panic. Now, with the immediate danger gone, it had become a waiting game. The baby—he or she—was calling the shots, determining when to make an entrance.

He or she? During the last ultrasound, the doctor had asked again, "Are you quite certain you don't want to know the baby's sex?" She studied the grainy monitor screen while I peered over her shoulder. Rebecca shook her head firmly. "I want to be surprised." I stepped back. How could I argue with a woman who'd been sentenced to bed rest, her head perpetually tilted downward as if gravity itself were the enemy?

How could I resent spending every waking hour in this medical prison when she was the one suffering? This should have been my week with Sofia before baby duty consumed my life. Nothing about impending fatherhood felt real yet—at least not for me. For Rebecca, it was already pretty damn real.

"What do you think of Jennifer if it's a girl?"

Had I ever mentioned my sister to her? I vaguely recalled telling her that Jennifer had died as a teenager, but I may have lied, saying she had a serious illness. It wasn't an actual lie. Drug addiction was an illness, but it came with a negative connotation, unlike cancer, which only elicited sympathy.

I sank into the upholstered chair beside her bed, the steady rhythm of monitoring equipment creating a monotonous soundtrack. Rebecca watched for my reaction, but words eluded me. Would this baby become a painful reminder of loss, or could it be a way to honor Jennifer's memory, giving this child the life my sister never had?

Finally, I managed, "That's thoughtful of you. Let me think about it." Then, almost as an afterthought, I added, "What if it's a boy?"

"Then you get to choose. Unless it's something dreadful like... Irving or Otis."

"Really? Because Irving was at the top of my list."

She smiled—more grimace than grin, but it was the first time I'd seen her face lighten all week. I was beginning to understand the toll this ordeal had taken on her. Even when we were dating, Rebecca had been more stoic than expressive, never one to wear her heart on her sleeve. Still, I could see how this experience had changed her.

"Bloody hell!" she squealed, her face contorting as her hands clutched her basketball-sized belly.

I shot out of the chair. "What's wrong? Is it a contraction?"

She nodded, teeth clamped down on her bottom lip.

"I'll call for the nurse. Don't panic," I said, though the directive was more for myself than her.

I hammered the call button repeatedly, and when seconds passed without response, I bolted into the hallway toward the nurses' station. My sneakers squeaked against the polished tiles as I ran, nearly sliding into the plexiglass partition. "Rebecca—room 104," I gasped, catching my breath. "I think she's going into labor."

The seasoned nurse glanced up from her computer screen with practiced calm. "A nurse is on her way to check on Rebecca." She gave me the look of someone well-versed in handling panicked expectant fathers. "Don't fret yourself, love. We'll take proper care of her."

By the time I sprinted back to the room, a middle-aged nurse in blue and white scrubs was checking the monitors. I forced myself to appear calm and positioned myself by Rebecca's head while the nurse draped a sheet over her legs, snapped on gloves, and began her examination. "That's it, dear. Open up a bit more for me, please."

The monitors suddenly erupted in rapid beeping, and Rebecca released an ear-splitting scream—deep, guttural, and absolutely heart-wrenching. Her fingers clawed at the bed rails while every muscle in my body went rigid.

"Rebecca, love," the nurse began, her voice steady as stone, "I think this little one has decided today's the day." She assessed Rebecca's pained expression with experienced eyes.

"No." Rebecca shook her head vehemently, finally drawing air deep into her lungs. "It's too early."

"Not to worry—you've made it to thirty-six weeks. Perfectly safe to deliver now." She patted Rebecca's knee reassuringly before turning to leave. "I'll page the doctor straightaway."

Rebecca's eyes found mine, wild with fear, her face as pale as the hospital sheets. I absently wondered if I was the same color. "Don't leave me, all right? I can't do this on my own."

I forced myself to breathe before responding. "You're going to be fine, and so is the baby. I'm not going anywhere." Until this moment, I hadn't felt the weight of the responsibility so acutely, nor had I realized how helpless I would feel. Now that it was happening, I had no idea what to do.

Rebecca writhed through another contraction, and instinctively I grasped her hand. She squeezed my fingers until my knuckles went white. I found myself mimicking half-remembered movie scenes, puffing out rapid breaths. She caught on quickly, synchronizing her breathing with mine until the wave passed.

"Well done. See? That wasn't so difficult."

She shot me a look that could have melted steel. "No, not bloody difficult at all—for you! You're not the one with a spasming uterus trying to eject a human being through what feels like a ruddy keyhole!"

"True, but my hand is killing me."

I was laughing now, which made her laugh too, though tears streamed down her cheeks. I couldn't tell if she was laughing or crying—maybe both simultaneously. Before I could ask, the room was flooded with white uniforms, nurses bustling to check vitals and monitor readings. Blinding light from an overhead lamp bathed everything in harsh brightness as hands positioned her legs apart.

"I'm Dr. Miller, and you must be Ryan. We spoke on the telephone." She glanced up, meeting my dazed eyes briefly before refocusing on Rebecca. It made me uncomfortable imagining her embarrassment. I knew her to be modest, always wrapping herself in towels or robes. Now, her legs remained splayed wide, her vagina the center of attention.

I flashed on how I would feel if that were me on the table and cringed. If men were responsible for having babies, the human species would be doomed to extinction.

"How are we doing, Rebecca?" Dr. Miller popped up from behind the sheet, tugging off her gloves. "If you want an epidural for the pain, now's the time. You're dilating nicely—won't be long now."

"Fuuuck!" Her scream could have shattered glass as another contraction wracked her body. "Give me the bloody injection! Knock me unconscious if you have to!" Her face flushed in angry red blotches.

My stomach clenched in sympathy, and nausea hit me like a rogue wave. I swallowed hard. "Yes, please—do something!" My eyes darted desperately to the nurse.

"First-time father?" The question clearly didn't require an answer because she continued immediately, "She's doing brilliantly, but don't worry—we'll give her something to ease the discomfort." I felt heat creep up my neck. Thousands of babies were born daily; women had been bringing humans into the world since time began, but I couldn't begin to understand how they endured what was obviously excruciating agony.

I stepped back as the nurse moved past me, gently helping Rebecca roll to her side. "Would you wait outside for just a moment, sir?" Relief flooded through me as they drew the curtain around her. I hated needles even more than hospitals. The smell of disinfectant reached me in the hallway, making my knees nearly buckle as I paced back and forth between the stark white walls.

Medical staff brushed past me, but I barely noticed. I caught sight of another man in his thirties, pacing at the far end of the corridor. Our eyes met briefly, exchanging a worried glance. Both of us turned away quickly, as if seeing ourselves in the mirror image might cause a total meltdown.

Part of me still couldn't believe this was happening. In theory, from a distance, I knew I was the father. But it had seemed like merely a donation of sperm. Now, with the impending arrival of an actual baby, I couldn't wrap my mind around the reality of being a father.

When I finally gathered enough courage to return to the room, I found Rebecca fitfully drifting in and out of consciousness. The doctor had left, but the nurse remained, eyes focused on the monitors. "Jane, how much longer do you think?" I asked, reading her nametag.

"These things are difficult to predict. The medication might slow labor a bit, but she's quite close to delivering." She offered me one of those knowing smiles reserved for anxious fathers who realized they had absolutely no control over the situation.

Before settling into the chair beside Rebecca, I picked up a towel from the bedside tray and wiped sweat from her forehead. Without makeup and with her hair matted and disheveled from the ordeal, she still looked pretty. Her eyes remained closed, but a faint smile crossed her lips. I felt a surge of affection for her—after all, she was about to give birth to a baby I'd helped create, even if it had been an accident.

Still, I knew I was capable of feeling so much more than simple affection for a woman. I missed Sofia, though a twinge of guilt hit my gut. Picturing her face, the way her eyes broadcast her emotions even without words... I had to wonder how she felt about me now. I clung to that image in my mind, pushing away how she'd looked at me—the hurt she couldn't hide when I left her.

An urgent alarm on the monitor jolted me from my thoughts. Jane immediately responded, running her hands over Rebecca's belly before examining between her legs. Rebecca bolted upright with a moan.

"What's wrong?" I asked, my chest clenching in a tight knot.

"The baby's heart rate is dropping." Her eyes met Rebecca's, now wide with panic. Despite Jane's practiced steadiness, my mouth went dry. "We need to get this baby out now. You'll need to push soon, dear."

Sounds penetrated the buzzing in my ears—voices calling for the doctor, footsteps racing down the hall. Dr. Miller burst through the doorway and went straight to Rebecca. From my angle, it appeared she was reaching inside her while manipulating her belly with the other hand. Jesus, was this normal? Rebecca let out a blood-curdling scream that made every muscle in my body contract.

"It seems this baby is determined to come out backward. The distress stems from the umbilical cord being tangled. Hold on, Rebecca—I'm going to sort this out. I'll need to turn the baby into the proper position."

The next few minutes were gut-wrenching as I watched in horror. Her belly shifted, and something round and sharp protruded. I flashed back to an alien movie buried in my memory and forced my gaze back to Rebecca's face. She screwed her eyes shut and pressed her head deep into the pillows. I barely breathed while Rebecca gasped and blew out bursts of air through pursed lips.

Two more doctors appeared—I didn't see their faces but gripped Rebecca's hand and held her gaze, anchoring her so she wouldn't notice the frantic activity surrounding us. I told her to hang on, that she was doing great, trying to drown out the voices: *The BP rate is dropping, doctor. Should we take her to the delivery room? No, there's no time to move her—we'll proceed here.*

Metal instruments clattered against trays, and the incessant *beep... beep... beep* of multiple monitors chimed in competing rhythms. I didn't know if Rebecca noticed them, but my heart was racing to keep time as the pace accelerated.

"Right then, we've got you sorted. Time to push, Rebecca," Jane declared with unexpected brightness in her voice.

I felt utterly useless as a bystander, watching in awe as Rebecca doubled over each time the doctor commanded, "Push!" again and again. There wasn't much I could do except place my hand on her back to support her position and encourage her with my voice. She dug her fingernails into my other hand, her screams drowning out my words. I'd planned to videotape this miracle of birth, but it seemed like an incredibly stupid idea now amid all the chaos.

"One more time, Rebecca. You can do this," the doctor called out.

Everyone in the room went still. A second later, a tiny human being lay in the doctor's hands. She held the baby up, and I saw her for the first time.

"Congratulations—it's a girl."

The first rays of dawn streamed through the window, gradually illuminating the darkened room. Finally, all was quiet—except for the occasional sound of sneakers shuffling in the hallway and Rebecca's rhythmic breathing as she slept. I held Jennifer in my arms, pushing off the floor with my toes each time the rocking chair swayed. Instead of harsh lights, medical equipment, and sterile walls, this room felt soothing, designed like a nursery, with soft pastel colors warming the walls, and a bassinet sitting beside the bed.

Though she'd been sleeping peacefully in her bassinet, I'd carefully lifted the tiny, swaddled bundle without waking her. There hadn't been time to hold her after the birth—she'd been examined, weighed (six pounds two ounces), cleaned, and Rebecca had attempted to nurse her. Now it was my turn.

I gazed down at her face, unable to determine who she resembled yet, but she had a full head of dark hair and the smoothest, most perfect skin imaginable. I'd noted earlier that her eyes were blue, though they'd told me the color might change. I wanted to believe she had my eyes. In my estimation, she was the most beautiful baby ever born, even though I had enough sense to guess that all fathers must feel that way.

I lowered my face until it was next to hers and breathed in her sweet scent. It completely undid me. I wanted to capture that new-baby smell forever, to bottle this moment in time.

"Hi, Jennifer," I whispered. "I'm your dad." The words sounded surreal, but holding her filled me with joy I'd never experienced. My eyes unexpectedly welled again as I watched her eyelids flutter and her lips pucker in sleep. I was a father. The reality was finally sinking in. Warmth spread across my chest, my heart swelling with unfamiliar emotion. I already knew I loved her, yet...

My head fell back against the chair as I released a heavy sigh.

"Oh, my goodness, a baby girl! I have a granddaughter! Have you told your father the news? I can imagine he's got strong opinions about your, er, situation." My mother's voice still echoed in my ears. I'd dreaded making that call, but she'd made me promise to let her know the moment the baby arrived. She'd barraged me with questions: *Is the baby healthy?*

How's Rebecca? Oh, the poor thing. What a scare she gave us all! Maybe I can fly to London to meet my granddaughter—do you think I can get a direct flight from Boston?

When I told her the baby's name, her voice cracked with emotion. But soon her tone grew serious, launching into the lecture I'd expected. "Ryan, dear, a child needs her father. I know you're not in love with Rebecca, but the fact remains—you've made a baby with her." I filled my lungs with air, preparing for the battle. "Is Sofia making you choose between her and your new family?"

"God, no, Mother. She would never do that. Sofia supports whatever decision I make. The point is, Mother, I don't want to be with Rebecca. I'm in love with Sofia, and nothing will change that fact. I can't lock myself into a traditional family—not with Rebecca. You, of all people, know what it's like to stay in a loveless marriage far too long."

My mother had sputtered, searching for arguments to change my mind, but finally conceded it was my decision. Even now, I couldn't imagine staying with Rebecca to be close to Jennifer. Of course, I wanted to tuck my baby in bed every night, read her stories, and watch her sleep. But then what? Climb into bed with Rebecca? I'd grow to resent that she wasn't Sofia. Eventually we'd split anyway, and meanwhile, I'd lose Sofia.

The agony of that decision felt like my heart being torn in half.

I bent and planted a gentle kiss on Jennifer's forehead. "It won't be easy, but we'll find a new way to be a family. I promise to always be there for you," I whispered softly.

Still rocking her, I rose from the chair and carefully lowered her into the bassinet. She squirmed, her pink lips parting in a tiny yawn, just as a voice crackled over the hallway loudspeaker: *Paging Dr. Miller.* Thankfully, she didn't wake.

Now I understood why new parents took endless photos and videos of their babies doing absolutely nothing noteworthy. I couldn't take my eyes off her. I pulled out my phone and snapped a photo of Jennifer. The sunlight danced across her sweet face, and oh my God, she looked like an angel. My heart melted, and there was only one person I wanted to share this moment with.

> *Isn't she beautiful! Today I became a dad, and I'm already smitten. I miss you so much and can't wait to see you again. I'll call this weekend. Love you...*

Chapter Twenty-Four
Sofia

There's a particular kind of panic—one that sends you bolting out of bed—when your phone pings with a message alert late at night. It had been a week since I'd returned to San Francisco, and I still blamed my disorientation on jet lag. Suspended between consciousness and deep sleep, I reluctantly surfaced to the insistent sound of *ding... ding... ding*. My feet hit the floor, panic sending adrenaline shooting through my body as I leapt out of bed. Halfway to the front door, my brain finally registered the sound had stopped, and it wasn't the doorbell at all. Stumbling in the dark, I shuffled back to my bedroom and reached for my phone, steeling myself for an emergency. *Who texts in the middle of the night unless someone is in the hospital?*

Ryan's photo flashed on the screen. Chest pounding, it felt like tennis balls crashing against my ribs until I realized it wasn't a middle-of-the-night text for him. In London, it would be early evening.

I clicked on the first text, a photo. Though I was poised for the news, my fingers trembled as I stared at the evidence—the baby was real.Instead of just a bump in Rebecca's tummy, she was now a living, breathing human being—Ryan's daughter. And oh my God, she was beautiful.

Tears leaked from my eyes, landing noiselessly on my pillow as I read his message. *He still loves me. He hasn't forgotten me.* I read and re-read his words, consumed by an avalanche of emotion; my thoughts tumbling over feelings, changing one second to the next. Joy, hope, fear, longing, despair... chased themselves in circles in my sleep-deprived brain.

Despite the love encased in his text, the photo of his baby felt like a punch to the stomach. He had the chance to fulfill a dream I couldn't give him—he could have his family, just not with me. If only a fairy godmother could turn back my aging process just ten measly years, to a time when my ovaries weren't shriveled up. Sure, the end of monthly periods was a relief, but it was pretty damn inconvenient now.

Rebecca had given him the gift my body no longer had the ability to create, and I had no doubt that would make her the special woman in his life. I didn't need a crystal ball to see where this was headed. My brain already knew the answer, even though my heart was still screaming in protest. I couldn't tell him, not when he was so happy. It was easier to pretend when he couldn't hear my voice; see the answer in my eyes. Swiping my palms across my cheeks, I chose my words carefully and sent him a reply.

> **Congratulations! She is beautiful!! Loving you - always.**

At the risk of hurling Madison into a panic, I forwarded the message to her, adding approximately ten exclamation points. Within seconds, her text appeared:

> *OMG! She is seriously precious. But how are you doing?*

My fingers hovered above the keyboard. That was a loaded question.

> *Me? My brain feels like the inside of a bat cave at dusk—chaos—which doesn't make any sense since I knew it was coming.*

> *Babies are always easier to deal with in the abstract. Ryan must be figuring that out too. Will you tell him this weekend?*

> *Not sure. We'll see how the conversation goes.*

> *Well, you'd better give him a heads-up before you board a plane to Barcelona.*

> *I don't even have a flight booked yet. There's time. Anyway, thanks for listening. Now, go to bed. It's a work night. Xo*

> *Oh, and guess what? Today is day sixty of our contract.*

> *And she chose to be born today? What are the odds...*

I stared at his message a while longer, then at the swirling patterns of plaster on the ceiling. Every time I closed my eyes, I pictured his daughter and imagined the expression on his face when he held her. I twisted in the covers, burying my face in the pillow, trying to stop the images—trying to deny the significance that she was born on the day our contract ended. As much as I loved him, it was wrong to be wedged between his love for me and his baby. Something had to give, and I knew it had to be me.

I'd already made a decision. This time, I'd be setting the terms, risking total devastation—for me as well as Ryan.

It came that week in the mail, an inconspicuous envelope that held the letter approving my visa to live in Spain. The man at the consulate had told me it might take a month or more. Only a few months ago, it had taken Madison practically hammering me over the head to convince me to make the trip to Barcelona alone. Now, I'd already wired a deposit to hold the apartment, risking everything—betting they'd approve the visa. I didn't even recognize myself anymore.

I'd completed the documentation in record time, fueled by the prospect of my new apartment—my new life. I'd fast-tracked the background check; even the medical exam to certify that no, I wouldn't bring any communicable disease into the country, and that I wasn't out of my mind—although that was debatable. The income verification was trickier. In the end, they were satisfied with the money I transferred to a Spanish bank account. Thank you, severance package.

My mother had taken the news better than I'd expected. "If this is what you truly want, dear, then go, have the time of your life. I'll be fine. Your brother is just around the corner if I need anything." She patted my knee and leaned back against her overstuffed couch, propping her swollen ankles on the coffee table. I swallowed the golf ball-sized lump of guilt in my throat, knowing that if I didn't make the leap now, I might never have this chance again.

But then she asked if Ryan was going too. I could have remained vague, skipping over the details, but it didn't matter that I was a grown woman; I needed my mom just then.

"Life isn't fair, is it?" She handed me a tissue from the box she kept on the sofa, her eyes softening. "I so hoped you'd find some happiness, especially after the divorce. Does Ryan make you happy?"

I nodded, blowing my nose and feeling pretty pathetic.

"From what you've told me, Ryan cares about you. Don't throw the whole thing in the garbage just yet. You never know, maybe things will work out this time."

That was the last thing I'd expected her to say. My practical mom (yes, the apple didn't fall far from the tree) who had long since given up on the fantasy of romance, had thrown me a lifeline of hope. It was a tenuous rope, but still... She'd planted a speck of a seed, and I had to decide if it was worth watering.

My son was another matter. I texted Ben and Callie, attaching a photo of the visa followed by an assortment of emojis. Hours later, of course, he responded with exclamation marks and his own set of emojis. Callie communicated in actual sentences, saying she was SO excited for me.

To be fair, Ben and I had already spoken on the phone about my plan when I arrived back from Barcelona. He could have at least pretended he'd miss me. "Are you sure you're okay with my leaving the country?" I'd asked, my enthusiasm tempered with a healthy dose of motherly angst.

"Mom, I'll be fine. Callie and I have each other. It's time for you to go live your life. Besides, it will be a great excuse to come back to Europe—this time, to visit you." Callie must have had a talk with him, because this was a far different response than I expected.

I recalled the brief moments we'd spent together in Barcelona when our travel plans accidentally collided; he and Callie on their own romantic adventure through Europe. The next time, I hoped we'd spend time as a family. Just me, Ben, and Callie. My family. Every time I thought of Ryan and his new family, it felt like an electric shock striking in the pit of my stomach—a zing back to the new reality.

Despair didn't have a chance to claim a foothold while I was making preparations, at least during the day. But the nights... that's when the darkness descended, wrapping me in a blanket of doubt, sorrow, and loss. Each time we'd parted ways before, I'd been running away from the pain—the loss of the greatest love of my life. Fear had forced me into a corner, and I'd sprinted away from the danger as if my survival depended on it.

Now, I imprisoned myself, as if knowing that cell was waiting for me, so I grabbed the keys and stepped inside. The pain still waited for me every night, but this time, I wasn't running. I'd face Ryan and make the impossible decision so he wouldn't have to.

Chapter Twenty-Five

Sofia

"She doesn't usually cry this hard. She must be hungry or wet. I haven't figured out which cry means what." Ryan's voice was swallowed by the baby's screams, proving she had a set of healthy lungs. I heard the clatter of his phone as it tumbled to the floor, then Ryan's apology. "Sorry, Sofia. Her foot knocked the phone out of my hand. Hey, Robin, can you take her for a minute?" The sound of her crying became more distant. "There, I'm back."

"How is everything going? Are you getting any sleep?" I tried to sound cheerful, my voice lilting a little too high.

"She's up every few hours, and I'm trying to help so Rebecca can get some rest. So, no, I'm not sleeping much, but I don't mind. I love holding her. Sometimes she falls asleep on my chest, and while I'm listening to her breaths, I drift off."

My throat squeezed at the sound of his gentle tone, and I swallowed against a lump the size of a boulder. He'd already fallen in love with his little girl. I searched for words, something supportive, but they stalled in my constricted throat.

"Rebecca's sister, Robin, arrived a few days ago, so I've scheduled a flight back to San Francisco next week." He lowered his voice, the words barely a whisper. "Babe, I miss you so much. I'll text my arrival info. Will you meet me at my place? I know I'll be too dead to drive anywhere."

"Of course. I'll be waiting for you," I said, my voice husky.

He knew. The silence between us lasted only seconds, but it felt interminable—awkward—unspoken conversations hanging in the airwaves between us.

"Well... I'd better go," he finally said.

"Right. Of course. See you soon." Abruptly, I hit the button to end the call. Something in me lurched, and for a moment, I considered running for the bathroom in case my lunch was about to erupt from my stomach. I fell back on the bed, the pain in my heart reverberating through my entire body as if loss was a disease, spreading from one organ to another. *This is really happening,* I thought. Nothing would ever be the same. Even though I'd resolved to go forward with grace and my dignity intact, the sense of loss was crippling. I had no idea how I'd face him when he returned and admit we were over.

The hills of San Francisco were known for being steep, but as I climbed the sharply inclined sidewalk to Ryan's apartment, I had to wonder if this was the highest point in the city. My feet felt leaden, my whole body weary. I'd slept little last night, consumed with a mixture of elation at the thought of seeing him again and the dread of what today would bring. When I reached the top and stared up at the Victorian building that held his apartment, the sun was setting over the bay, a blazing peach-colored ball of light casting a glow across the blue water. I paused for a moment to marvel at the beauty of this city and wondered briefly if I would miss it. Only time would tell if I was making the right decision.

"It's me." My voice wavered when he answered the intercom. The door popped open, and every cell in my body vibrated at the sight of him filling the doorframe. Our eyes locked, and with each step up the staircase, I tried to read his thoughts. He was dressed in sweatpants and a T-shirt, looking like he hadn't slept in days, his eyes half-open slits. A slow smile swept across his face. The dimples on his cheeks melted me in an instant. And then his arms stretched out, pulling me to him when I reached the last step. The sound of his breath on my ear, the feel of his broad back under my hands, the familiar scent of him—caused a corkscrew of longing to unravel in my core. It didn't take more than a second to remember everything. Tears springing in my eyes, I bit hard on my lip to stem the tidal wave of grief. He was my home, and without him, I was lost. I tried not to think about how his skin felt on mine when we were naked, but all I wanted to do was rip his clothes off and make love with him—reconnect and let everything else disappear, as if going back in time.

"Oh God," I whimpered, my breath so jagged that I thought I might hyperventilate. I was headed toward a panic attack—heart racing, a pulsing beat thumping in my ears. No, no, no. Not here, not now. *Pull it together.*

When he held me at arm's length and scanned me with his eyes, the smile slid off his face. "What's wrong, Sofia?"

It was useless trying to hide my emotions. "We have to talk."

Drawing his brows together, he nodded, laced his fingers through mine, and led me to the living room. The last rays of sunlight poured through the large windows, the view of the cityscape gleamed below—an ironic contrast with the darkness that settled over me. This time, there were no lit candles or soft music, only the weighted silence as we found our places on the couch.

Ryan cleared his throat. "How are Madison and Roger? I didn't get to say goodbye," he said, ignoring the ominous black cloud perched above us.

Were we really doing this? Pretending things were... normal? It took every bit of strength I had left to slip on a mask that resembled a smile.

"They fell in love with Barcelona and are planning a trip back already. I wouldn't be surprised if they moved in together soon."

"They make a great couple. I'm happy for them," he said, but his eyes weren't radiating *happy.*

I continued the charade, asking how the birthing process had been for him and if the baby was doing well.

He answered with details, although I wasn't sure if he was giving me the whole picture. "I don't know how women do it. I have a newfound respect for mothers."

When he talked about the baby, his eyes grew bright despite the fatigue, his face glowing with a smile that looked a lot like pride. "I know that babies mainly eat, poop, and sleep, but when she opens her eyes and looks at me..." He rubbed a hand over his dark hair, pushing it off his face. "It's like she is imprinting my face on her little brain, folding me into her. When they are your own flesh and blood, babies are an irresistible force."

I nodded. "I know." I really did know exactly what he was feeling.

"Jennifer is her name," he said, his voice almost cracking on the word. "Rebecca named her Jenny after my sister."

"That, um... is really touching." I was going to lose it. This was the final nail in the coffin of our relationship.

Just like that, I felt as though the cloud was engulfing me in darkness—the eye of the storm.

"I've been thinking—" we both said simultaneously as if on cue.

"You first," I offered, my breathing all but stopped.

It took a moment for him to start, first shifting in his seat to face me. "Meeting my daughter has changed me, no doubt. We already have a bond, and I can't believe how quickly I've fallen in love with her." A lump the size of a boulder rose in my throat, and I looked away, pulling at a loose thread on my jeans. "Being a good father is important to me; you know that. I won't repeat my father's mistakes. But I also won't repeat the agony of my parents' relationship." He tipped my chin with his finger, pulling my gaze to his. "I love you in a way

I never imagined loving a woman. I'm happy when I'm with you, and I can't conceive of my life without you in it."

My lips parted, but the words lodged in my throat. "How?" was the only thing I was able to utter, but he was already finishing my sentence.

"How can I manage to be a father and be with you at the same time?" He blew out a heavy breath. "I've had this discussion with Jennifer." He smiled then. "She knows I'll always be a presence in her life—her father forever. I just won't be there twenty-four seven."

"Wait." I catapulted off the couch, my feet pacing back and forth against the hardwood flooring. "You're telling me that you're not going to stay with Rebecca? Why not?"

"You didn't seriously think I'd leave you for Rebecca?"

"Hell yes." Sweat was congealing under my arms, caused by the hot flash ripping up my chest to my head. "I came here prepared for a goodbye. Our sixty days are up, and now you have a good reason to move on with your life." My words fired into the air as if fueled by ten cups of espresso. "If there ever was a reason to terminate a contract, I'd say this would be right at the top of the list."

"Sofia, I—"

It didn't matter that a grin was curving his lips, I plowed ahead on my predetermined course—still pacing, my arms flailing in the air for emphasis. "No. I'm giving you your freedom. Why would you turn that down? You can finally have the family you've dreamed of."

Ryan caught me mid-stride, a ray of sunlight angled at my face, his hands on my shoulders. He was smiling. How could he smile at a time like this? "Sofia, haven't you heard a word I've said?"

My head was spinning, his words tangled and lost in my emotional web—the web that held only one solution to this dilemma. "I'm not sure. Which ones?"

His voice was so gentle, I thought I might break. "I love you. I choose you."

My mind captured his words this time, savoring them, lodging them forever in my memory like a squirrel stashes nuts away for the cold winter—just in case.

"What about you? Do you choose me, Sofia?"

Those gorgeous blue eyes probed mine, and I saw the very thing that made me fall for him the night we met. I saw his heart. "I choose you," I admitted. "There's no one else in the world I want to be with."

"Okay, then we'd better start planning."

A laugh barked out of me. It all seemed so surreal. "What happened to being spontaneous? Now you're planning?"

"A baby does change things; I've learned that much. I want to be near Jenny, and she's in London, so your being in another country so far away presents some logistical problems."

"I think we'd better sit down for this. And while you're at it, I could really use a glass of wine. Maybe the whole bottle."

He eyed me suspiciously but shuffled to the wet bar and returned with a fresh bottle of red, then joined me on the couch. I downed several gulps of the cabernet, feeling the liquid courage slide across my palate, still unsure if our paths were compatible or if my plans would derail everything.

"I had to make a decision for myself—for my future—separate from any decision you might end up making for yours." His eyes went wide. "No, it's not a bad thing; in fact, it might be the best decision for us. I'm moving to Barcelona. There's an apartment waiting for me in the Born."

He shook his head, stammering out, "When... how?"

While I recounted the sequence of events—from seeing the apartment all the way to obtaining my visa—the expressions on his face passed through like the seasons, from surprise to wonder, and finally excitement.

"I'm impressed, Sofia. Totally in shock but impressed by how you've pursued this move and how quickly you could pull everything into place."

When he brought his hand to cup my face, stroking his thumb across my cheek, I grabbed onto that lifeline of hope. Could I really have it all?

He leaned back against the couch as the idea registered. "But what about your house?"

"I want to keep my options open, so I'm storing my furniture and renting out my house. I have a property manager lined up, and she's already found some good prospective renters."

"I think I've just fallen in love with you even more. Like I said before, I admire your determination. It's funny, but remember when we talked about moving to Europe on our first date in Barcelona?"

Nodding, I said, "I told you it had been a dream of mine."

"Yes, but you blew off the idea. You couldn't imagine actually taking that leap."

Sensing my opening, I blurted, "That's just it, I've changed. Maybe largely because of you, but now, I need to do this on my own. I need to discover myself as an independent woman—discover who I am, or who I want to become, in the second part of my life." By the time I'd expelled the words in one long breath, my insides were quivering.

"What are you saying? You don't want me in your life?" He reeled back as though I'd slapped him, and I couldn't bear the look on his face. I lunged, gripping his thighs with my hands.

"No! Of course I want you in my life. But hear me out." I took a deep, calming breath. This wasn't a decision I'd come to lightly, but it was one that the warring factions in my brain could live with. "You need time to bond with Jennifer and figure out what it means to be a father. I need time to figure out what I'm going to do with the rest of my life. What if our new contract allows for both of us to experience our respective paths without losing each other?"

His head cocked to the side, my words falling like fairy dust on that gorgeous hair. He brought the glass to his lips, holding a finger in the air while he drank. I got the message.

"Sofia, slow down. You're firing this at me at warp speed, and I need to understand exactly what you mean."

"Look, I was prepared for a whole different conversation, but I like this plan B. Plan B is a solution." I took a breath, followed by more wine. "A sixty-day break is plan B, and I know it wasn't our original plan, but the way my brain works... well, I need a plan. We can still communicate, but seeing each other would be too distracting. We come back together at the end, and depending on how we feel then, we can create a new contract."

"Sixty days without you?" He shook his head vigorously. "No. That's a terrible idea. It's too risky. We could fuck this up, lose what we have."

I set the glass on the coffee table, climbed into his lap, and wrapped my arms around his neck. No mask this time, only honesty. "Do you really think I'd give you up? You're the best thing that's ever happened to me. You are my person—the only man I want to be with."

It took a little time to convince him. He might have come around after I slid my hands against his taut muscles, pulling the T-shirt over his head—then kissed my way down his chest, his stomach... Finally freeing him from the sweatpants, my lips moved down his skin, his muscles contracting involuntarily with each kiss.

"Wait," he muttered breathlessly. "Not here." He took hold of my hand and led me to the bedroom, his bare feet shuffling against the floor, my heels ticking behind. The scent of him consumed me the moment I walked in the doorway. It permeated his bed linens and drifted from the clothes hanging neatly in his closet, filling the room with the essence of him. Memories of us flooded me, my skin prickling with goosebumps. Images and sounds were magnified, seeming to come to life.

I stood waiting as he took a match and lit candles across his dresser, all the while gawking at the magnificence of his naked body glowing bronze in the dim light. I waited while he unbuttoned my blouse and slowly stepped me out of my boots, then my jeans—all with the reverence of someone unwrapping a piece of fine art. Slowly, deliberately, with adoration.

He walked me backward toward the bed, his lips never leaving mine. I sat down, then sprawled across the duvet, my skin exploding at the feel of his touch. The kisses he planted down my breasts, then my stomach, felt like divine torture. My stomach contracted violently, and my body arched, longing for my release yet never wanting this to end.

When he lifted his head, his eyes locking on mine, any remaining doubts vanished. "I love you. Don't ever forget that."

It was then I knew we'd made a new contract. We were going to be fine, even if separated for a time. The love wasn't going to disappear; it was in itself a binding contract.

My hands laced through his curls and guided him so that his body rested on mine. I kissed him hard, our tongues entwining in a perfect dance, silently telling him how much I loved him, how I could never forget him no matter how hard I tried. When we broke apart, he gazed into my eyes with such intensity, it was as if we'd just had an entire conversation.

A gasp rose from deep in my chest at the sensation of him pushing inside me—uniting not only our bodies. I lost sight of where I began or ended, his very being flooding my veins in a river of warmth. The night became a blur of mind-blowing sex, seamlessly blended with gentle caresses and tender words. Sometime during the early morning hours, when the candles burned low, I gratefully wrapped myself around the bulk of him and fell into a peaceful sleep for the first time in weeks.

During the next few days, we cocooned ourselves away from everyone and everything. In light of the impending time apart, we indulged in lovemaking whenever the moment struck us, luxuriating in the freedom. My body ached in unfamiliar places, but every time I looked in the mirror, a rosy glow beamed on my face.

We stayed in for meals; me padding around the kitchen in nothing more than his T-shirt, him ordering delivery when there was nothing left in the refrigerator. We talked, saying everything we'd held inside without worrying what the other would think or if we'd lose each other. And we negotiated the terms.

"Thirty days apart, and I want the option to see you, with daily video calls," he said, while we sat on the couch eating Thai food from the containers. When you were wearing nothing but your boyfriend's shirt and he'd satisfied you every which way to Sunday, it was pretty hard to take a tough stance. "Obviously, we remain monogamous," he added.

"Obviously! I took that for granted. After thirty days, we can renegotiate. No in-person contact, and texts every day," I countered. "And you must send me photos of you and Jenny together."

He side-eyed me, chewing another bite of pad Thai. "You send me naked selfies, and I'll think about it."

"What?" I coughed out a laugh. "You just want me for my body."

"Men are visual. I'm not apologizing."

Between his adorable smile that made his dimples pop and the Thai-flavored kisses, I was putty in his hands. In the end, we agreed on sixty days, renegotiable at the thirty-day mark, daily phone or video calls when possible. I'd consider his selfie request. The contract held our promise. I felt more secure than I ever had with a marriage certificate.

Chapter Twenty-Six

Ryan

"Mate, do you know how much work I'm covering for you while you're skipping around continents? Look at my desk. Go on. Oh, wait, I'll shift the camera."

The view on my laptop screen shifted from James' face to the wall of his office. There were coffee stains on the beige paint. I wasn't even going to ask. Now I saw the top of his desk, though "top" was a generous description, as I couldn't actually see the desk because it was hidden under towering piles of paperwork and stacks of files, their corners jutting out like a miniature cardboard cityscape. Yellow sticky notes peppered the chaos, each one no doubt containing some urgent task with my name on it. I had taken advantage of some paternity leave and a little extra to come back to Sofia, but it was crazy how the work had multiplied in my absence. I was already anxious about juggling my job plus helping with the baby, my stomach knotting tighter with each passing second, and this visual evidence wasn't helping one bit.

"James. James," I yelled, my voice cracking with frustration. His camera was upside down now, the bright fluorescent light blinding me. He could have dropped the damn laptop, because that would be totally on brand. "Get back on screen."

"Now do you get me?" Finally, I could see his face again, and this time I noted the dark circles under his eyes, purple half-moons that made him look ten years older than when I'd left. His shirt was wrinkled as if he'd been sleeping at his desk. Maybe I felt a little guilty, the weight of it piling another few stones on my shoulders.

"I'm sorry, buddy, but you know the situation with Rebecca, and I had to sort things out with Sofia. But I'll be back there soon, so keep your shirt on, or whatever you blokes say over there."

James slumped in his chair, and I could see the relief wash over his face like a wave. "Thank God," he breathed, running a hand through his hair.

"No, thank me, because I'm coming back to the London office full time."

James moved so close to the camera I could see the stubble left where he'd missed shaving, little patches of ginger bristles standing out against his jaw. His bloodshot eyes widened. "You're moving to London?!"

"What did you think I was going to do, leave Rebecca and Jenny on their own? They're my responsibility now. And by the way, how the fuck do you manage work plus marriage and kids?"

"Wait, just hold on. What are you saying? You're back with Rebecca?" James's voice rose an octave, his forehead creasing like an accordion. "You can't do that to Sofia. I really liked that bird, and well, we both know that Rebecca is just a touch—"

"James," I interrupted, "if you'd stop rambling, I'll tell you." I had to take a breath as I tried to figure out how to explain this to him, knowing already it was going to sound crazy, like one of those convoluted plotlines from the soap operas my mother used to watch. "It's complicated, but I'm still with Sofia. She'll be moving to Barcelona, and I'll be living in London for a while so I can help Rebecca and bond with my daughter."

"Okay, that makes sense. London isn't far from Barcelona, so you can pop over anytime you feel like... you know, hanging out with Sofia." His eyebrows wiggled suggestively, a flash of the old James breaking through his exhaustion. I must have grimaced because James caught it, his smile faltering. "What? Hey, I didn't mean to get in your business."

"It's not that. Sofia thinks it would be best if we didn't see each other for a month, maybe two. We're on a... break." As soon as the words came out of my mouth, I knew it sounded ridiculous, like a teenager trying to explain that he really did have a girlfriend, but she just went to another school. Yeah, right.

"Ohhh, mate. Are you ruddy crazy? Bad things happen when couples take a break, if you know what I mean." He shot me a warning stare that made my stomach go queasy, because his words were the same ones whirling in the back of my mind.

This plan had made a lot more sense when Sofia had pitched it, her logical arguments painting a picture of separate but parallel lives temporarily diverged. "We're going to be fine," I said, probably as much to convince myself as him. "Sofia needs this time to start a new life in Barcelona, and she thinks I need the time to figure out how to be a dad. She's not wrong." The truth of it stung, though I hated to admit it.

James was quiet for a while, his eyes drifting away from the screen, focusing on something I couldn't see, the silence stretching between us. Then he chortled out a laugh, starting deep in his belly and exploding all over his face.

"What the hell are you laughing about?" The irritation in my voice didn't cut through his amusement.

"I was just picturing you..." He threw his head back, practically howling with laughter, tears forming at the corners of his eyes. "I'm sorry, mate, but you have no bloomin' idea what you're in for. Explosive poops and projectile vomiting, not to mention the crying that goes on forever. And that's just the baby." His laughter subsided, replaced by a knowing smirk. "Rebecca will be going through her own shit and will blame you for it. And Sofia? She'll be off having fun in Barcelona, sipping sangria on the beach while you're knee-deep in dirty diapers."

"Thanks, man. I really needed to hear all that." I shot him a look, and he instantly threw up his palms in surrender, his chair rolling back a few inches as if physically pushed by my glare.

"I'm sorry. You're right. There are a million great things about having a child. I love my two kids to death and wouldn't change a thing." His voice softened, and his brows drew together in a worried look. "It's just that I've always seen you as a bloke who has it all together—totally in control of everything. Unattached, you know? Flying solo. You're diving into the deep end without much prep time, and without your girl."

"Okay then, thanks for the pep talk. I'm signing off now. Maybe I'll go talk to someone a little less depressing, like a funeral director." My finger hovered above the key to end the call.

"Wait. Ryan, you're my mate. I'll lend a hand whenever you need me, except for the diapers. I never want to change another diaper for the rest of my life." His face scrunched up in remembered disgust. "But I'll keep things running smoothly at work until you get here."

"Thanks, mate. I appreciate that." The sincerity in my voice surprised even me.

After I closed my laptop, the sudden silence in the apartment was deafening, broken only by the ticking of the wall clock. I tried to focus on the million things that needed to be done before my flight, my mind buzzing in too many directions. The apartment seemed like a good place to start, I decided, given that it was a visual task that didn't require too much stress on my fatigued brain.

Wandering from room to room, I confirmed that the moving company had packed up my personal things in boxes, each one neatly labeled in black marker with contents that suddenly seemed trivial, except for the photos. The framed shot of Sofia and me at the beach in Barcelona, her hair wild in the wind, was carefully wrapped in bubble wrap, the sound of it popping under my fingers oddly satisfying. Even before

Sofia and I had talked, I'd decided to keep my apartment and rent it out furnished, so the hassle of moving was minimal, but the emotional weight of it all was anything but light.

James's words kept playing in my head like a broken record as I padded into the kitchen in my socks, the tile floor cool against my feet, determined to find a bottle of wine. It took me five minutes of rummaging around in the half-light of dusk to realize it would be a lot easier if I turned on the light. The switch clicked on, and there it was; a box clearly marked in red letters: WINE.

I uncorked one of my favorite bottles, a Spanish Rioja, its rich aroma immediately filling the kitchen with notes of cherry and oak, used a glass that was in the dish drainer, and leaned against the counter while I tasted it. What I wouldn't give to let the wine relax me and chill out, but a hamster wheel was spinning in my head.

Again, I tried to focus, the to-do list in my head shifting and rearranging like tiles in a sliding puzzle. What else needed to be done? The last thing I wanted to do was think about what I was getting myself into—the warning bells James had just set off, the clanging reverberating through my skull—but the thoughts kept circling my brain like buzzards over a kill.

In the silence, I heard the neighbors upstairs, their footsteps trailing across the wood floor, each step a sharp reminder of life continuing around me. A gay couple had moved in a few months ago and I'd met them in the elevator, but I couldn't recall their names. Then the sound of a baby crying pierced through my ceiling, high-pitched and insistent, like a drill through concrete. Not that I had much experience, but it resembled the newborn cry of Jenny, except it was a lot louder, more desperate somehow. God, this kid had a set of lungs that would put an opera singer to shame.

Before, I probably wouldn't have given it a second thought, but now, it made me curious. Did they adopt or have a surrogate? I wondered how they were adjusting to this big change in their lives, their once orderly existence now dictated by this tiny tyrant. The baby's cry was escalating to Defcon 1, a primal wail that seemed to vibrate the very walls, and it was reaching my ears from another floor. I couldn't imagine how that decibel level wouldn't blow out the eardrums of any living thing in a 750-foot radius, let alone the poor parents trying to soothe it.

The uneasy feeling in the pit of my stomach intensified with every wail, a growing knot of dread that expanded with each passing second until I couldn't ignore the impulse to get the hell out of the apartment. I grabbed my coat and keys by the front door and stepped into my trainers, the laces still tied from the last time I'd kicked them off. Then I sprinted to my car, the night air cool on my face, carrying the scents of the city—exhaust fumes, restaurant kitchens, salty air blowing in from the ocean.

My only goal was to escape; it was fight or flight, and I never would've believed a tiny baby could make me run. I had faced ruthless business competitors and angry board members without flinching, but the idea of managing the needs of a baby had me freaking out.

After driving aimlessly through city traffic, the streets a blur of neon signs and shop windows, drunken groups of tourists staggering from bars, I spotted a shopping center, its vast parking lot half-empty this late in the evening. I needed to do something to fix this—take action and calm the fuck down. My palms were sweating on the steering wheel, and I was sure my heartbeat was beating faster than normal. When I spotted a children's superstore, with its cheerful sign featuring a cartoon giraffe glowing against the darkening sky, a lightbulb ticked on and I knew what I had to do.

At first, I piled things in the cart like an impulse buyer on speed, the metal basket filling rapidly with items in bright primary colors. A car seat, padded with cushions that promised ultimate safety, a state-of-the-art stroller with more features than my first car, a giant stuffed bear with glass eyes that seemed to watch me suspiciously. Would Rebecca need a breast pump? And toys! There were so many aisles of toys, each one promising to make my child smarter, happier, better somehow. Before I came to my senses, I even considered loading a tricycle on top of the heap—because didn't dads buy this kind of stuff for their kids?

In the middle of the diaper aisle—sweaty, heart racing, and overwhelmed with the options, the different brands and sizes making my brain hurt—I realized I was acting like an idiot. Me—the man who was responsible for multi-billion dollar deals, who could read a room of hardened executives and know exactly how to play them—was having a meltdown in a children's store, surrounded by other parents who seemed to know exactly what they were doing. First, there was no way in hell I was getting this stuff on an airplane, and shipping would cost more than the items were worth. There were baby stores in the UK. It wasn't like I was going to raise a child in a third-world country.

When I was growing up, my family had the resources to provide whatever we needed. I hadn't lacked things; our house had always been filled with the latest gadgets and designer clothes, but they were a substitute for love and attention—my parents' way of saying "sorry we missed your soccer game" or "we'll be back from Hong Kong next week." Maybe therapy had done some good, because suddenly the fog receded and everything was clear. I was trying to prove to myself that I could provide for my kid—that I could be a good dad. But was this the way to do it? The bottom line was my child needed to know she was loved by her father and that I'd be there for her. My presence was worth more than all the toys in this massive store. Sofia was right. I had to put in time and effort to figure this out with Jenny. I knew I'd work it out, while holding on tight to the promise of a future with Sofia. We would make it through this challenging period because, as Dr. Webber had pointed out, Sofia and I were equally committed to the relationship; our connection ran deeper than the challenges we faced.

Now that things were making sense, a wave of exhaustion hit me, bone-deep and overwhelming, and I eyed the rocking chairs on display. If only I could get a beer or a glass of wine and chill out right here. They really should sell alcohol in these stores, maybe a little bar tucked between the baby clothes and the diaper bags? I considered leaving my cart in the middle of the aisle, abandoning my retail therapy experiment, when CRASH. The cart's metal frame vibrated with the impact, but since I'd built a mountain, I couldn't see what hit it. My tower of baby paraphernalia went flying, the stuffed bear landing with a soft thud at my feet, and the rest scattered throughout the aisle like detritus from a shipwreck.

"What the..." I heard the sound of frantic breaths first, then I was face to face with a man staring straight at me, wearing a horrified expression, his skin drained of color, eyes wild with panic.

"Have you seen my little girl?" His hands shook violently as he shoved a phone screen in front of my face with a photo of her, the image slightly blurred but showing a smiling child with missing front teeth. "She's five, and her name is Rachel." Before I could answer, he yelled, his voice cracking with desperation, "RACHEL. RACHEL. If you're playing hide and seek, please come out. Daddy needs you to answer right now."

"Where did you last see her?" I asked, my voice sounding almost as urgent as his. "How long has she been missing?"

The man ran a hand down his sweat-drenched face, leaving streaks in the sheen of moisture that covered his skin. "I think it's been ten minutes. I turned my back for a few seconds, and she was just... gone." His voice broke on the last word, a sound of pure anguish that cut straight to my core, and panic began to course through my body. "It was... in the toy aisle, I don't know which one." His eyes darted around wildly, as if praying she might suddenly appear out of thin air.

"What's your name?" I needed to anchor him, to pull him back from the edge of hysteria.

He hesitated, as if it was too much pressure to remember something so basic in this moment, his mouth working soundlessly before the word emerged. "Charles," he managed to cough out.

"Okay, Charles, we're going to find her. Come with me to the front of the store so you can show them her photo." My voice was calm and authoritative, a tone I usually reserved for board meetings, but it seemed to work. Charles nodded, then we were sprinting through the aisles, dodging shopping carts and wandering toddlers, the cheerful music playing over the loudspeakers a sharp contrast to the scene we were creating. Shoppers stopped and stared, their faces a blur of confusion and concern as we raced past, and I heard a few say, "Slow down..." but there was no time to lose. Breathless, we arrived at the cashiers, and my voice boomed over the din at the checkout counters, startling a grandmother who dropped her purse.

"There's a five-year-old girl who's gone missing in the store. Her name is Rachel. This father needs help finding her. Is there a manager here?"

All eyes shifted to me, worried expressions on the other parents' faces, some clutching their own children closer, as if Rachel's disappearance might be contagious. One woman shouted, her voice piercing through the sudden buzz of conversation, "What does she look like?"

Charles held up his phone, the screen's glow illuminating his tear-streaked face, and though his voice shook, he managed to describe her: brown hair, wearing a blue dress and jean jacket with an embroidered kitty on the back. From the far side of the store, a bald, overweight man wearing a shirt and tie headed our way, doing his best to walk-run across the slick floor, his face flushed from the exertion. As he approached, I saw the tag attached to his lapel had the title "Manager" in bold letters.

"There's a lost child?" His voice was gruff, but his eyes widened when he saw the faces at the checkout line.

While Charles gave him the rundown and answered his questions, everyone in the checkout lines began scanning the surroundings for the little girl, necks craning and eyes darting to every corner. It occurred to me that twenty or thirty years ago, losing a child in a big store wouldn't be considered a crisis, and hopefully it wasn't now. Kids didn't play all afternoon in the streets anymore, free to roam until dinnertime, and education about stranger danger was commonplace, taught in schools alongside math and reading. Why had the world become a more dangerous place for children? And would I be panicking along with Charles if I hadn't just become a dad? Every cell in my body was engaged in the protection of this little girl. With sudden clarity, I knew I had the instinct, if not the knowledge, to be a father, the realization both terrifying and exhilarating.

The manager assembled a team to go with Charles to search, barking orders like this wasn't the first time he'd had to run this drill. He locked the exit doors, the electronic click audible even over the store's ambient noise. There were some groans and complaints from customers ready to leave, but for the most part, people were more concerned about the child than their own schedules, which in itself was a small miracle.

A voice came over the loudspeaker, tinny and distant but clear enough: "Rachel, your dad is looking for you and he's worried. Please come to the front of the store." Then came the announcement to everyone to be on the lookout for her, the manager's voice sounding official, but I knew he must be in a panic with the weight of the responsibility for a lost child.

I went with the team to search; men and women checking the respective bathrooms, the smell of industrial cleaner filling my nostrils as I pushed open each stall door, and everyone stooping to view potential hiding places from a tiny person's perspective. Calls of, "Rachel," could be heard throughout the enormous store, echoing off the high ceilings and bouncing back distorted, and as customers were alerted, the search party grew—strangers united by a concern for a child none of them knew. Charles was choking back tears, his panic increasing with each minute, his movements growing more frantic, less coordinated, as if his body was running on pure fear.

We lost track of time, but it seemed like forever before a customer cried out, her voice slicing through the tension like a knife, "I've found her!" Footsteps thundered across the hard floor as we raced toward the sound of the voice. A mom and her child, a girl about the same age with pigtails, stood near a row of clothing racks, their faces a mixture of relief and concern. Rachel was crouched on the floor, partially obscured by the dresses for older girls, their sequins catching the light and casting tiny rainbows on her tear-stained face, clinging to the metal base as if it were a life raft. My heart lurched in my chest when Charles scooped her in his arms, his tears flowing freely now, soaking into her hair.

Everyone in the search party sighed with relief, the tension slowly draining from the air. Although Rachel buried her head against her dad's shoulder, I caught sight of her face, pale and drawn, her eyes wide with an emotion I couldn't quite name. What would make this five-year-old look scared to death? Quiet sobs escaped her while her dad rubbed circles on her back, asking, "What happened? Why did you hide?" His voice was gentle now, as if he could take away her fear if he stayed calm. I watched Charles, how he shrugged off his own emotion to soothe his daughter. He was an amazing dad, but maybe that's what all good parents learned to do?

Then I noticed a back exit door wide open, not twenty feet from where we found her, the night air rushing in and creating a cold draft. The skin on my back prickled, and hot rage shot through me. I bolted through the back door, the manager following behind me, our feet crunching on the gravel. We exchanged a knowing look, then scanned the loading area, the darkness broken only by a single security light casting long shadows. Aside from several large garbage bins, their contents spilling over the edges, and a stray cat scavenging for food, its eyes reflecting the light like tiny lamps, the area was deserted.

While the manager went to call the police, his footsteps shuffling a little slower now, I checked in with Charles. Understandably, he was a wreck, his entire body shaking as he tried to comfort his little girl, whispering reassurances into her hair. "Is she okay?" I asked, keeping my voice soft.

"I don't know. I've never seen her like this. She won't talk, but I know in my gut something happened."

"I believe you. The exit door was wide open, but there's no one out there now. The police should be here soon, and maybe when she calms down she can give them some information." I put a hand on his shoulder, feeling the tremors running through his body. "I'm so sorry, Charles, but I'm glad she's safe. Everything is fine now. Is there someone I can call for you?"

"My wife is on the way." He wiped his face on his sleeve, still clutching Rachel against him as if afraid she might vanish again if he loosened his grip. "Thanks, man. I appreciate your help."

"No problem, I'm just relieved she's safe."

As I turned to leave, I didn't care that my shopping cart stood deserted in the middle of the aisle. Jenny didn't need all those things—she needed me. And right now, I needed Sofia, my person, her steady presence the only thing that could calm the storm of emotions raging inside me.

Chapter Twenty-Seven

Sofia

Dear Ryan,

This will be my last entry for now, and I don't have much to share with you because we've already discussed our deepest fears, our greatest hopes, and exposed all our secrets. But someday, when you read my notes and look back over this time together, I hope you realize how much I appreciated you taking me on this wild adventure. I'm not going to say it's always been easy, because the challenges have sometimes felt insurmountable. But here we are, on the other side of the mountain, still together. Life doesn't turn out like the fairy tales would like us to believe, but that's fine by me. I'd rather struggle through life's ups and downs with you than live an uneventful life alone or settle for less than the love I've found with you. You are my prince, not because I need you to rescue me but because you're the finest man I've ever known—your love the greatest gift I've ever received. And while happily-ever-after can be elusive, I believe our love will stand the test of time—even separation—because the fates brought us together for a reason.

Someday, we'll understand the grand plan. In the meantime, I'll keep hanging on, standing strong as the next part of our story unfolds. Yours... always.

"This house is a classic, Sofia. You've kept it in good condition," Roger said, maneuvering around the stacked boxes to inspect the kitchen. "I hope you got a good price for the lease."

Madison swooped in from behind and swatted his ass. "Do you need a tour, or are you going to get to work? Sofia needs this place cleaned out today."

Roger turned to me. "Has she always been this bossy?"

Crouched on the floor, I finished writing a label and slapping it on a box before looking up. "What you see is what you get with Madison. Don't pretend you didn't know what you were signing up for."

Roger hooked an arm around Madison's waist, pulling her away from the box she was packing. Whatever he whispered in her ear had her giggling. "Alright, alright. Later," she said, planting a kiss on his lips before directing him to grab a box and haul it to the van.

Ryan picked up a stack of boxes, those lovely biceps bulging. "These go to the van?"

"Um, let me think." Seconds ticked by while I enjoyed the view.

"Sofia, some direction here?" He followed my gaze straight to his arms.

"Oh, right. Yes, to the van. Madison's only taking my clothes to her place. The rest goes into storage."

He nodded, a smile unfolding on his lips that didn't quite reach his eyes. "Okay." He carried the boxes outside. Neither of us could ignore the tension hanging in the air like static electricity, little shockwaves pinching us as we worked through the day's tasks. Each box emptied from the house was a reminder of the monumental shift taking place.

By evening, even Madison and Roger were sensing it, the four of us sitting on the floor holding plastic cups. "Spanish wine. Fitting for my send-off, right?" I forced a cheery tone as I filled the cups to a round of unenthusiastic nods.

"Okay, truth time," I announced, leaning back against the wainscoted wall. "I'll go first." In unison, their gazes swiveled toward me with expressions that read, *What-in-the-hell do you mean?* "I used this technique when I worked with kids in group sessions. Humor me. We'll each take a turn. No rebuttals to what someone else says."

They shrugged, and I continued. "My truth is—while I've been so excited about this move, when it comes right down to it, I'm nervous. I'm not only leaving my home, I'm leaving my friends." Madison and I exchanged a look. "And though Ryan and I have concocted a solution, I'm going to miss the hell out of him." I peeked at Ryan. The look in his eyes was so soft I had to fight back tears.

After a few moments of silence, Madison volunteered to go next. "My truth is simple. I know in my bones you need to do this, but I'm going to miss my best friend, so I'm a little sad today." Eyes fixed on the ceiling, she added, "You're my hero, so don't fuck this up." I heard a few snickers, including my own.

"My truth is, I'm going to miss you both," Roger said. "I was just getting to know you guys, but hey, we're going to visit as often as we can." He swung an arm around Madison's shoulder, both of them nodding.

My body stiffened when Ryan began. "My truth is complicated. Moving boxes today made it real—this is the end of an era for you, Sofia, and a transition into a new phase for us." He brought the cup to his lips and took a swig. "Like I said, it's complicated."

I crawled into his lap, wrapped my arms around his neck, and laid my head on his shoulder. "Yep. Complicated. We can unpack that later," I whispered in his ear.

Madison, in true form, piped up. "The truth is, we need to toast new beginnings and down this wine."

We complied, raising our glasses. There was nothing left but the goodbyes, and after Madison and I stood in the doorway locked in a hug, laugh-crying, Ryan asked, "See you at my place?"

"Soon. I need a little time alone here."

He gave me a nod. The look in his eyes told me he understood. I watched until Madison and Roger got into her car and Ryan fired up the van, then I closed the door and surveyed the empty room.

Everything was gone. All that had defined me had surreptitiously disappeared. The years of accumulated stuff—the things that identified my history over decades of marriage and raising a son in this very place—had been packed away, stored, or sold on local Craigslist over the last several weeks. After the divorce, I'd been given custody of the dishes, furniture, books, and countless things we'd picked up on a whim. I'd never realized how much stuff I'd accumulated, or how hard it would be to reduce my possessions down to three suitcases.

It was different for Ryan. He hadn't spent his life in California. He'd opted to rent out his apartment to a co-worker based in San Francisco, packing up and storing only his personal things. I'd spent the weeks before he came back sifting through the entire contents of my house. For me, the decision-making had been agonizing. I couldn't part with the porcelain vases circa 1940 that my grandmother had left me, even though I'd never use them again. They had fit nicely here, placed on a built-in shelf in a room constructed in the same era—a room with wainscoted walls and china cabinets painted over so many times they barely closed. Now, the vases were wrapped in bubble plastic, along with the dainty tea set with pink flowers that had been prominently displayed on her kitchen shelves, a reminder of my childhood. They certainly wouldn't fit in my new apartment.

The photos, the furniture, even the china set I'd picked out for my wedding registry—they'd all vibrated with memories as I'd decided each one's fate. All part of the fabric of my life, the multicolored threads woven in random patterns that vividly depicted each phase, each mark of passage, each road I'd traveled.

As I walked from room to room, the wood floor creaked under my feet, and memories echoed from every corner. A lump grew in my throat, but I let each one have its turn, listening to the sounds as they gave rise to a slideshow of images. The ghosts of Christmas past—the laughter and jokes, tables stretched across the length of the room for holiday dinners. The cries of a newborn swaddled in my arms, his eyes radiating up at mine in the purest reflection of love. Shouting, vile voices spewing words that could never be retracted. Then, the slam of the front door that rocked the house almost off its foundation. Me losing my foundation.

For a long time, a hush had fallen over the house. A lonely silence—a table set for one, the television burbling in the background—until one day, I opened the door again. It hadn't been easy to let Ryan into my life, but now the thought of two months without him made my heart ache. But if we had a shot at making it, this was the only way forward. We still might not have forever, but no one ever knows how long a relationship might last. At least we could count on a series of sixty-day commitments. Hopefully, they'd add up to years in the end.

"Goodbye," I whispered into the emptiness. It was the last of the goodbyes. There had been so many in the last week or so—to family, friends, ex-coworkers. So many tears and hugs and excited happy dances. Especially with Madison.

One evening we'd sat side-by-side on the steps of my front porch, watching the fog roll in overhead like a giant gray wave enveloping the city. "I'm coming for a visit as soon as I can," she'd promised, punching me in the arm. "I know where you live, so don't even think about dodging me. Call me whenever you need to talk." She wiped her nose with a tissue. I'd come prepared, already clutching a pack in my hand.

"Same. You'd better call me at least once a week." I passed her the bottle of wine. She pulled a face.

"Girl, how did I let you talk me into drinking straight from the bottle?"

I shrugged. "All the glasses are packed. And I seem to recall that time in Vegas—"

"Oh, no. What happens in Vegas stays right there."

"Ha. Ha. Now pass me that bottle," I said, side-eyeing her. I took a swig, then let my head drop onto her shoulder. She let me rest there and didn't lecture me about being too emotional. In silence, we stayed like that—I wasn't sure how long—until the streetlamps clicked on, light penetrating through the haze.

"I'm going to miss you." Madison's voice was soft and so unlike her, it made the back of my eyes prickle.

"Who knows, maybe I'll be back sooner than we think."

"Nope." She bumped my head off her shoulder and pulled back to look at me. "You're going to stay over there and finish what you started."

"Are you saying 'carpe diem?'" My grin was enough to make her shake her head. "I haven't forgotten how you started this whole thing. And thank you."

"Yeah, well, if I'd only known how far you'd take it..." She paused. "No, I'm not going to complain. This was the path you were supposed to take, so make the most of it."

I didn't argue. As usual, she was right. "Fine." Neither of us moved from that spot, nostalgia holding us hostage, until the chill of the night air soaked into our bones. There would be no goodbyes—we'd made a pact that night. This wasn't an ending. It was a door opening, a new chapter for both of us.

Since I'd returned from Barcelona, the planning had moved so quickly I'd barely had time to think about what I was leaving behind. It wasn't until this moment that it became truly real. A part of me was reassured by the thought that the house was still mine. I could come back if I changed my mind. I'd rented it to another family. A mother and her ten-year-old boy would weather their own storm of life after divorce in a house that knew the story all too well.

Through some motherly instinct, she'd known this was where she belonged the moment she pulled into the drive-way. I knew the house would take care of her, shelter her and bring her comfort, just as it had for me. But I also knew deep down that I was letting go—not only of the place that had been my home, my anchor, but also of the past. I'd outgrown it, and like a college student stepping into her newfound independence, I was ready to spread my wings and fly.

Keys in hand, I made my way to the front door. I breathed in the scent of familiarity—of newly refinished hardwood floors and a hint of my perfume lingering in the air—inviting one last wave of nostalgia to break over me before closing the door.

Chapter Twenty-Eight

Sofia

"We're really doing this?" My question sounded rhetorical as we lay in bed, arms and legs wrapped around each other so tight, we looked like a couple of contortionists. Ryan's flight to London was scheduled a day after mine, so although we were surrounded by boxes, he still had a bed.

He lifted his head off the pillow, scanning the sparse surroundings. "Looks like it." Sighing, he said, "It is complicated; you can't argue with that." I nodded against his chest. "But change is a good thing, for both of us. I want this day to be exciting for you—no negativity, no worries."

We'd taken full advantage of our last night together before my flight to enjoy every minute. No long conversations, because the time for talking and decision-making was in the past. It didn't mean I hadn't second-guessed everything in my mind several times over, and by the look I'd caught on his face, he'd had doubts too. But this train was already moving, and there was no jumping off now.

I tipped my mouth to his, peppering his lips with kisses. "Thank you," I said, just as both our phone alarms beeped in unison, in harmony with our mutual groans.

"On the count of three, we get up. Okay?" Ryan's tone sounded serious, until he rolled me onto my back, the weight of his body pressing me to the mattress, his mouth holding me hostage.

Though I was a willing participant in one last shag for the road, it meant I had to rush through showering, makeup, hair recovery, and finally getting dressed. After he'd helped me downstairs with my load of suitcases, we faced each other while waiting for the Uber driver.

"No goodbyes, right?" Ryan said.

"Right. We'll see each other soon," I confirmed. We'd already agreed on this, but once everything was loaded in the car, I climbed into the back seat and a heaviness settled over me.

He leaned halfway through the window. "Promise me you'll text the minute you arrive."

I gave him a thumbs up, then my eyes stayed locked on his until the car finally pulled away, and he was out of sight.

"Sofia Drake?" the Uber driver asked, confirming my identity from the app.

I pulled the seatbelt across my shoulder and secured the buckle. "That's me."

"Which terminal are you flying from?"

My fingers rubbed at my temples as I tried to focus. "Terminal three," I mumbled.

At this early hour, the car easily rolled through the city streets, and by the time we reached the crowded freeway, my heavy eyelids succumbed to the weight of far too little sleep. When they closed, I saw Ryan's face, the sadness lurking behind his eyes. Childbirth notwithstanding, leaving him even temporarily was one of the hardest things I'd had to do.

"I'm booking your flight business class," he'd announced promptly when he'd finally grasped I was serious about the move.

Despite my useless protests of independence, he had insisted. I was secretly relieved, because once you've traveled business class, returning to the cattle section of economy on a fifteen-hour flight amounted to cruel and unusual punishment. Besides, I'd be testing my independence soon enough once I started living in Barcelona.

"So, are you going on vacation?" The driver's voice reached me in the back seat, an unwelcome interruption.

I pried open one eye.

"No, not exactly. I'm moving." Before he could ask the obvious next question, I answered, "To Barcelona."

"You are moving to Barcelona, Spain?" His voice lilted with an inflection of incredulity. "Well, ain't that something." He paused long enough to shake his head, then raised his eyes to the rearview mirror and peered back at me. "I've never been to Barcelona. What's it like there?"

I wanted to be excited, to share the wonders of the city I had come to love, but exhaustion had dampened my enthusiasm. Besides, I was grappling with too many emotions. My brain felt like a tumble dryer where fear, anxiety, grief, hope, and elation bounced around like mismatched socks.

I straightened in my seat and took a deep breath. "It's an amazing city. Vibrant and so alive, yet it's filled with an old-world charm." I repeated a phrase that had stuck in my head when I was in the city. "There are surprises around every corner on those cobblestone streets."

"It sounds awesome, lucky you."

Lucky me, I thought, except that I was headed there without Ryan. We rode the rest of the way in silence. I didn't have it in me to make conversation. As we pulled up to the departure curb, my airport anxiety spiked. I wondered if I'd ever get used to traveling alone.

Struggling to maneuver two large suitcases, which weighed nearly as much as me, plus a carry-on and a backpack, I quickly realized that the job required a third hand. While I sent one rolling with a push and ran back for the others, I heard a woman yelp. Even before I turned around, I had a hunch my plan had backfired. My apologies didn't do much to ease the damage to her foot or stop her from looking at me like she considered ramming her suitcase at my leg.

When I finally reached the check-in desk, I sent up a silent prayer as I hoisted the bags onto the weight scale. *Please don't be overweight. I can't remove one more thing.* Then I slid my passport across the check-in counter. The cheery, round-faced attendant examined it, and her fingers flew on the keyboard, pulling up my reservation

"You have a one-way ticket to Barcelona? When do you plan to return?" She peered at me over the rim of her glasses, her expression less jovial now. I knew the rules all too well. The automatic visa to visit Europe was extended to Americans for only three months. I reached into my bag and produced a set of papers, sliding them over the ledge into her hands.

"This is my visa to live in Spain," I said confidently.

She rifled through the papers, then walked away, leaving me with my jaw hanging open. The muscles in my back tensed into a knot when she handed them to a man in an official-looking uniform. Possibly a supervisor? He examined the documents, flipping each page before giving them back to her with a nod.

"This looks to be in order," she said, returning the papers into my waiting hands along with a boarding pass. "Have a pleasant flight, Ms. Drake."

I veered into the ladies' room after passing through security, but with my phone at the bottom of my purse, I neglected to check the time. It was while I casually strolled down the corridor toward my gate that I heard on the loudspeaker: *Last call for flight 112 to Barcelona.* I swore loud enough to cause a couple to scoot quickly to the side, leaving me room to bolt. My carry-on suitcase wobbled on its wheels as I zig-zagged around passengers darting in front of me to grab a snack at the concessions. The thought crossed my mind that I really should improve my time management skills since this wasn't the first time I'd had to dash to the gate, although in this case I could blame Ryan for making me late. As it turned out, I wasn't the last person to board the plane. A man with a walker was being assisted onto the gangway by an attendant.

Once more, I was sweating, tearing off my leather jacket and scarf when the flight attendant pointed to my seat. When I grabbed hold of my suitcase and prepared to hoist it into the overhead bin, I stopped in midair at the sound of his smooth, deep voice.

"Can I help you with that, Miss?"

"Ryan!" I dove at him, landing squarely in his lap. It didn't matter that he wasn't supposed to be here. It wasn't in our contract.

I kissed him until I heard the flight attendant come up behind me and say, "I'll just put your bag in the overhead bin."

Barely glancing over my shoulder, I replied, "Thank you." I didn't want to take my eyes off him, still unable to comprehend how he was here.

"Surprise," he whispered, his brows bouncing. "I'm glad you're pleased to see me. A part of me wondered if you'd be mad."

"You did lie to me, telling me your flight was tomorrow."

"Yes, but only so that I could see you one more time before my flight to London. Then you'll be on your own, I promise."

"You are so bad." I stroked his cheek with my fingertips. "But I'm so happy to see you."

The only downside of his plan was that we had to part all over again when he walked with me all the way to the door at baggage claim. But the time we spent on the plane was precious. Once he had reclined his seat into a bed, I'd climbed in next to him—well, practically speaking, I was pretty much on top of him, as his frame took up the entire space. This resulted in a suggestion—possibly mine—about a rendezvous in the bathroom.

Remembering our first encounter in an airplane bathroom, I had to rethink my earlier assumption that it would be impossible to have sex in such cramped quarters. At least this time, my nose didn't bleed when a misdirected elbow came at my face.

Granted, it involved some creative maneuvers, but still it felt gratifying that I'd finally joined the *Mile High Club* for the first time with him. Although the flight attendant did eye us suspiciously when we came out of the loo. Ryan attempted to suppress a grin. I squared my shoulders and smiled at her. It was the kind of smile that could have meant anything at all, but when she diverted her attention to the drink cart, I attributed it to my new air of confidence.

"I'm going to miss you," I whispered in his ear, my arms locked around his neck. We stood to the side in one last, desperate embrace, only vaguely aware of the stampeding feet inches away—impatient passengers headed for the exit. I memorized everything about him, concentrating on the way his body felt against my own, the softness of his hair between my fingers, the smell of his minty fresh breath as he laid his cheek against mine—all while a twinge of panic fluttered in my chest. I didn't want to let him go. I didn't know how I was going to manage without him for sixty days, or worse... *Oh God.*

His arms held me tighter against him, as if he felt the fear rise in my throat. "I'll miss you too," he said, his voice husky. When he finally broke away, he blinked hard, then held my hands in his. "Sixty days, or thirty days if I get my way. No sweat. We've got this." His voice strained with the effort to sound excessively confident. "*You've* got this. You're ready to test your wings and figure out who Sofia is as an expat in Barcelona."

I gave a slight, unconvincing nod and wiped my cheeks with the backs of my hands. God, this was going to be harder than I imagined. He must have seen me tremble, noticed the way my face was crumpling, because he pulled me to him and kissed me. The kind of kiss that was meant to imprint his lips on mine, meant to reassure me, to make me believe everything would be okay.

"The universe brought us together for a reason," he breathed against my ear. "A little distance is no match for our contract. This is just a slight detour."

It took superhuman strength to turn and walk away from him. When I looked back, pausing just as I reached the no-return doors to baggage claim, he was still standing there. A young couple with a toddler in a stroller hurried toward the exit, and I briefly stepped aside to give them room; an unbidden ache in my stomach rising at the sight of the family.

"Meet me in Barcelona in sixty days, okay?" Then, sounding more desperate than I meant to, I added, "Promise me."

He nodded and gave me a thumbs-up. "Nothing could keep me away." A reassuring smile blossomed on his face. Even if he was forcing the smile, still, it gave me courage.

I turned, took a deep breath, and willed my feet to move. The automatic doors shut behind me. There was literally no going back. I propelled myself forward to baggage claim, tugging my wheeled case, uncertain of what might lie ahead for my future. But I was certain about Ryan. In a world where relationships were tenuous—fragile—I knew that no matter what, I would never stop loving him. This time, I wasn't running away. I was running headlong toward a new version of myself. And if the fates were still on our side, we'd most certainly be together again, creating a new version of us.

The End

Bonus Chapter

Ryan

I watched her walk away and couldn't help wondering if we were going about this in the right way. Could she sense my doubt? Oh, I covered it well, and the encouragement I gave her was all true. She deserved that much, considering what she'd had to put up with. What girlfriend stuck around after they learned you'd fathered a child with another woman?

One last look back at me, and she disappeared beyond the door that would separate us for at least thirty days, if not sixty. It wasn't the first time that I'd questioned my sanity in agreeing to this new contract. Pretty much every day, I'd regretted it, but was there any other choice? Sofia had come up with a plan to save our relationship by going in different directions, and on some level, it made sense. But then why did I feel like shit now?

"Excuse me."

I turned to the sound of a woman's voice, jolting me from my thoughts. American, by the sound of it. She was attempting to wrangle two toddlers, boys nearly the same age, along with backpacks and carry-on luggage to baggage claim.

"Sorry," I muttered, stepping out of the way, just then clocking the line of passengers waiting to exit. Since Jenny, I'd started noticing kids now, or more accurately, the parents trying to manage their kids. Finally turning to head for my flight to London, I tried to imagine myself rolling Jenny around in a stroller, armed with a diaper bag full of whatever supplies you put in there. Who the hell was going to teach me these things? James came to mind, if I could put up with all his jokes at my expense. My mother? No chance of that happening. Her mothering instincts weren't exactly on point. I couldn't imagine her changing a diaper, much less taking the night shift with a crying baby. Yeah, she said she wanted grandchildren, but she'd be the kind of grandma that showered the kid with things and posed for photo ops. Her specialty was delegating—to babysitters, nannies—or just leaving the kid to fend for himself. Okay, I was a teenager before she pulled that. Would she be different as a grandmother? I guess I'd find out.

I caught sight of a children's store out of the corner of my eye. Funny, but I'd never noticed it before, and detoured to check it out. What the hell, my carry-on had some room, and Rebecca might appreciate it if I picked up a few things, but the first rack I saw held cutesy stuff, like T-shirts that said *Daddy's little princess*. No way was I going to perpetuate that fairytale crap. I'd teach her to be a strong, independent girl—not a princess like her grandmother, and certainly not dependent on some boy to validate her worth. I cringed internally at the idea of boys and shoved that right out of my mind. *Fuck*.

Then I spotted the Barca team merchandise. This stuff I could get behind a hundred percent. I picked out a bib, then found a T-shirt that was several sizes too big, but she'd grow into it in a year. The soccer ball, even miniature sized, would have to wait. She'd be into soccer, right? I'd introduce her to it early, maybe when she turned two. I could already see myself going crazy at her games, standing on the sidelines, or maybe coaching?

"How old is yours? Boy or girl?" My head swiveled toward the voice—a dude about my age, maybe older, his arms loaded with team stuff.

Jesus, this felt weird. "Girl, only a few weeks old. Guess I'm getting ahead of myself here."

"No way. It's never too soon to start indoctrinating them with team spirit. I've got a boy and a girl, seven and ten. You a fan?"

"Barca all the way, right?" I confirmed.

"But losing Messi was a blow, not gonna lie."

"Win or lose, you gotta stay loyal though."

"Damn right," he said, reaching for his wallet. "I've gotta get to my gate. Good luck with the newborn, man. It gets real now." He shook his head in a way that told me I wasn't at all prepared for what I was walking into.

When it was my turn at the checkout counter, I grabbed a few things that were marked for infants—a teething ring (when did babies grow teeth?) and a rattle.

After jamming the stuff in my suitcase, I glanced at my watch and picked up the pace, since the gate was all the way at the end of the corridor. But of course, when I arrived, an image flashed on the board: *Flight delayed thirty minutes*. It never failed to floor me how often this happened. With all the seats taken, I had to search for one at the next gate. I realized that focusing on Jenny had helped take the edge off watching Sofia disappear through that door. It would be sweet if we were all in Barcelona. I'd prefer to stay here, not in London, but Rebecca and my job were there.

London. The letters scrolled in white above the counter—taunting me—the distraction of the baby store gone now. I'd probably be boarding the plane before she'd have a chance to respond, but I pulled out my cell and texted Sofia anyway.

> *Hey, babe, just thought I'd shoot you a text while I wait for my flight. Apparently, there's some kind of delay, so I have another 30 minutes to prepare for my meeting or think about you. I'll let you guess which one I'll be choosing. Anyway, I hope you love your new apartment. Call me when you get in, okay?*

Instead of putting it back in my pocket, I held the phone in the palm of my hand, waiting. Just in case. Five minutes later, I stowed it away and prepared to force my feet to walk down the gangway and onto the plane.

"Thank God you're here. She's been asking for you, and you're, like, two hours late." Robin greeted me with a tone that was simultaneously relieved and pissed off when she opened the door.

Stepping into Rebecca's apartment, an uneasy sense of familiarity made my skin crawl. The same Victorian hard-as-a-rock couch sat in the living room, flanked on all sides by her grandmother's flowered wallpaper still plastered on the walls—an unfortunate testament to Rebecca's resistance to change, bad taste in design, or, more generously, preservation of her grandmother's memory. But one thing was noticeably different: the smell permeating through the apartment. If I had to describe it, dirty diapers were probably the big offenders, but puke and spoiled milk most likely had roles in the assault on my nose.

"Nice to see you too, Robin," I responded, a grin softening my sarcasm.

"Whatever. Shoes off."

"I remember the rules," I said, wedging them into the shoe rack by the door next to the lineup of her boots.

From behind the closed bedroom door, Jenny's wail reached my ears like a siren call, piercing my chest, gripping my heart in a chokehold. I froze in place. It had only been a few weeks, but I'd recognize that cry anywhere. I whipped around, eye to eye with Robin. "Is there something wrong? With Jennifer? Rebecca?"

A laugh bubbled up from her throat but quickly died out. She gave me a look that said, *you idiot*, her expression telling me the story of sleep deprivation and frustration. "Babies cry, Ryan. For that matter, so do new mothers. Honestly, I may have joined in a few times. Everything is fine as far as I can tell."

"Should I go in there? I mean, is she decent?"

"Besides having one tit out almost all the time, yes, but nothing you haven't seen before." Robin pulled a pair of trainers off the rack, and slipping them on, she continued. "That baby nurses like a bloody camel. I don't know where she puts it all."

"Wait. You're leaving? Now?"

She let out a huff. "I've been pulling twenty-four-hour shifts here, and I need sleep so that when I return to work tomorrow, I might actually have a ruddy functioning brain."

An ominous feeling hit me in the gut. If Robin was trashed after a couple of weeks, what hope did I have of surviving? "You must be tired, I get that, but isn't there an instruction manual you can leave with me?"

She gave me that look again as she shrugged on her coat. "Rebecca can tell you what she needs. I left breast milk in the fridge if you need to feed her a bottle, and there are clean sheets for the guest room. You'll figure out the rest."

She must have noticed the deer-in-the-headlights look I shot her, because she paused as she opened the door. "You'll do fine, Ryan. Jenny is a good baby, really. Rebecca's just worn out, and this is all new to her."

"Hah. It's new to me too. If neither of us knows what we're doing, this setup doesn't look promising for Jenny. What if—"

Robin cut me off. "No new parent knows what they're doing, and believe it or not, the human species continues to survive. Now, get in there and hold your daughter for a while. For starters, that's all you bloody have to do."

And then she was gone, leaving me to man up and take charge. I told myself, *you've got this,* as I approached the bedroom. Rebecca lifted her head off the pillow when she saw me in the doorway, Jenny cradled in her arms. "I thought I heard you come in. Is my sister gone?"

"Yeah, she needed to get some sleep. Sorry I'm late. The plane was delayed."

I didn't know if I was reading too much into it, but as soon as I spoke, Jenny opened her eyes, shifting her gaze in my direction. Did she remember me?

"Speaking of sleep, I'm knackered. Would you mind taking Jenny for a while? If she's not being held, she starts wailing." Rebecca didn't resemble herself at all. She was wearing a worn-out jogger sweatshirt with baby puke stains on both shoulders, and her hair looked like it hadn't seen a brush in a week.

I extended my arms, my hands motioning for her to give me the baby. In two seconds, Jenny was against my chest, all bundled up in a pink blanket, and Rebecca's eyes had already closed. As I made my way to the living room, I noticed a new rocking chair in the corner. The modern Ikea design was totally out of place in the room, and I wondered whose idea it was to buy it. As far as I knew, Robin and Rebecca were estranged from their father, and the mother had died a few years ago, although I didn't remember Rebecca telling me much about the family history. *Unfortunately for her*, I thought. *She could use a mother for support about now.*

"It's just you and me now, Jenny. Are you good with that?" I asked, sliding back and forth on the rails of the rocker. Her eyes surveyed my face, studying me with the intensity of a scientist examining a new species. Then her little lips puckered, and I swear they broke into a smile. I had done some reading on the plane about babies and timelines of development. Smiling was not on the chart for at least several more weeks, but right there, I convinced myself it was a sign—an answer to my question.

My phone pinged inside my pocket, and shifting Jenny, I managed to dig it out. Sofia. Finally, a response to my text.

> *I'm on the way to my apartment and will call as soon as I can. I love you! Xoxo*

Calm spread through me like a wave. Everything was going to be okay, I was sure of it now. The love we had was solid—unbreakable. "You hear that, Jenny? She loves me. You're going to love me too once you get to know me." Jenny let out a squawk. "Why, you ask? Because I'm your dad, and I'll love you forever, no matter what. Period." Maybe it was gas, but those little pink lips curved into a smile, and I melted. I suspected this was only the beginning of the way her smile would always affect me—not unlike the way Sofia's gaze made me feel raw with emotion. Now, with my heart about to burst with love for this woman and my baby girl, I realized I had free-fallen off that cliff in a way I never could've imagined. It seemed crazy that I'd been so afraid to fall.

There was always a chance I could still hit a few rocks because that was life, but I had faith I'd survive. There was no turning back now.

THANK YOU FOR READING *THE RELATIONSHIP CONTRACT!* It would mean a lot to this author if you would leave your honest review on the retailer's book page.

Other books by this author:
THE VACATION BUBBLE
TO BARCELONA WITH LOVE TRILOGY, BOOK 1
E-book Amazon. Paperback on Amazon or your favorite retailer.
https://www.amazon.com/dp/B0FF2VMQFD

The Vacation Bubble

Also an audiobook! You can find it on Audible, Google Play, Kobo, Apple Books, Spotify and more.

COMING THIS SUMMER: BOOK 3, TO BARCELONA WITH LOVE TRILOGY
To receive bonus material from the author, including behind the scenes tips on Barcelona, recipes, and information about the release of Book 3 of the trilogy, check out this link!

Marcellasteele.com/bonusbook2

Follow me on social media. I'm always happy to hear from readers!

Instagram @marcellasteele.writer

TikTok @writerMarcellaSteele

Facebook @Marcellasteelewriter

And subscribe to my newsletter for new releases, giveaways, and more!

https://www.marcellasteele.com